THE
ALLURE OF
Julian Lefray

R.S. GREY

The Allure of Julian Lefray
Copyright © 2015 R.S. Grey

Published: R.S. Grey 2015
authorrsgrey@gmail.com
Editing: Editing by C. Marie
Cover Design: R.S. Grey
Stock Photos courtesy of Shutterstock ®
ISBN: 1514673614
ISBN-13: 9781514673614

Monica,

enjoy!

xo

KS Grey

Prologue

Josephine

"You can take the girl out of the country, but you can't take the country out of the girl."

Who in the world came up with that shitty phrase? It's my least favorite quote of all time. I spent my entire childhood wishing I was somewhere better than my tiny hometown. Where I grew up, football reigned and being a vegetarian was on par with being a Satanist. Fortunately, it wasn't all bad. I had two doting parents and Sally's Thrift Shop. Sally's was my version of church, because it was where I found my bible: *Fashion 101 - A Girl's Guide to Dressing Fabulously*.

I remember one particular Saturday when my mother caved on the way home from my youth soccer game. I'd pleaded with her to stop into Sally's for a minute, and finally she gave in and pulled into a free parking spot right in front of the shop. I unbuckled before she finished parking, threw my car door open, and flew through the front door to the sound of her reprimanding me from her driver's side window.

Every trip to Sally's followed the same routine. I had about ten minutes to wander through the aisles—fifteen if my mom was feeling up to chatting with the clerk on duty—during which I would pile as many things into a small basket as I could possibly muster. The rule was always the same: I could pick one item and that was it. No ifs, ands, or buts about it, as my mom loved to say. Even still, I tested her resolve each time.

That day was no different. When I joined my mom at the front of the store I had two purses slung over my shoulders, a fedora resting on top of my head, two scarves, and a basket overflowing with clothes. My mother tsked and took the basket from me, preemptively apologizing to the clerk for having to return all of my unpurchased merchandise to the shelves.

"Mom, please! TWO THINGS, PLEASE!" I begged as she tipped the basket out onto the counter. My glittery tops spilled out in a sad display.

"Josie Ann, you had better pick one thing now or we're leaving here with nothing," she said with a stern voice and a hand on her hip.

I knew that look. I knew I wasn't going to get away with two items that day.

And then I saw them.

I swear a beam of light shined down from the heavens as I stared down at a pair of cheetah print flats on display beneath the glass counter. They looked ten sizes too big, but I had to have them.

I slid to my knees, pressed my hands to the display case, and fogged up the glass with my stinky child's breath. Then, having learned my lesson, I wiped the glass clean, held my breath, and stared at those flats like they were going to come to life and pounce at me.

"I want…those," I declared with utter decisiveness.

"Jo, those won't fit you. They're probably my size," my mom protested, bending down to join me.

"They're also quite expensive," the clerk said. "Vintage Chanel."

My eyes widened. Chanel—a label I'd learned from *Fashion 101*. I didn't know a lot about a lot of things (in fact I'd been pronouncing it "channel" in my head), but I knew that those Chanel flats were going to be mine someday.

I stared at them until my mom started dragging me out of the store. I dragged my hands on the carpet in protest.

"Save them for me! Don't let anyone buy them!" I begged. "Please!"

I cried the entire way home as my mom berated me for not appreciating the life I had. I didn't care that we had a roof over our heads and food on the table every night. What good are basic human amenities without a pair of faux fur flats? I wanted those shoes more than anything.

As soon as I got home, I ran to my piggy bank and counted out all the money I had to my name: twelve dollars and seventeen cents.

The shoes were $150.

For the next year and half, I saved every dime I got. Birthday money, allowance money, Christmas money, (attempting to be Jewish so I could get money for Hanukkah did not work on my parents)—it all went into the piggy bank until the day I could finally walk into the shop, take a hammer to my bank, and walk out with a pair of size 8 vintage Chanel flats wrapped up like Fabergé eggs.

Those vintage Chanel flats were my very first designer purchase, and they were the shoes I wore at twenty-three as I left my small life in Texas with hopes of tackling the fashion world in New York City.

Chapter One

Josephine

"Where to?"

I glanced up in time to watch the driver toss a hastily concealed cigarette butt out the window and cringed. I knew the stench of secondhand smoke would cling to my layered gown, but I was already running ten minutes late and the chances of finding another cab were slim to none.

"Upper East Side," I answered, sliding into the backseat. "Carlyle Hotel."

He pulled out into traffic and I tried my best to check my complexion in his rearview mirror. Our eyes met in the glass; I blushed and settled against the seat. *What does it matter?* It's too late to fix anything now anyway.

"Ah. The Carlyle," he repeated with a thick Italian accent. "Must be a fancy party."

Fancy didn't begin to cover it.

"It's the New York Fashion Gala," I offered, not sure if he was interested in talking or if he was just amusing me.

"Sounds like a party I'm happy to be skipping," he said, lazily turning back to check if the left lane was clear before swerving over sharply. I fell against the window before I could catch myself and scrunched my nose to ease the pain as I collided with the door handle.

"You look good though. Pretty dress," he offered with a lighter tone than he'd used the moment before. Maybe he felt bad for insulting the gala, or maybe I did actually look nice in my rented Dolce & Gabbana gown. Either way, I was happy to hear the compliment. I needed all the confidence I could get.

I still couldn't believe I was en route to the gala. When my invitation had arrived *(in a gold envelope smelling of baby angels, no less)*, I'd screamed with excitement for all of two minutes before the stress of attending such an illustrious event crept in. The gala was *the* fashion event of the year. Every big-time designer, model, socialite, and blogger would be in attendance. Normally I read about the juicy details of the event on blogs and celebrity websites the day after it happened, but for the first time ever I was going to experience it all firsthand.

"So why are you going to the gala? Are you wunna them models or something?" the cabbie asked, eyeing me in the rearview mirror as if assessing whether or not I could cut it on the runway.

I snorted. "No. I'm a fashion blogger."

He nodded as if impressed.

"My buddy Geno started a blog, but it's mostly about the best hoagies on Long Island. What's yours called? I'll tell my daughter to look it up," he said, reaching toward the console for something and swerving toward the car next to us in the process. I flinched and reached for the door handle, ready to jump for it and get the hell out of his death trap. *Just tuck and roll. You'll survive.*

"Whoops," he said, righting us on the road and reaching back to give me a paper and pen.

Aw man. He'd just about killed me, but it was because he wanted to pass my blog along to his daughter. *Am I prepared to die for the sake of my blog?* Oh hell. I jotted down the URL and passed the paper back to him.

"*What Jo Wore*," he said, reading off my blog name with his thick accent. "Clever. You Jo?"

Hearing him read my blog name with his heavy accent brought a smile to my face.

"Josephine."

He lifted up onto one side so he could slip the piece of paper into the back pocket of his pants. *I can safely say that's as close as my name has ever been to a cabbie's ass.*

"Well, Josephine, I'll be sure to tell my daughter I gave a ride to a famous fashion lady. She'll be impressed."

I nodded, not bothering to correct him. I might have been a "fashion lady" but I was far from famous.

For now.

● ● ●

When we arrived, there was a line of cars wrapped all the way around The Carlyle Hotel. I peeked through the window to see a string of sleek limousines with a few

7

Maseratis thrown in for good measure. Suited hotel attendants rushed to the limousine doors and whisked gala attendees out one by one. Meanwhile, my cabdriver tried to discreetly light another cigarette and then openly flipped off every limousine driver that tried to cut him off. *Pure class, people.*

I should have had him drop me off down the street, but it was too late. A hotel attendant whisked open the back door of the cab and I fumbled to pay the driver as quickly as possible so that I wouldn't hold up the line.

"Crap, I don't have any cash," I said, flipping through my purse and hating myself for not being more prepared.

"I take cards, lady," the cabbie said, pointing to the credit card machine in the center of the console. "I take numbas too," he said with a wink.

The hotel attendant cleared his throat, and I threw him an awkward smile as I swiped my card.

"Just a second," I said to the attendant, pretending not to hear the last part of the cab driver's sentence.

"Of course," the attendant replied with a curt, practiced tone. If I hadn't been about to make my debut at a ritzy party, I would have turned to the attendant and told him exactly what I was thinking. *You're a hotel attendant, not the King of England. Now be quiet and take my hand so I don't trip over my rented designer dress getting out of this smoke-filled cab.*

The driver handed me my receipt and met my eye.

"Well good luck anyways, Jo," he said with a quick nod.

I smiled weakly and nodded. *I can totally do this. Italian cabbie believes in me, and that counts for something.*

I exited the back of the cab with my head held high and

let my bright red dress flow down around me. The sweetheart bodice was so fitted that it had been hard to breathe during the ride over, but standing up seemed to help. I adjusted the strapless top and let the rest of the dress fall into place. Red was a bold choice for my first gala. There was no way I could blend in with the masses, but that's the way I'd planned it. There would be fashion industry bigwigs in attendance and I wanted to make a memorable impression.

I fell in line on the red carpet and pulled out my invitation in case they asked to see it, but when I scanned the line, no one else had their invitation out. *Rookie mistake.* I quickly rolled it up and tried to discreetly conceal it in my clutch.

Most everyone in line seemed to be arriving in couples or groups, but I was rolling solo. The invitation hadn't specified whether or not I could bring a date and I didn't want to assume it would be okay. *Also, who am I kidding?* I didn't have anyone I could have invited.

"Name?" the event coordinator asked in a clipped tone as I approached the front of the line.

"Josephine Keller."

She scanned down her clipboard, using a small penlight to illuminate a giant list of names. I saw a few surnames starting with K but she scanned over them, flipped the page, flipped another one, and then flipped back to the front.

"I don't see it, next please," she said, uttering the very words that had been my worst nightmare in the days leading up to the event.

I broke out in a cold sweat immediately.

"There must be a mistake," I said, holding up my rolled invitation—which now looked like I'd nabbed it from someone's curbside trashcan. *Dammit.*

I could hear the annoyed people muttering behind me in line, but I didn't dare turn around and show my face.

"Just step aside for a moment," the event coordinator said, turning on a radio attached to her shoulder strap and using it to summon an assistant to the front entrance.

This *would* be my luck. I was *this* close to really taking my career to the next level and then life decided to give me an ol' "not so fast, sister" slap in the face. Life is an evil bitch sometimes.

For ten minutes I stood to the side of the line, beneath the hotel awning, fidgeting from one heel to the other as guests rattled off their names and were ushered inside without a hitch.

Five more minutes and I'll leave.

Five minutes came and went and I stayed, growing more mortified by the second. *Where the hell is her assistant?* I made it a point to keep my face mostly hidden so that no one would recognize me inside as "that poor girl from the outer borough".

Finally, a petite blonde dressed in simple black slacks and a matching button-down ran through the front door clutching a clipboard with wide eyes and a frazzled look.

"Madeline!" the event coordinator snapped as soon as the blonde came into sight. "Check to see if there's a—" the event coordinator paused and turned to find me standing a few feet away. "What was your name again?"

"Josephine Keller," I answered, trying my hardest not to look past the coordinator. Everyone in line had turned in my direction to see what the commotion was about.

"I'm sorry. I couldn't hear that," Madeline replied, looking like she was on the verge of tears.

That's because I whispered it, you hard of hearing

whore. *Please stop drawing attention to me.*

I coughed and took a step closer. "Josephine Keller."

Madeline nodded and got to work, flipping through her notes.

"Just a second," she said.

I was crossing my fingers behind my back, repeating the phrase "Please find my name, please find my name," over and over again in my head, when I looked up and met the eye of a man standing in line.

My gut clenched.

HOLY GUACA-DO ME.

He was third from the front of the line and watching me with a bemused smile. Where all the other stares had been easy to ignore, his devoured my attention to the point of discomfort.

I swallowed slowly as I scanned over him. Handsome only brushed the surface. He was a vision in black. He had everything down to a T: a fitted tuxedo, silver cufflinks, and impeccably polished designer shoes. His arms were crossed over his chest and his wide shoulders blocked out the streetlamp behind him so that he seemed to glow against the bustling backdrop of limousines and hotel attendants.

I let myself glance over him for three intense seconds and then forced myself to look away.

Enough.

I'd stared too long.

But he'd been staring back.

I forced myself to watch Madeline scan through the list of names until the line moved forward again. I peered up from beneath my lashes, using the opportunity to see him one last time before he went inside and disappeared into the crowd forever.

I tried to memorize every feature as quickly as possible. His black hair was thick and styled flawlessly, a bit shorter on the sides with a smooth wave on top. His cheekbones were so defined that Webster's surely had an entry for them. As he spoke to the guests in front of him, a permanent pair of dimples framed his cheeks. His jawline was sharp, clean-shaven, and inexplicably alluring.

I watched him for another moment before he finally detected my stalker-stare and turned my way.

Hazel eyes locked with mine and I froze as my world slipped right out from under me.

"Ah! Josephine Keller! I finally found you," Madeline exclaimed. "Someone put your name down as 'Josephine Geller'."

Typical.

"Okay," she said, offering me a relieved smile. "Right this way."

I followed behind her as she beckoned me toward the hotel doors. I knew the man's gaze was following me as I stepped past him. I could feel his eyes on me, heating my cheeks to a cruel, rosy blush that I prayed he couldn't see.

"The step and repeat is there to the left," she said, pointing to a small section of the hotel lobby where a few celebrities were getting their photos taken by the paparazzi. "And the ballroom is just beyond the lobby."

I glanced past the black marble floor to where she was pointing.

I could see a glimpse of the party, hear the pulsing music streaming out, and smell the delicious hors d'oeuvres sweeping into the room.

For better or for worse, I'd arrived.

Chapter Two

Josephine

After I'd snatched a glass of champagne, spilled a bit of it onto the front of my dress, run to the bathroom to clean it off, and stuffed a few crab balls in my mouth, I was officially ready to party.

Oh, and by party, I mean stand by myself in the corner of the ballroom and pretend like I belonged. I was praying that the dim lighting made me look like a statue so that people wouldn't take pity on me. Either that, or for the sexy man from the line to come over and say, "Nobody puts baby in a corner." And then we'd perform that routine from *Dirty Dancing*, and everyone would clap, and Vogue would offer me a job because they were so impressed with my footwork.

I pulled out my phone and shot a text to Lily, my best friend back home in Texas.

Josephine: I'm standing in the corner by myself like the kid that pees his pants at a middle school dance.

Lily: Get out there and schmooze! You need a job!!

Lily: Also...nobody puts baby in a corner.

Josephine: Already made that reference in my head.

Lily: Classic. But, seriously, the longer you stand there the more you look like the pee-kid.

Josephine: Yeahyeahyeah. By the way, I submitted my resume to Lorena Lefray today.

Lily: Is that for the executive assistant position?

Josephine: Yeah, it's just something temporary while I keep building my blog following. NYC ain't cheap.

Lily: I'll be moving up there soon, don't worry.

I finished off my glass of champagne and cringed.

Josephine: Oh god, my drink's empty. What do I do with my hands now?

Lily: Snap along to the music.

Lily: No wait. Keep touching or pointing toward your cleavage so guys will get the picture that you're an easy lay.

Josephine: I hate you. Later, dweeb. The crab balls are coming back around.

Lily: Stop shoving balls in your mouth. You're at a gala. This is why you don't have any friends in New York.

I rolled my eyes at Lily's response and shoved my phone back into the glittery purse I'd thrifted a few years back. I missed Lily, but I really needed to find some friends in the city. In the two weeks I'd been there, I'd only made two, and that was counting the old Jewish man in my building and my landlady.

After finding a new glass of champagne to hold in front of the small stain made by my previous one, I ventured out of my comfortable corner and ambled through the party.

The gala organizers hadn't changed much of the hotel's original Art Deco décor for the evening. Ornate gold sconces and extravagant crown molding surrounded the party from above. Cocktail tables were spread throughout the room with small groups of people crowded around them. I was too intimidated to attempt to join a conversation already taking place, until I spotted a few women I knew from the blogosphere. I'd only met them once, at a small blogger conference, and they hadn't been the nicest women in the world, but a bitch in need is a friend indeed. *Or something like that...*

I was almost upon them, having worked up the nerve to reintroduce myself, when a hand reached out to touch my shoulder. I paused and turned to see a smiling older woman standing behind me. She had a chic gray bob, layers of colorful jewelry, and was clutching the "it" Hermès bag of the season. I had to resist the urge to snatch it and run.

"Excuse me, are you Josephine from *What Jo Wore*? The blog?"

I all but gaped at her, completely stunned that this regal-looking woman would know of my blog and recognize me from my posts.

"I am," I said, putting my hand on my chest before reaching out. "I'm sorry, I don't think we've met?"

She smiled wide and a few lines near her eyes hinted at her age.

"I'm Maxine Belafonte, the U.S. director of operations for House of Herrera."

I laughed.

I laughed because I was too stunned to do anything else. I was two seconds away from asking, "Are you serious?" when I remembered where I was. Of course she was Maxine Belafonte, because this was a dream that I would soon wake up from.

"It's such an honor to meet you," I fumbled quickly, proud of my brain for having acquired appropriate social skills some time during my several years of life.

"Likewise," Maxine said, smiling wide and shaking my hand. "I've been following your blog for several months and I think you have a real eye for fashion."

I stood there holding her hand for an inappropriately long time, then finally spoke.

"I'm sorry. I think my brain just stopped working for a second there. Could you repeat what you just said?"

Maxine laughed, patted my shoulder, and then gently extracted her hand from my death grip.

"I'm serious. I'd love to hear more about your story. Do you have a few minutes to chat?" she asked, gesturing toward a free cocktail table a few feet away from us.

I nodded. "For you, I'm free for the rest of the night."

She smiled. "See! That's why I wanted to meet you. I love your humor. It really comes across in your posts. I think a lot of fashion bloggers tend to take themselves much too seriously. But not you."

I nodded my head, unsure of what to say. After striving all night to just blend in with the herd, this request for individuality caught me off guard.

"How long ago did you start your blog?" she asked as we settled across from each other at the table.

"It's been five years." I inwardly cringed as I thought about her going back to read my very first posts. "But those first few years were rough. I was just starting college at the time."

"NYU?"

"Um, no," I corrected. "A small fashion school in Texas."

She smiled, and I hurried to change the topic away from the fact that my degree wasn't from a prestigious New York fashion school.

"I'm sorry, but may I ask how you even happened upon my blog in the first place?" I asked before taking a small sip of champagne.

She smiled wider, but before she could respond, a pair of dress shoes hit the marbled floor right behind me and I caught the scent of spiced cologne. There was a hint of fresh citrus with a unique blend of cinnamon and geranium. The combination was intoxicating.

"Ah, there you are Maxine," a deep voice said behind me.

Six of the sexiest syllables I'd ever heard gave me no choice but to turn and put a face to the voice. I shifted to look over my shoulder, trying to be as nonchalant as possible, and then openly gaped as I came face to face with the handsome stranger from earlier.

His eyes shifted to me and he nodded, the tip of his mouth lifting in a silent acknowledgment that he recognized me as well.

"Julian! I wasn't sure if you'd make it. I'd assumed things were too hectic with your family right now."

"It was a last minute decision. You know how I like to fly by the seat of my pants."

If I was a provocative temptress from a James Bond movie, I'd have picked up my champagne, held his eye as I took a sip, and then seductively whispered, "Is there room for two on that flight in your pants?" *or y'know, something equally as seductive*. But since I am Josephine, weird-girl-from-the-country, I stayed silent and took another sip of champagne.

Maxine cleared her throat and then held her hand out in introduction.

"Josephine, this is Julian Lefray."

My eyes widened in shock as I fought to keep from choking on my champagne.

Julian Lefray. Julian Lefray, as in the brother to *Lorena Lefray*, the designer I'd submitted a resume to just that afternoon. He was the silent partner of her brand, heir to his family's old-money fortune, and apparently keeper of all my hopes and dreams.

I pulled it together and held out my hand.

"You look nothing like your sister," I noted, trying to reconcile the fact that they were related. Lorena was a lithe, pale woman, all skin and bones. Julian was...the polar opposite: tall and tan, with a captivating smile and those bright, hazel eyes.

"I got more of the Spanish blood," he said as he took my hand. "She took after our mother."

I nodded as I let his strong grip encase my hand. His touch was hard to reconcile, and for a moment, I glanced down at where our hands met, surprised by the connection.

"Do you have a last name Josephine?" he asked as he dropped my hand. I gripped my fist after losing contact with him, trying to maintain the fading warmth in my palm for as long as possible.

"Keller."

"Josephine Keller," he repeated, testing it out on his tongue. "Well, it has been a pleasure." He motioned around the room. "Unfortunately, I have to keep making the rounds."

To his credit, he didn't look too pleased about it, but before I could come up with a reply, he excused himself to greet other party guests. I was left staring out after him, trying to understand how someone could possibly be that gorgeous.

"He's quite a lot to take in, no?" Maxine asked once we were alone again.

I laughed and brushed off her question, careful to keep my silly feelings under wraps.

"So anyway, I believe you were saying something about how awesome my blog is…" I joked, letting the laughter rescue me from the ether of Julian's presence.

It wasn't until I was in the bathroom later, fixing my red lipstick, that I realized my mistake. I'd had Julian Lefray right in front of me and I hadn't even mentioned my desire to work for his sister. He probably didn't have much say in the hiring process, but I'd been a fool not to mention it. *Wasn't this how it worked?* Insider jobs were given to people willing to go the extra mile, to put themselves out there.

I clasped my clutch and evaluated my look. The rented gown had only been available in a size smaller than I normally wore, which meant my chest was a bit more on display than I would have preferred. *Thanks a lot for the boobs, Mom.* I pulled up the strapless bodice and tried in vain to hide a bit of my cleavage. Yeah. Nope. Not happening. They had minds of their own.

I blew out a puff of air, checked that I didn't have any red lipstick staining my teeth, and then finally exited the restroom.

After a few minutes of searching, I finally spotted Julian in the middle of a discussion with a group of men near the bar. They were older, with thick beards and hard lines across their foreheads. They looked like a stock photo of investment firm big wigs, but I couldn't let that stop me. I just needed a moment to speak with Julian.

I subdued my nerves and waltzed up to the group. I inhaled his cologne as I stepped close; it was just as captivating as the first time. He was in the middle of a conversation, but I didn't want to take the chance that I'd lose him again. I ignored the curious stares from the other men in his group and cleared my throat.

"Mr. Lefray, do you have a moment to speak with me?" I asked, reaching up to tap his shoulder.

One of the men stepped forward, sloshing his drink over the brim of his glass.

"I'm available to speak sweetheart, if Julian here is too busy," he said with a leering smile and a roaming gaze that never quite met my eyes.

Chapter Three

Julian

My eyes flicked from Patrick to the younger woman I'd met earlier in the night. She looked stunning in her red gown—a fact I knew the men nearby were all too quick to pick up on as well.

"That won't be necessary, Patrick," I replied.

She shot me a thankful smile.

I nodded and stepped away from the group, gripping her arm just above her elbow. Her arm was slim and toned, and I found it far too easy to lead her away from the group of investors. A moment alone with her would far outweigh another five minutes of suffering the company of old men with older money. I led Josephine toward a private corner of the ballroom, consumed by the subtle scent of gardenia that followed in her wake.

"This won't take long," she promised, her bright green stare meeting mine. A blind man wouldn't have missed the hope poorly hidden behind her faltering smile. My alarm bells rang loud and clear, but I tried to quell them. *Not every girl wants to fuck you, asshole.*

"It's fine. You saved me from another ten minutes of a boring pitch," I replied, slipping my hands into my pockets and doing my best to stare anywhere but her chest. I'm no saint, and she had an unbelievable body. Nothing like the fashion girls I usually saw around Lorena's office. Emaciated seemed to be the desired look as of late, but Josephine had curves.

"Oh crap. You were doing a pitch?" Her eyes widened and then she covered her mouth. "Ignore the fact that I just said crap."

I smiled.

"Twice," she said, uncovering her mouth and seeming to regroup. She rolled her shoulders back and stared up into my eyes. She looked so young, much too young for me.

I laughed. "It's fine."

"This whole event is making me a little nervous to be honest," she offered, glancing up at me from beneath her long lashes. She blushed, a rosy tinge dotting her cheeks— the same blush I'd appreciated outside earlier.

"Is this your first big event?" I asked, tilting my head to the side with a curious smile.

"Is it obvious?" she asked, touching her curled hair self-consciously.

I shook my head. "No. The event coordinators tend to memorize faces after a while, so their guest lists are more of a formality."

She laughed, interpreting my subtle reference to her delayed entrance earlier.

"Well, my face is far from being memorable."

I resisted the urge to insist otherwise.

"Should I get us a drink?" I offered, trying to figure what her game was. Most women were a little more forward, but Josephine seemed to be working up the nerve to ask me something. I thought perhaps I could make it a little easier on her.

She held up her hands to stop me. "No thank you. No drink."

Her gaze drifted to the party as she took a deep breath and then she met my eye with newfound conviction.

"I wanted to speak with you because I'd like a job at Lorena Lefray Designs. I actually submitted my application this afternoon—before I realized you'd be at this event—and I was hoping if I got a chance to speak with you, maybe you could put in a good word for me."

Son of a bitch.

She wanted a job, not a night in my hotel room.

I narrowed my eyes and studied her: delicate features, bee-stung lips. She was practically lethal.

"What position did you apply for?"

Her back straightened as she replied, "Executive assistant. I think it would be for Lorena, but the job description didn't specify."

Of course.

I stared out at the party, trying to regroup for a moment before glancing back to her. This was dangerous territory. The feeling of being near her in public was tempting enough; would I really want her working alongside me every day?

When I glanced back, the glimmer of hope hadn't faded from her eyes. God, she was so young. Couldn't have been a day over twenty-five. Was I willing to dash her dreams just because I found her attractive?

I cleared my throat.

"Actually, the position isn't with Lorena. It's with me. Lorena is ill and I'm stepping in to help with the company for the time being. I'm hiring an assistant to help me for a few weeks."

I was feeding her a lie, but the truth was too personal to explain at the moment. The paparazzi were already hounding Lorena's every move and it was my job to protect her as much as possible.

Josephine's red lips formed a small "o".

"I'm sorry to hear that," she said, nodding and brushing a strand of light brown hair away from her face.

Was she disappointed she wouldn't be working with Lorena? I couldn't tell.

"You can retract your application if you've changed your mind," I offered with a quirked brow.

Her eyes widened and she reached out to touch my forearm. I ignored the desire to wrap my hand around hers.

"No! No. I would still like to be considered for the position," she reiterated. She stared down at her hand on my forearm as if to nail the point home, then quickly pulled it away, clasping it with her other hand in front of her trim waist.

"But now that I have to interview with you this just seems…"

She hesitated and I smiled.

"A bit awkward?"

She laughed. "Well, yes."

I watched her try to collect her thoughts. The light tan

covering her clear complexion made her bright eyes stand out even more. The freckles dotting the tops of her cheeks were a refreshing sight.

I smiled. "Don't worry about it. I can hardly fault someone for showing initiative when opportunity strikes."

"Okay well, um, I hope to hear from you about an interview," she smiled. "But y'know, don't feel like you have to give me one because of tonight, and me now practically begging for it."

I choked back a laugh.

Her eyes widened.

"That didn't sound right, I admit," she laughed and covered her face for a moment.

I wanted to bail her out of the hole she was digging, but it was too damn cute to watch her squirm.

"Let's just ignore the fact that I've made a fool of myself, all right? I'll just walk away and you can pretend that I was very charming and put together."

I bent to catch her eyes and smiled.

"I assure you that there won't be any favoritism during the interviews. I'll evaluate everyone with a clean slate."

She smiled. "Okay good!"

Her gaze darted out to the party and then back to me. "Well, it was a pleasure to meet you, Mr. Lefray, and I really hope your sister gets well soon."

She backed up a step, taking her sweet scent with her.

"I look forward to the possibility of *maybe* hearing from you about the interview," she said coyly.

With that, she nodded and spun on her heels. She was swallowed up by the crowd within a few moments, and it wasn't until she fully disappeared that I realized I'd been watching her walk away, focused on the curve of her hips in her red gown.

Chapter Four

Josephine

An hour after I'd returned to my apartment, I was still wearing my rented designer gown as I browsed Facebook on my computer. My hair had mostly fallen out of my up-do (it was more of an up-don't by that point) and my thrifted Jimmy Choos were lying on the floor beside my coffee table after I'd haphazardly kicked them off when I'd gotten home.

Josephine: I made such a fool of myself tonight.
Lily: Spill. It's probably worse than you think it is.
Josephine: I told my could-be-future-boss that he

didn't have to give me an interview just because
I was "practically begging for it".

Lily: So...you came onto him. Bold move,
Casanova.

I thought back to the way Julian had tried to conceal his laughter. It hadn't worked. His dimples were there, the smile was there, and I knew he'd caught the unintentional innuendo.

Josephine: Oh god. I don't want to talk about it anymore. I'm going to bed.

I went through my nighttime routine, finally peeling off the red gown in exchange for a soft nightshirt. I kept my makeup on as I brushed my teeth, admiring the way the Nordstrom counter girl had applied my eye shadow earlier in the night. The gold tones made my green eyes pop and it was a pity to have to wipe it off.

Once I'd checked that my one tiny window was locked and my apartment door was double bolted, I sauntered over to my bed and pulled my phone from where I'd set it to charge. I already knew there were two voicemails waiting for me. I'd ignored the calls earlier in the day, praying they'd both disappear by the time I got around to checking them.

Unfortunately, they were both still there waiting for me.

The first message was from Janine, my loan adviser and least favorite person in the world. I pressed play and stared up at my ceiling.

"Hello Ms. Keller, this is Janine Buchanan from Forest Financial. I'm calling because we didn't receive your student loan payment last month. This is the second month in a row that we've had a late payment from you and I want to remind you that one more missed payment means you risk defaulting. Also, please be advised that after a third late payment we will have no choice but to hire a collection agency and notify the credit bureau—"

I hung up. Ms. Buchanan wasn't telling me anything I hadn't heard before. Yes, my payments were late, yes I was dangerously close to defaulting on my loan, but unless I could start paying them back with Monopoly money, I was shit out of luck. I could either pay rent or pay my loans, and being homeless in NYC wasn't cute.

My phone automatically started playing the second voicemail message, and as terrible as Janine's had been, that one was far worse.

"Josephine, this is your mother." *As if I wouldn't recognize her voice.* "Listen, I know you aren't going to take this well but I just have to tell you one more time. It's my job as a mother to make sure you're making good decisions and I can't help but feel like you're headed down the wrong path. Your father and I have talked and we think you should come back home to Texas. You've only been in New York for two weeks. No one will even have to know that you left. We'll help with your loans and you can get a job in town. I'm not sure what you could do with that fashion degree of yours, but we'll figure it out. I was talking to Beatrice when I was shopping and she said her sister is the manager at the TJ Maxx—"

I pressed end on the message before it was over and dropped my phone onto my bed. Throughout high school, I'd overheard hushed conversations between my parents that often followed the same pattern: my dad would worry that I was being bullied at school for the way I dressed, then my mom would do her best to settle his nerves, but nothing helped. "Why can't she just be like the other girls?" might not have ever been said aloud, but it was the undertone of most of my adolescent years.

My parents had a way of cowing me so easily, so swiftly, that for a moment I almost considered moving home. How easy would it be to live with them and have them help me with my loans? How easy would it be to give up on living my dream in New York City for a quiet life in Dullsville, Texas? Sure, I'd managed to find a tiny apartment, but how long would I be able to afford the rent? How long could I pretend that anything was going according to plan?

I let the nagging self-doubt sink in. If my parents didn't believe I could make it, then how could I believe in myself? After all, New York wasn't for everyone. Right?

But then I remembered Julian and the promise of a job interview and I decided that first thing in the morning I was going to march down to the Lorena Lefray offices and demand an interview.

I had nothing to lose, and I knew no one needed the position as badly as I did.

Chapter Five

Julian

As soon as I returned from the gala, I ripped off my bowtie and tuxedo jacket and threw them on the desk beside my computer. My hotel room was dark, but I didn't bother flipping on any lights. I was thirty floors up and there was enough light seeping in from the city that I could see just fine.

I fixed a drink from the mini bar and settled in by the window, staring down at Central Park. I'd hated hotel rooms for years. I'd had to travel a lot in my twenties, helping to expand the Lefray family companies to the global scale they now enjoyed. At thirty-one, all I wanted was to be back home in Boston in the bed I'd picked out and far, far away from the realities I now faced.

The week before, my baby sister had finally entered herself into a rehab facility after years of trying to fight her addictions alone. It was a bold move, one that the media were already suspicious of, but if she had any desire to see her thirtieth birthday, it was the only option she had. I'd promised her I would step in and keep the ship on course for the time being. She had detailed plans to overhaul the entire place, to get rid of the toxic employees and the clock-punching deadbeats while she had the strength to do it. That was where I came in. Unfortunately, that meant I was in New York, holed up in the penthouse suite of some hotel, alone and tired. I loved the power and responsibility, but I resented the monotony of corporate politics. It reminded me too much of my family.

My father died young in a car crash, and neither my sister nor I trusted my mother with the responsibilities of running Lorena's company, which conveniently left everything on my shoulders.

I took a sip of my drink and mulled over the list of people I still knew in the city other than my family.

There was Dean, an old college buddy who'd settled down in New York after school, but I couldn't call him at midnight just to announce that I was back in the city for the foreseeable future. I made a mental note to give him a call the next day just as my computer dinged with an incoming email.

I turned toward my desk and contemplated waking it up. Opening my laptop at midnight was a slippery slope—as with any workaholic—but I was far past the point of pretending I had any work-life balance. Answering emails helped me put my world in order, and if anything, I'd sleep easier knowing I had everything prepared to begin work the following morning.

I pulled out the chair from behind the hotel desk and took a seat. I had twenty-two unopened emails, most of which were filled with resumes and cover letters pertaining to the executive assistant position I'd posted around the web earlier that day. I'd posted on the Columbia and NYU alumni pages and I knew I'd have a number of applicants more than interested in the job.

An image of Josephine flitted through my mind. I'd promised her that all the applicants would be judged fairly, but the memory of how she'd looked in that red dress would be impossible to forget. Even still, I knew how to conduct a professional interview. Just because she was beautiful didn't mean she was the person most suited for the job. If anything, it'd make my life a lot easier if she wasn't a qualified applicant.

Curiosity won out.

I scrolled down the list of emails until I found one sent from JBKeller@gmail.com. She'd sent her resume about an hour after I'd first posted about the job.

I scanned her resume, attempting to stay as impartial as possible. She'd done her undergrad at a small fashion school in Texas with a focus on fashion marketing and branding. She'd interned for a few local fashion brands while in school and had started a blog a few years before blogging had really caught on everywhere. I clicked the link to her site and smiled at the name. *What Jo Wore* was a simple website. It was user-friendly with a clean layout and professional graphics.

My interest was piqued as I scrolled down and realized her last post had been about the gala.

What Jo Wore

Post #1248: You'll never get anywhere by staying in your comfort zone.
Comments: 34   Likes: 309

Tonight, ladies and lads, I will be attending the New York Fashion Gala. That's right, little ol' Josephine Keller from way down yonder in Texas (that's the wild wild West for those of you who've never ventured past Fifth Avenue) will be rubbing elbows with New York's elite. I rented a gown from renttherunway.com. I highly recommend using this site if you're someone like me and have designer tastes on a beggar's budget.

I promise to give you all the juicy details about the event as soon as I wake up tomorrow, but in the meantime, here are the top three trends I'm seeing around New York as of late:

- Chunky overalls. I'm serious, people. Moms everywhere are pairing them with white converse and Berkin Bags. I've linked a few pairs below. **BEWARE**: as with all 'kitschy' trends, this can go south, fast. Be sure you aren't pairing your overalls with any of the following: chunky tennis shoes, baggy t-shirts, or—god forbid—a fanny pack.
- Bright lip stains. (I'm wearing <u>this</u> red shade tonight. It's a little bold, but I want to stand out.)
- Big, loud statement necklaces. Pair 'em with

a jersey dress or layer them over a J. Crew tee. These necklaces will be trending for multiple seasons, I guarantee it.

All right, I have to go get ready for the gala! I'm already nervous, but I'm going to think back to the title of this blog post every time I feel like giving up: you'll never get anywhere by staying in your comfort zone!!!

Until tomorrow,
XOJO

I was impressed enough by her wit to browse through a few more pages of her archived posts. Her writing was approachable and real. Most of the women who worked in New York fashion would never admit to thrift shopping, but Josephine had a freshness about her that her readers seemed to appreciate and connect with.

After scrolling through a few pages, I clicked back to my email and attempted to run through a few more resumes. There were plenty of well-qualified applicants, lots of graduates from Parsons and FIT. There were applicants who had interned with Tommy Hilfiger and other top brands, but as I finished off my drink, I was still thinking of Josephine. She had hardly half the work experience of some of the other applicants, but I found myself already imagining her in the position. She and I could work well together. She'd make me laugh. Wasn't that important? And sure, maybe I was also craving another glimpse of those lips. *Every man has his weakness.*

Before closing down my computer for the night, I

opened a new email window and started typing away before common sense set in.

Subject: Interview Request from Julian Lefray

Chapter Six

Josephine

I woke up bright and early the morning after the gala, ready with a full cup of coffee and chock-full of false optimism. I was planning on checking my emails, finding my most businesslike outfit, and then waltzing down to Lorena's office for an interview. The fact that I had no clue where her offices were seemed like a negligible detail.

Unfortunately, my go-get-em attitude wasn't needed. The first email, sitting right at the very top of my neglected inbox, was from Mr. Fuck-Me himself. *Er, I mean, Julian Lefray.* It had been sent at 1:14 AM, which immediately made me wonder if he'd been up late thinking of me, but I knew better. *Nope. No. Don't go there*. You need a job and he's looking for a new assistant. Nothing more, nothing less. Ignore the tall, dark, and handsome vibe. Book boyfriends exist for a reason.

Julian needed an assistant, and while being organized wasn't exactly my forte, I needed this job badly enough to pretend it was. One look at the mountain of bills sitting on my kitchen-turned-bathroom counter drove that point home.

I immediately replied to his email with my availability, and then dragged my laptop right back to bed to type up my next blog post.

What Jo Wore

Post #1250: Job Interview Attire (Or how I pretend to be much more professional than I actually am...)
Comments: 55   Likes: 513

Tomorrow I have a super important job interview. I know, YIKES. Send some positive vibes my way!

You guys are always asking me to do posts about workday attire, so I thought I would share three of my favorite interview outfits with you all. Most of the items are thrifted or from a few seasons ago, but I've linked to the few items you can still find around the web.

Also, disclaimer: I snapped these photos using a timer on my camera so please excuse the poor composition. I've yet to find someone to help me with photographs in New York. I used to bribe my best friend Lily to take my photos back in Texas. Let's hope for y'all's sake I find someone soon! For now, just squint and pretend these are awesome photos!

Until tomorrow,
XOJO

• • •

The day of my interview, I woke up extra early and slipped into a pair of fitted navy slacks and a cream long-sleeved blouse. The day before, I'd researched Lorena's company while watching a marathon of murder mystery shows. Sure, I was now highly paranoid about getting kidnapped, but at least I felt prepared for my interview.

Julian wanted me to meet him at Blacksmith Coffee at 9:00 AM, sharp. Once again, I tried not to read too much into his choice of venue. Late night emails, coffee shop interviews...sure, most interviews were conducted in a boardroom with stuffy, boring businessmen, but maybe Julian liked to stretch his legs.

I was nearing the coffee shop, giving myself an internal pep talk, when my phone buzzed in my hand.

Lily: Good luck with your coffee date. Oh, I'm sorry, "interview". ;)

Josephine: STOP. Seriously. There is no hanky panky happening. I'm a professional career woman.

Lily: I looked him up last night per your email... Y'know, maybe you should have mentioned the fact that he is a 10/10 on "Josephine's hot guy scale"?

Was he?

Josephine: I hadn't noticed.
Lily: I'm so calling bullshit on that.
Josephine: Lalalala. Can't hear you over the sound of my future calling. Oh, and it's Vogue. I better take it.
Lily: You are so lame.

I pocketed my phone, pushed my shoulders back, and held my head high as I pulled open the door to the coffee shop. I couldn't let Lily get into my head. I needed to get into business mode. *I am Josephine, hear me roar.*

The scent of roasting coffee overwhelmed me as I stepped into the shop. It was a small, intimate space. One wall had been left with exposed red brick and another was covered in shiplap wood. Mercury glass chandeliers hung overhead and two antique green velvet couches sat at the front of the shop for people to sit and wait for their coffee.

I kept walking, past the start of the coffee line, scanning the room for Julian. There was a small, secluded room in the back and when I stepped past the central brick archway, I spotted Julian at a table against the wall. My stomach dipped at the sight of him. He was dressed down compared to the tuxedo he'd worn for the gala, sporting a crisp white shirt, sans tie. The top button was undone and he'd rolled the sleeves to his elbows. He adjusted on his chair and reached down to smooth the thigh of his charcoal gray pants. I studied his hand and its placement on his thigh before he glanced up at the girl in front of me who was bee-lining for his table.

She giggled as she sat, saying something annoyingly cute, I'm sure. I was fifteen minutes early for our scheduled appointment and it appeared he wasn't yet done with the interview before mine.

Why did that bother me so much?

I turned to move away, feeling like a weird voyeur just standing there and watching them, when Julian held up his hand.

"Just give us ten more minutes, Josephine," he said with an apologetic smile.

Oh god, he saw me standing here.

I forced a polite nod and moved to join the coffee line. The entire time I waited for my vanilla latte I wondered just how much Julian could get away with when he used that apologetic smile of his. Those deep-set dimples. The genuine look in his hazel eyes. The man probably hadn't heard the word "no" since he was five years old.

By the time I had my drink in hand, the seat across from Julian was empty and I made my way over. *Was the girl before me qualified for the position? More qualified than me?* Julian was typing away on his iPhone as I approached, but when he caught me out of the corner of his eye, he pocketed his phone and stood to pull out my chair for me.

"Why, thank you," I joked.

He smiled.

"Sorry that interview ran a little overtime. I hope you weren't waiting long," he said, bending forward so that I could hear him over the background noise of the coffee shop.

My body was interpreting the entire situation wrong. The way he'd pulled my chair out and leaned in close so that we were only a small table away from each other. The way he scanned over my features before taking a sip of his coffee. My heart thought, "Wow this date is going well!" while my brain screamed at me to remember that this was a job interview.

"I'll admit, I sort of thought I'd be the only applicant meeting you here today," I said, unsure of where the honesty was coming from.

"Why would you think that?" he asked with a bemused smile.

I shrugged, glancing at the table beside us while I processed my answer. "I guess because this seems like kind of a strange place to conduct interviews."

Julian frowned, scanning over the shop. "Ah, I admit, that's my fault. Lorena was operating her business out of a dilapidated warehouse in Brooklyn. I had to decide whether to have you all drive out there and risk getting tetanus from a stray nail or line you all up outside of my hotel room."

An image of him in his hotel room, sans suit, instantly jumped to the front of my thoughts. I pushed it aside and tried to ignore the hint of blush I knew was now very prominent across my cheeks.

"Well, for the record, my tetanus shot is current," I said with a smile, still attempting to quell naked Julian thoughts.

He laughed and I took the opportunity to pull out my resume and slide it over to him.

"I read a few of your blog posts last night," he offered before leaning back in his chair and studying me, completely ignoring my resume.

"Really?" I asked, shocked by his admission.

He nodded. "They were charming. Very real. I liked them."

I don't think my eyes could have been any wider.

"Wow." I nodded, tucking his words away in my mind so I could extract them later when I needed a little pick-me-up. "Thank you."

"Do you think your blogging would get in the way of this job?"

What?

"Oh. No! No. I write my posts at night and take my outfit photos on Saturday mornings. I'm very flexible."

He nodded, seemingly pleased by my answer.

"Tell me a little bit about your background."

I smiled. I loved talking about my home. Growing up in a small town in Texas made for quite a few interesting stories. I decided to leave out the cow tipping and bonfires in favor of my family life and college years.

"I loved it, but as soon as I could, I moved here."

"So you came to New York a few years ago?"

My hands twisted together beneath the table. "Uhh, actually it's been about two weeks."

"Wow, so the move is still fresh," he said.

"Very fresh," I admitted. I was still learning how to handle the big city. As soon as I thought I'd seen it all, I'd step off the subway and in the span of three blocks I'd see a couple fighting, breaking up, and then getting engaged. On any given day, half of the subway cars smelled like urine, and attempting to get anywhere on time was nearly impossible. It was stressful to live in the city and I still hadn't found my niche, but I had dreams. One day when I'd paid off my massive pile of student loans and was working for Vogue, I'd move to the Upper East Side and get to experience the city in a whole new light.

"So you studied at a fashion school in Texas?"

He was doing his best to withhold judgment, but I could tell he was less than impressed by my lack of experience.

"I assure you, I had a great education there. Very hands on classes and I interned with Kendra Scott while in school.

She's a Texas based jewelry—"

"I know who she is," Julian interjected, scanning down to my resume.

"I might not be as qualified as some of the other applicants, but what I lack in experience, I make up for in commitment and work ethic."

He studied me intently as I spoke and something in his gaze forced me to glance down at my coffee to regroup. Having his attention on me, his eyes on me, was hard to stomach. It felt like a rare treat, something not every woman was fortunate enough to experience in her lifetime. I wanted to savor his attention while I had it.

"I'd like to offer you the position."

My gaze shot back up to him to see if he was kidding. The dimples were there, but the smile was gone. His eyes were bright and clear. His sharp features were relaxed and focused. He wasn't kidding.

How many people had he interviewed before me? Two? Three, tops?

My mouth opened but it took a few seconds before words finally spilled out. "You're offering me the job right now? What if someone better comes along this afternoon?"

SHUT IT. He's giving you the position.

"My gut says to go with you and it's yet to fail me." He smiled, brushing off my concerns so easily.

Well that's because your gut is probably made up of rock hard abs; they wouldn't fail anyone.

"I have one condition," I said.

His brow arched.

"I think I could use my skills as a blogger to rejuvenate your brand's image. For the last few years, Lorena has been focused solely on her designs, not the branding side of things. She's not utilizing social media like other fashion brands. I mean Rachel Zoe and Diane Von Furstenberg have camera crews following them around 24/7 for reality TV. We need to get Lorena Lefray out there in the public eye."

"And you think you can help with that?"

I straightened my back. "I have a pretty large following on YouTube and Twitter. I know I can do it."

"Excuse me," a sweet voice said from behind me. I twisted in my chair to see a woman about my age, standing with a padfolio clutched in her arms. She was pretty, angelic really.

"Are you almost done?" she asked, flitting her gaze between the two of us. "I don't mean to be rude. It's just that the other interviews only lasted about five minutes and I have to run back across town for an appointment in fifteen—"

Julian waved his hand, silencing her and standing at the same time. He reached for his suit jacket and looked out toward the other few applicants who'd gathered in the room without my notice.

"I think we're all done here." He paused and glanced my way. "That is, if you're ready to accept?"

I had two seconds to make a decision. Two seconds of staring into Julian Lefray's fuck-me eyes and deciding if I wanted a job where I could stare at him all day, every day.

Easiest decision of my life.

I nodded and stood to shake his hand. "I accept."

I tried to conceal my megawatt smile as his warm hand engulfed mine once again.

He nodded and glanced back to the small group of applicants. "Thank you all for coming today, but the position has been filled."

I smiled.

Now if only he could fill something else...
And so the sexual fantasies begin. Lovely.

Chapter Seven

Julian

"I think they're trying to poison me here."

What?

I glanced over at Lorena to see if she was serious. My sister, the eccentric artist of the family, sat up in her bed and crossed her arms. She pointedly stared at the food in front of her. It looked decent enough to me, albeit a little bland.

"Relax, Lorena. You're in the top rehab facility on the east coast, not with Nurse Ratchet."

She sneered.

"Well it feels like I'm in the loony bin. Look at this

stuff! It looks like lettuce with a bad perm!"

I rolled my eyes. "That's kale, Lorena."

She waved me off as if I wasn't making any sense.

"I can't fit into any of my old clothes either," she said, redirecting her glare to the overflowing closet, grimacing at the piled garments she hadn't cared to hang up after trying them on.

"That's a good thing," I assured her. "You were way too skinny before. A little bit of added weight means you're getting healthy."

For a long time my family never spoke of Lorena's drug problem. The hints and warning signs were dust to be swept under the rug, along with the other skeletons that my mother believed should be kept locked away in the closet. Lorena would have probably sought help years earlier if only she could have spoken up about her problems.

"I brought you something," I said, reaching for the brown bag behind my chair.

Her hazel eyes lit up and I knew I'd done the right thing by bringing her a gift.

She made grabby hands as I handed over the large bag. She ripped it open without hesitation and pulled out the large black frame I'd picked up on my way over.

There were three photos framed side by side. One photo was of the two of us when we were little, all big teeth and dirty faces. The second photo was of the two of us the year before at Christmas. The third was a photo of our father and us before he'd died. I'd purposely picked photos that didn't include our mother.

"Aw, I love it!" she said, holding it out in front of her for a better view.

I took in the sight of her for a moment. She'd been in rehab less than a week and she already looked better than she had in years. Her cheeks were flushed with a healthy glow and she'd started to put a little meat on her bones.

I promised her I'd hang the frame on her wall before I left, knowing it would add some personality to her room. Each "guest" at The White Dunes had their own small room. It was the most expensive rehab facility on Long Island, but even her lavish room still looked like a sterile cell, and I knew that to Lorena, it felt like one as well. The walls were white. The linens were white. The desk, doors, and dresser, all white. The colorless aesthetic was not her style, and I intended on helping her decorate as much as I could.

"Now enough stalling, how's my company?" she asked, dropping the frame on her lap and staring at me with expectant eyes.

"I'm in the process of cleaning house," I declared, cutting through the bullshit. For the last year, she'd done everything in her power to run her company into the ground. If there was any hope for revitalization, it needed a major overhaul, beginning with the staff.

"Geoff? What about Gina?" she asked with hope in her eyes.

"Everyone will be replaced."

I had zero remorse for the employees I'd already let go. There were only a handful of them, all under qualified, all enablers of Lorena's drug addiction. Their expulsion from the company had been a long time coming and she knew it.

Lorena rolled her eyes and went to work twisting her hair into a knot on top of her head. She'd taken the brown hair we shared and bleached it a pale blonde, verging on white, a few months back. Her roots were showing now that she was stuck in "rehab hell", but I knew she'd color it back as soon as she could.

"And my space in Brooklyn? Are you planning on dumping that as well?"

I frowned, unsure of how honest she wanted me to be. I had plans to overhaul her entire company, to get rid of the employees and slim down on expenses. I'd wanted to step in years ago, but it was Lorena's baby, and I respected her need to make decisions on her own. At the same time, I owned 49% of the company and that 49% was about to be worth nothing if something drastic wasn't done.

"The Brooklyn warehouse is still under lease for the next two months, but I'd like to move the company to a space in Manhattan."

She groaned, but I pushed on.

"While I'm running the company, I'm not commuting out to Brooklyn every morning. I'll find a space in Manhattan and set up shop there."

"And you're the only employee right now? Just great." She threw her hands in the air in defeat.

"No, actually. I hired someone just this morning."

She slid her gaze to me, curiosity and skepticism fighting for control over her features.

"And who, pray tell, did you hire to help run MY company? Some idiot straight out of fashion school? So help me god if they think they can come in and take over my designs—"

"Relax. I hired someone you'd like. Her name is Josephine Keller—"

"Wait. Josephine from *What Jo Wore*?"

"You know her?"

Lorena nodded. "I don't live under a rock. She's that pretty blogger chick from Texas, right?"

I hesitated before nodding and then told myself I was only confirming that she was from Texas, not that she was pretty, though she was. Gorgeous even, but I shook the thought away.

"She'll be my assistant, but she'll also help me with the branding and marketing side of things."

"Where will the two of you work while you look for a new place?" she asked.

I swallowed before answering. "My hotel."

Lorena nodded with an arched brow. "Interesting. I mean, convenient."

"What?" I asked.

"Nothing." She shook her head. "Do you have any office spaces for me to take a look at yet?"

"I'm meeting with a realtor tomorrow morning. I'll bring over information about the prospective properties after that."

"Assuming I'm still alive tomorrow." Lorena frowned just as a knock sounded from her door.

A moment later, a "recovery and wellness concierge" popped her head in and smiled. "The group activity is starting in the main room in fifteen minutes. We'll be screening *Sixteen Candles* while lighting sixteen lamps filled with different aromatherapy oils."

She smiled and closed the door after her announcement and Lorena's eyes widened in horror. "Do you see what I mean? They're poisoning me with cheesy 80s movies and yucky lettuce."

I laughed and stood to leave. My baby sister had made her bed of kale, and now she had to lie in it.

Chapter Eight

Josephine

I'd just finished shoving the last bite of a donut in my mouth when my phone buzzed in my hand. I wiped the chocolate icing from my mouth and discarded the donut box in the trash. I took extra care to get rid of all the evidence of the sweet doughy deliciousness because that's how denial works. No proof, no calories. Ha!

After I wiped my hands, I swiped my finger across the screen and answered the call.

"Hello?" Yeah, my mouth was still pretty full. *Attractive, I know.*

"Josephine?"

The deep voice sent a slight shiver down my spine. I swallowed slowly.

"Julian?" I asked, pulling the phone away from my cheek to check the number. I didn't recognize the area code.

"Yes. Sorry to call you so early. I just wanted to let you know that we won't be meeting at my hotel like we originally planned."

"Oh."

I sounded sad. Why did I sound sad? Had I been looking forward to seeing the inside of Julian's hotel room? Had I wanted some alone time with him?

"Is that all right?" he asked, sounding worried.

"Oh! Yeah. Of course. Where are we meeting instead?"

"My realtor has lined up a few properties for us to take a look at. I'll text you the first address after we hang up."

"Okay, cool. I love looking at real estate."

He laughed. "Really?"

"Yep."

"I can't tell if you're kidding."

I laughed. "I'm borderline addicted to HGTV. It's not healthy."

"Ah, I see. Well, we'll be going into some unfinished job sites, so make sure you wear closed-toe shoes."

"Oh, don't worry. I'll dress the part," I quipped.

"Are you getting ready as we talk? I'm already on my way to the first address."

Oh crap. "Let me go so I can map it."

"All right. Good luck."

I dropped my phone and scrambled to finish getting ready. Last night Julian had emailed me a few details about my first day on the job. I'd planned on meeting him at his hotel—where we'd be working until we found a space to rent in Manhattan—but if we were going to be running around town all day, I needed to change my shoes. My feet would be screaming by the second listing.

I slid into some black leather flats and peeked at the mirror before dashing out the door. A stray chocolate sprinkle was lurking in the corner of my mouth from the donut I had allegedly eaten a minute before. I wiped it away and reassessed my makeup. *Not bad. Not bad at all.*

It was warming up nicely in New York City, but there was still a morning chill lingering in the air, so I walked to the first listing instead of taking the subway.

Julian was standing near the entrance of the building, chatting with a short, balding man in a three-piece suit. The man had on a blue paisley tie that coordinated with his pocket square and a Bluetooth thing sticking out of his right ear. *Ah, he was definitely the realtor.*

"Josephine," Julian said with a smile as I approached.

I scanned over his outfit quickly, pushing away the swell of lust that accompanied the sight of him. Black slacks—not cute. White button-down—not cute. Fitted black jacket—ew. Who thinks defined arms and a broad chest are attractive? No one.

He reached forward and gripped my arm just above my elbow as he leaned in to kiss my cheek. JESUS CHRIST. He smelled divine, like he'd spent the morning in the woods building me a log cabin. I hated him.

When he pulled back after our kiss, he kept his hand on my arm and introduced me to Sergio, our realtor. Taking it as a cue, Sergio leaned in to kiss my other cheek. I flinched, and my nose knocked his earpiece to the ground.

"Oh, I'm so sorry, let me get that!" I sang, trying to allay the awkwardness.

I bent to grab it before either of them could get it, then

handed it to Sergio with an apologetic smile.

"Let me just grab the key from the lockbox and then we'll head inside," Sergio explained.

I nodded and wet my lips, trying hard to work up the nerve to glance at Julian. I'd felt so confident during our phone call, but in person my courage dwindled away as if it'd never been there at all.

"No overalls? I'm a little disappointed," Julian quipped as he turned toward me.

I laughed and glanced down at my outfit. *He read that blog post!*

"I figured overalls were more of a second-day-on-the-job kind of look," I said with a smile.

Julian laughed. "What's a third-day-on-the-job look then?"

"Jorts."

He laughed, but furrowed his brows. "Jorts?"

My smile fell. "Oh c'mon. You don't know what jorts are?"

He shook his head with a bemused expression.

"They're cut-off jeans, made into shorts." I made a cutting motion across my thigh. "Mostly worn by hipsters with handlebar mustaches."

"I guess I'll see them on Wednesday," he laughed.

"Got it!" Sergio explained, motioning us forward and sweeping the door open with enough razzle-dazzle to give Vanna White a run for her money.

And so began our tour of really crappy New York real estate. Julian and I quickly learned the lay of the land. Any spot worth renting cost enough to purchase a small island in the Mediterranean, and if the property was priced reasonably, well, there was a reason. Rats, poor plumbing, no windows—the list went on and on. By the time we were walking through the sixth listing, we'd both all but given up hope of finding something quickly.

We were touring the final property of the day, an apartment that was listed on the market as a commercial office space, but it didn't look any better than the previous listings. The entire apartment couldn't have been more than 400 square feet total, and the floor plan was incredibly odd. Right when we walked in, we were led into a small room with three chairs lining the walls. An ornate black chandelier hung from the ceiling, but there was no artwork on the wall. It looked like a stark waiting room of sorts.

"Is the space vacant?" I asked the realtor.

"No. Their lease is up in two weeks and the landlord wants to get a new tenant in right away."

I nodded and continued into the space, skeptical of what we'd find. There was a once-functioning kitchen to the left, and off to the side there were two small doors that branched off the main hallway.

"How could someone classify this as a commercial space?" Julian asked, following after me. He seemed just as disappointed as I was.

I stepped toward the first door and turned the knob so I could peer inside. The room was small and dark, no larger than a walk-in closet. Yikes.

"We could each take a closet and pretend they're actual offices," I joked.

Julian came to stand behind me so that he could see into the space. I stepped forward to turn on the light, but it was out of my reach. Even still, I could tell that the walls were covered in a dark crimson wallpaper with a damask print. First the black chandelier, now red wallpaper? Had I just stepped into Dracula's lair?

"No, clearly this will be the employee break room," he

added dryly. "I think the lack of windows is a real plus."

I smiled and took another step inside the closet, curious about what the tenant used the space for. Surely it wasn't someone's office, right? As my eyes adjusted to the lack of light, I saw that directly across from me there were built in bars running horizontally across the walls. They looked like they'd be used as clothing racks, but they were at odd heights, a foot too tall for most people to reach. Then I saw that in the center of the space, near the back wall, there was a pole that ran from the ceiling to floor. It almost looked like a fireman's pole, but that didn't make sense…

And then it hit me.

Holy shit.

I scanned the space and realized all my fears had come true. Sitting on the floor near the base of the stripper pole were a couple of unused condoms and a stray pair of handcuffs, leather and all.

"Julian."

"Is that a stripper pole?" he asked, taking a step closer. Poor, naive man.

"I think we're standing inside a sex dungeon," I said.

He barked out a laugh and took another step inside.

"How would you know what that looks like?" he asked as he stepped up behind me and pressed his hand to my lower back, trying to get a better look at the space.

I blushed, though he couldn't see it. "I've read about these things."

I turned to see his brow quirked with interest as his hazel eyes met mine in the darkness.

"For purely scientific reasons, of course," I said, holding up my hands.

"Oh, I'm sure," he nodded with sarcastic reassurance. "Why do you think we're in a sex dungeon? Because of that pole?"

I pointed toward the pile of forgotten items on the ground. He stepped closer in the darkness to get a better look and then I heard an audible squelch, followed by Julian momentarily losing his footing. I squeezed my eyes closed to keep my composure though I knew I was seconds away from full-on hysterics.

"What the?" he asked.

He lifted his foot and glanced down.

"Julian, I'm pretty sure you just stepped on anal beads."

Chapter Nine

Julian

"Wait. Wait. Wait. You're telling me that you spent the day touring sex dungeons while the rest of us punched the clock?"

Dean groaned as he waved the cocktail waitress back over toward us.

"Can I help you?" she crooned, eyeing Dean with blatant interest.

"Yeah." Dean pointed toward me and I watched the waitress stare back and forth between us, unsure of where she wanted to focus. "This bastard here would like to buy me another beer," he said, throwing his hand onto my shoulder and squeezing hard.

I rolled my eyes but nodded for her to go ahead with the order.

After a few days of playing phone tag, Dean and I had finally managed to meet up for drinks at the lounge on the first floor of my hotel. I hadn't seen him in years, not since an old college friend's wedding, so the least I could do was buy him another beer.

"So any girl in your life? Anyone you can take to the sex dungeon you discovered?" Dean asked with a cheeky smile.

I thought of how much work had dominated my time lately—and then out of nowhere, Josephine popped into my thoughts. I shook my head clear of the memory of her standing in the dark closet, of her laughter as we fled from the apartment as quickly as we could.

I realized Dean was still waiting for an answer.

"Nah, I left them behind in Boston," I said with a shrug.

A basketball game was playing behind Dean's head and I snuck a quick glance at the score before meeting his eyes. His skeptical glance told me he didn't believe my answer.

"Julian fucking Lefray doesn't have a girl following him around like a horny puppy?" Dean asked, clutching his hand to his chest like he was having a heart attack. "What has the world come to?"

I smiled. "Times have changed."

He smiled smugly but didn't challenge my declaration.

"What about you? How's business?" I asked, hoping to steer the conversation as far away from me as possible.

At thirty-two, Dean Harper was a well-known restaurateur in New York City. He'd already opened five successful restaurants, one of which—a burger joint—had turned into a franchise that spanned from Brooklyn to the Upper West Side. He had a gift when it came to creating unique dining experiences. Food was his forte and I knew he was probably hard at work on his next project.

"Business is good," he nodded. "I have a soft opening for Provisions this weekend."

"Already? I swear I remember you talking about the idea for that place just last week," I said.

He smirked—a classic Dean move—and then reclined back in his seat. "Yeah well, the restaurant world moves fast. Seems like as soon as I start working on a project another idea pops up in its place."

Our waitress returned with our drinks and she bent to hand us each a cold brew. "Can I get you boys anything else?" she asked with a little wink at Dean.

I laughed.

"We're all set," I said, saving myself from having to watch Dean flirt with her for the next half hour. He threw her a smile as she walked off and I took the chance to watch another few seconds of the basketball game.

"Anyway," Dean said, ruffling his blond hair. "This new place is awesome. We tried to make it a little oasis in the heart of the city. There's a courtyard in the center with a grove of trees. It'll be where most of the action takes place."

"Let me guess what the waitstaff will wear," I chimed in.

He smiled. "We're in New York, my friend. Skin sells."

"You know what else sells?" I said, narrowing my eyes. "Good food."

Dean laughed. "Why not both?"

I laughed and took another swig of my drink. We watched the last few minutes of the basketball game as we finished our beers. Dean talked my ear off about his new restaurant and I did my best not to think of Josephine.

"I hate to cut the night short but I've got to get up for work in the morning," I said, finishing off my beer with a long drag.

"Are you serious?" Dean protested. "You work for yourself dude, c'mon. Have one more drink. No one will notice if you're late in the morning."

I smiled. "Actually they will."

"What? You already hired an employee?"

I shrugged, trying to downplay the situation. "Two days ago."

"Where'd you find him?"

I decided not to correct his pronoun choice.

"On the web."

"He wasn't a friend of Lorena's or something?" he asked.

Why the hell did he care about my employee? I kept my focus on the TV and gave him the shortest possible answer.

"No. She doesn't know Lorena."

"*She?*"

I held my hands up in defense. "It's the fashion industry, what do you expect? Most of the applicants were women."

Dean sank back in his chair with a shit-eating grin. "I guess I know the real answer to that question from earlier."

"What?" I stared at him. "What question?"

"Who the almighty Lefray is le-fucking."

"She's my employee!" I argued. "I hardly know her."

"What'd she wear to work today? What color eyes does she have? How many times have you stared at her ass?"

I ignored his questions, threw some cash down on the table to cover our tab, and walked toward the entrance.

"See you at my opening this weekend," Dean yelled. "Oh and be sure to invite the girl you *aren't* sleeping with!

I still need a date!"

I flipped him the bird as I walked out of the bar.

Chapter Ten

Josephine

After our day of looking at lackluster properties, Julian and I decided that we should take a day to reconvene and get some work done from his hotel room. Working with him in his private space was a strange setup to say the least, and when I knocked on his door on Wednesday morning, I tried to quiet the swell of butterflies in my stomach.

He's not inviting you up for an early morning romp in his bed.

This is work.

I shifted on my heels, waiting for the inevitable turn of the door handle, but my knock went unanswered. I leaned forward and pressed my ear to the door, listening for any sounds of life. Nothing.

I hummed and turned in a circle, trying to figure out if maybe I'd knocked on the wrong door. A quick glance at my phone confirmed that I was at the right room number, so I knocked again and waited.

Still, no one answered.

I was debating whether or not to head back down to the lobby when a cleaning woman turned the corner, pushing her cart of supplies in front of her. She was humming along to the music playing from her headphones and nodding her head back and forth. Her dark brown hair had touches of gray springing up around her temple and her uniform stretched across her hips as she walked.

When she looked up and saw me standing there, she paused and narrowed her eyes. Her gaze slid from my head to my feet and then she shook her head and kept on pushing her cart toward me.

"Mhhmm." She tsked as she approached me. "These hoochies think they're gonna catch them a rich man by fishin' in hotel rooms. Shoot, this one's early, not even close to noon yet."

"Uhh, ma'am?" I said timidly, trying to make her aware that I could hear every single word she was saying.

When our eyes met, she pursed her lips and propped her hand on her hip.

"You're better than this, honey. Go on down to the lobby and get some coffee. Go find you some Jesus."

My eyes widened. *What did she think was going on?*

Oh.

Oh.

She definitely thought I was a prostitute.

I glanced down at my fitted wrap dress and kitten heels.

Sure, the neckline of my dress wasn't exactly a turtleneck, but I'm not a freaking nun. I'm allowed to show my clavicles for Christ's sake.

"I'm here to meet Mr. Lefray for business," I explained, offering her a smile to let her know I didn't take offense to her judgment.

"Oh, I'm sure it's business all right. Oldest business there is." She tsked again, moving on along the hallway past me.

I opened my mouth to set her straight just as I heard Julian yelling in his hotel room.

"I'm coming! I'm coming! Sorry!" he called.

His hotel room swung open, and a second later I was greeted with the most beautiful view of my entire life: Julian Lefray naked. Well, naked except for an itty bitty hotel towel wrapped around his waist. He could have been the Eighth Wonder of the World. Every single inch of his defined arms, chest, and abs were right there for me to see. Tan, toned, and still dripping wet from his shower.

My mouth fell open.

"You're early," he said, his hazel eyes widening.

"You're naked," I replied.

I blushed the moment the words left my mouth. A quick glance to my left confirmed that the cleaning lady had stopped pushing her cart and was standing there gawking at the two of us.

"Ah, sorry," Julian said with a bemused smile aimed at the maid. He didn't even know the effect those dimples had on my girly parts. One word: Ijustgotpregnant. *Yeah, that's one word*.

"Well it's clear you two have *business* to attend to," she said, wagging her finger at him and stepping closer.

"Oh jeez."

I huffed out a breath and pushed past Julian into his hotel room before the woman could start giving me pamphlets from her church.

Our shoulders brushed as I stepped past Julian and I inhaled the scent of his body wash: clean, masculine, fresh. It was just what I'd expected and the last thing I needed as I tried to piece together my resolve.

"I swear this isn't how it will be," he said, closing the door behind him and holding his hands up in an innocent gesture.

I dropped my laptop bag on a lounge chair in the suite's living room and then spun around to face him.

Abort! Abort! Staring at him when he was only wearing a towel was not good for my sensibilities. Before I could help myself, my gaze followed the contours of his chiseled torso, down over his abs, until I found myself staring at his hand gripping the towel right in front of his crotch.

Welp, I just stared at my boss' crotch for like a solid ten seconds. *That'll help the situation*. I gulped and looked away.

"I really thought we would have an office space by now," he said.

"Don't worry about it, I understand," I said, admiring the fine art on the hotel room walls. Yes, oh how very nice. I love sailboats. They're much better to look at than Julian's naked torso.

I saw him run his hand through his damp hair out of the corner of my eye and then he took a step forward.

"I worked out a little longer than usual so I'm running a bit late."

I squeezed my eyes shut.

"Okay, well..." I waved my hand to silence him. I was two seconds away from embarrassing myself, and I really needed to prevent that from happening. "It wasn't that awkward before, but now we're just standing here talking and you're wearing nothing but a towel, so maybe you should go get dressed already."

"Right." He laughed, then spun to head into his room.

"Make yourself at home!" he called as he shut himself in his room.

Only after his door was closed did I let my eyes wander around his space. It was remarkably tidy for a single guy's hotel room. No pizza boxes or beer cans littered the floor. A half-read New York Times sat beside an empty coffee cup on the living room table. He'd even taken the time to refold his newspaper as neatly as possible.

"Did that woman outside think that you were a prostitute?" Julian yelled through his door.

I smiled. "Yeah, is she used to a parade of them lined up for room 3002?"

"Ha ha. Sadly, my only visitor is Gary from room service."

I smiled as I stepped toward the window to admire his view.

"Okay, so I suppose I just look the part," I joked as the door to his room swung open.

He stepped out wearing gray slacks and a crisp white button-down. He was still finishing buttoning his shirt, so I was momentarily graced with one last glimpse of his chest. Buff—check. Tan—check. Just a sprinkling of chest hair that made my mouth water—check.

I glanced up to see him eyeing me with curiosity. He'd shaved away the stubble I'd grown familiar with the day before and had taken the time to style his hair after he'd gotten dressed. He looked like a consummate business man. Too bad the rest of him didn't fit the bill. He'd developed a tan from our time spent outdoors while looking at properties, which only made his features more appealing. He had a devious glint in his eye as he inspected me from across the room, but I captured my thoughts and pushed them away before my silence became too noticeable.

Julian laughed. "Between you and my sister, I don't think I can handle any more women in my life at the moment."

I sat down on the couch and pulled out my laptop.

"I'll take that as a compliment."

"You should," he said, meeting my eye for a moment before picking up the hotel phone. "Have you eaten already?"

"Some toast before I left the house."

"What an inspired meal," he said sarcastically, just as a voice on the other end of the line picked up.

"Hey!" I argued, trying to defend my love of toast, but he held up his hand to silence me with a smile.

"This is Julian Lefray in suite 3002. I'd like to place an order for French toast with a side of sausage."

"Oh gross. Everyone knows bacon is better than sausage," I whispered over the back of the couch.

"And a side of bacon," he said with a touch of amusement in his voice. He held his hand over the receiver and turned to me. "How do you prefer your coffee?"

"With a splash of almond milk, please."

"Yes. Two cups of coffee, and could you bring some almond milk on the side? That will be all. Thank you."

He dropped the phone back onto the receiver and I stared down at my laptop as I typed in my password.

Out of the corner of my eye I caught his bare feet and smiled. He'd styled his hair, shaved, and put on business attire, but apparently wearing shoes was asking too much.

"I figured if I'm going to force you to work in a hotel room, the least I can do is feed you," he said, grabbing his laptop from his desk and joining me in the suite's living room. There were two small couches that faced each other and a modern armchair that looked about as comfortable as a rock. He picked the couch across from me and met my eye.

"Will this do?" he asked, his tone a bit more vulnerable than I was used to.

Sure the situation was unorthodox and I'd just seen my boss in nothing but a towel, but nothing with Julian seemed awkward or strained. Working across from him and joking about whether he employed any *ladies of the night* seemed like normal water cooler talk.

I smiled up at him. "Perfect," I said, looking to see if my laptop was finished booting up yet. It needed another few minutes.

"Now tell me how your boys' night went before you make me get to work."

He glanced up at me. "Oh! That reminds me."

I tilted my head and waited for him to continue.

"I have an unusual request," he said with a nervous smile.

"Oh?" I asked, my interest already piqued.

His stare met mine and he hesitated for a moment as if determining whether or not he wanted to continue.

"How do you feel about ribbon cuttings?"

Chapter Eleven

Julian

In truth, I already knew that my feelings for Josephine weren't 100% platonic; the memory of her figure in that red gown from the gala had ensured that. She had curves and grace, such a classically beautiful face that over the last week, I found myself trying to memorize every detail. Despite all of that, she was also down to earth and humble, a contradiction that made me wonder if she knew her effect on men or if she'd somehow skated through life without yet realizing it.

I told myself I noticed these details and thought about her beauty not because I wanted to sleep with her, but because she and I had become friends. Besides Lorena and Dean, Josephine was my only friend in New York. Plus, after only a week of working with her, I was fairly certain that out of everyone, I enjoyed her company most of all.

She was smart and witty, different than the women I'd surrounded myself with in Boston. My life there was cold, a boring routine I'd tried to think of as something more. I hadn't realized it at the time, but there was definitely an emptiness in my life there. Yes, I'd achieved quite a lot: I had an investment portfolio that guaranteed I didn't need to work another day in my life, three cars, and a house in the most expensive part of the city, but then I thought of Josephine's smile, and everything I'd built before just seemed…hollow.

How?

How could she have done that to me so quickly?

"Jesus! It's like the zombie apocalypse over there by the bar," Josephine said from behind me as she rounded our cocktail table, balancing four drinks in her hands. I reached out to help her, but she had a delicate balance going.

"I recommend nursing your drink for as long as possible. The chances of getting another one are slim to none."

After we'd arrived at Provisions, Josephine and I had decided to divide and conquer. I'd found the table Dean had promised us and she'd headed to the bar to grab our drinks.

I eyed the tequila shots she set down beside our sangria.

"Shots?" I asked with a smirk.

Josephine smiled up at me and it felt like a punch to my gut. She was so fucking beautiful. Her dress was short and black, the straps barely there and the neckline verging on dangerous territory for me. When she'd climbed into the car earlier I'd fought the urge to maul her. Thankfully the driver had been there to keep the peace.

"And sangria! I figured since you have some Spanish blood, you'd approve," she said with a wink.

I smiled. "My grandfather was from Spain."

Her eyes lit up. "So that's where you get your whole 'Latin lover' look from. I was wondering," she said, waving up and down my body. "You could totally be in a soap opera."

I laughed. "Thanks?"

"That's a good thing! Seriously, every girl likes that look."

I wondered if "every girl" included her. Instead of asking, I licked the patch of skin between my pointer finger and thumb and then sprinkled some salt over it. Josephine did the same, but before she could reach for her shot, I grabbed her hand and held it in front of my mouth.

Her eyes widened as she stared up at me.

"Is this how you Spaniards do it?" she asked, a slow smile peeling across her lips.

I could feel her arm shaking against my hand and instead of answering, I bent forward and licked the salt off her skin. Her nostrils flared as she watched me and then a moment later she realized she was supposed to follow suit. She leaned forward and licked along the inside of my hand. She might as well have been giving me a blow job by the way my dick stirred in my pants. Her lips were just as soft as I'd imagined them to be and I had to resist the urge to pull her mouth to mine.

I released her hand, we reached for our shots, and we downed them in one go. The lime slices followed and I laughed as Josephine's features contorted from the burn of the alcohol.

"Jesus, that was strong!" she said, reaching for her sangria. I watched her lips wrap around the brim of the glass just before hearing my name from across the bar.

"Julian!" a voice called from behind me. "I've been looking all over for you man."

I glanced to my right to see Dean approach our cocktail table, eyeing Josephine with curiosity. There was another guy with him, a friend I didn't recognize.

"What's up Dean? You just missed the tequila shot," I said, holding up the empty shot glass.

He smiled. "There will be plenty more, I'm sure," he replied, letting his gaze fall on Josephine and then back to me with a question lingering in his stare.

"You must be Julian's new employee," he said, stepping forward and extending a hand. "I'm Dean, and this is my friend, Lucas."

I nodded to the newcomer and then glanced back at Josephine. Her pale green eyes lit up and an unfamiliar shot of jealousy wound through me as their hands touched.

"Dean as in Dean Harper?" she asked. "This is your restaurant?"

Dean smiled, obviously pleased that a beautiful woman knew of him. I resisted the urge to burst his bubble. *I explained who you were on the way over.*

"How do you like the place so far?" he asked, stepping another foot closer. My fist clenched under the table.

"It's amazing," she said, waving her hand over her head. "The courtyard is beautiful."

Dean caught my eye and quirked his brow. I shrugged. We'd just communicated an essay's worth of content in the matter of a second.

"Let me show you around. There's another courtyard up front that I bet you'll love," Dean said, extending his elbow for her to take. "Although—you're not on the clock right now, are you?"

My mouth opened, but no words came out. What was I going to do? Forbid her to go with him?

She glanced over at me from beneath her lashes, a silent request lingering between us. My eyebrows rose as I took a sip of my drink. *By all means, let Dean sweep you off your feet.*

They strolled away together and I resisted the urge to sneak a glance at her walking away in her little black dress. I already had the image burned into my memory anyway. Her waist was tiny and her curves were impossible to forget. Fuck.

"So is that your friend?" Lucas asked, filling the spot where Josephine had just been sitting. I didn't really feel like explaining myself to a stranger, but it was better than sitting alone.

I nodded and took another sip. Josephine had advised me to nurse the drink, but there was no way that was possible now.

"She's gorgeous," he said, waiting for me to contradict him.

I narrowed my eyes and stared at Lucas. "She's my assistant."

He laughed and nodded. "Of course. Of course."

I ignored him and downed the rest of my drink.

"Do you think you could put in a good word for me?" he asked with a crooked smile. "Y'know, if Dean doesn't end up going for her?"

I scooted my chair back from the table and ignored him. I'd rather wait for Josephine at the bar than deal with the rest of that conversation.

I found Josephine and Dean over in the courtyard,

talking beneath a canopy of trees. He was pointing out various features of the restaurant, waving his hand around to the trees and the fountains beneath them. She had a smile perched on her lips as she listened to him talk and for a while I kept my distance, watching them together. She'd tied her hair up at the base of her neck, revealing the slope of her back in her black dress. I couldn't see them, but I'd learned earlier in the week that she had freckles sprinkled across both of her shoulders. They were faint, hardly there at all unless you looked closely. They'd be almost impossible to see in the dim light of the courtyard, but I knew I'd be able to find them if I got closer.

I wasn't sure where to compartmentalize that desire. It wasn't as if I'd never worked with a beautiful woman before. I'd had plenty of experience with tempting women throughout college and my early years working in investment firms. So why was I leaning against the arch of the courtyard, studying Josephine from a distance instead of wandering through the party, looking for a beautiful woman to take home for the night?

Josephine peered over her shoulder, scanning the crowd until her gaze fell on me. My gut clenched as her smile spread even wider.

She waved me closer with her hand and I resisted at first. My body warned me to keep my distance from her. That yearning in my chest? The tight twist of my gut when she was focused on me?

Those symptoms held all the makings of my demise if I wasn't careful.

Chapter Twelve

What Jo Wore

Post #1254: Apartment Reveal!
Comments: 66   Likes: 789

Hello you beautiful people! Many of you have asked for an apartment reveal ever since I moved to New York a few weeks ago. I've been mulling over whether or not I wanted to do one because well...I'll be honest. My life in New York is not quite as glamorous as most of you probably believe. I don't even let the takeout guy in.

The rent here is insane (no really, I could sell all of my organs and still not come close to making next month's rent), but I think it's important for you all to see the honest side of my life. 98% of the time, I'm not standing in front of some adorable street mural wearing a cute outfit, posing for the camera.

My life is filled with bugs, tiny closets, Ramen Noodle dinners, and wacko neighbors. So, in an effort to be transparent, I've uploaded a few photos of my apartment.

Yes, the kitchen and bathroom and living room are essentially all combined, but as you can see, I've tried my best to decorate it as best as possible.

Let me know what you think!

Until tomorrow,
XOJO

• • •

Josephine

About once or twice a month, the voice inside my head convinces me that I need to get off my lazy bum and do some form of exercise. *It turns out that Nike shorts and leggings were originally intended for cardio, not Ubering to the cupcake shop.*

It was during one of these half-assed attempts at working out that I stumbled upon a rental space that would be perfect for the new Lorena Lefray headquarters. I'd been walking along, trying to decide if I'd burned enough calories for a donut yet, when I saw it. The storefront had sidewalk access, and when I pressed my face to the glass, it looked like the space went on for miles. We'd have plenty of room to set up a clothing shop for Lorena's designs in the front and then build out offices in the back for her team.

I kept my face pressed to the glass as I dialed Julian's number.

"Hello?" a sleepy Julian murmured into the phone. I glanced down to read the time. Oops. It was 6:45 AM on a Sunday and we'd been up late the night before at Dean's opening.

"Oh god, sorry to wake you. I didn't realize how early it is."

He groaned.

"But, now you're awake anyway. Get dressed and meet me at the address I'm about to text you."

He groaned again, louder this time, and then I heard something hitting wood.

"6:45? Do you realize I only went to sleep four hours ago?"

"Four hours ago?" I contested.

We'd both stayed at Provisions until closing and then Julian had hailed a cab for me. I'd assumed he had headed back to his hotel after that, but apparently he hadn't called it a night when I had.

"What exactly did you do after I left in the cab? It was already really late."

Oh god.

I knew the answer to that question. Dumb, dumb, dumb. There was definitely a girl lying next to him in bed, probably sliding down his body at this very moment. Oh, gross.

"Wait. Don't answer that. That's a breach of privacy. Just wake the girl up, get her some coffee, and get your butt down here. I found a good property I want you to look at."

I heard him shuffling around his hotel room through the phone. Cabinets opened and closed and then I heard the distant sound of his bathroom sink.

"There's no girl. Dean wanted to go to this diner for some food after you left."

I scrunched my brows. "But we ate at Provisions. You had a giant burger and then wolfed down half of my fries too."

"Yeah, but Dean and I were both hungry again by the time the restaurant closed. Don't you have guy friends? You should know that we require constant feeding."

I mulled over the question. I had Lily, and sometimes she had a mouth like a sailor. That was pretty much it.

"Nope. Just you," I answered.

Silence hung between us for a beat too long and I wondered if maybe I'd done something wrong by calling him my friend. Weren't we friends? Or did he only see me as his employee? I mean he'd licked salt off my hand the night before. Clearly, we weren't just acquaintances.

"Just give me a second to shower and then I'll meet you at there."

"Okay." I smiled.

"You owe me breakfast though," he added with a grumpy tone.

I laughed. "Fine."

I hung up, texted him the address, and then realized I was standing there, smiling down at my phone. *Weirdo.*

It wouldn't take him long to get to the building, but I still had some time to kill before he arrived. I wandered around the block in search of a street vendor serving hot pretzels, but the area was all but deserted. People were sleeping in and enjoying their Sunday morning. Meanwhile, I was walking around with a grumbling stomach and a yearning for warm dough.

I looped back around to the building and plopped down on the sidewalk, using the brick wall as a back support.

The city was quiet, leaving me far too much freedom with my thoughts. Usually I loved sleeping in on the weekends, but I'd woken up early with excitement settled in the pit of my stomach. Thoughts of Julian had lingered in the back of my mind as I'd fought to fall back asleep. I'd enjoyed hanging out with him and his friends the night before. I had no clue what Dean thought of me, but I thought he was really nice, and freaking gorgeous. He and Julian made quite the pair. Dean was a bit intimidating, with his own set of striking features to contend with. His dirty blond hair was cropped short, framing his sharp features and dark brown eyes. He was successful and driven. He'd given me a tour of his restaurant and I'd hung on to every word.

I wondered if Dean and Julian were best friends because they were both excruciatingly good-looking or if it was just a happy coincidence.

Speaking of best friends… I stared down at my cell phone and pulled up my text conversation with Lily.

Josephine: Are you awake?

I hadn't talked to her in two days and I knew she was probably going stir crazy back in Texas. *Or maybe I was the one going stir crazy without her?*

Josephine: Wake up. Wake up.

She wasn't texting me back, *the whore*. Then, finally, my phone buzzed in my hand.

> **Lily**: Are you kidding me?! Are. You. Kidding. Me? You're an hour ahead of me and it's ungodly early, even for NYC!!
>
> **Josephine**: Lil, I was just watching the sunrise over the Hudson and it reminded me of how beautiful you are.
>
> **Lily**: Enough with your false flattery, Slutilda. If you keep texting me, I will straight up kill you. LET ME SLEEP.
>
> **Josephine**: Last night was fun.
>
> **Lily**: Last night? It still IS night. Don't care. Don't care. ZZZZZzzzzzzz...

I rolled my eyes.

> **Lily**: Fine... Did you bang your boss or are you guys still pretending to be friends?

I narrowed my eyes at her text message. I hadn't told her much about Julian. I mean, I'd had her google him so she knew what I was forced to sit across from every day, but I hadn't told her that I had an itty bitty crush on him. Really, it was just a silly schoolgirl thing. I had no intentions of acting on it.

> **Josephine**: There's no pretending. We ARE friends.
>
> **Lily**: All right, then I'm going back to sleep.

"Waking the whole city up?" a voice asked from the corner of the street. "Y'know some people actually enjoy sleeping in."

I glanced up to find Julian strolling toward me with two cups of coffee, one clutched in each hand. Friends. Yup, just friends all right. He was dressed down in Nikes, workout shorts, and an old college t-shirt. I smiled at the sight; I'd won the bet with myself (the one where I'd put a million dollars on the fact that Julian would look sexy in anything).

I glanced over his legs. They were toned, long, and tan with the same dark hair that was sprinkled on his chest.

Just friends.

"Josephine?"

"Oh!" I glanced away. "Yeah. I thought it was only fair that I wake up my friend in Texas too."

He reached my spot on the sidewalk and I stood up to greet him.

"Coffee?" I asked, hopeful.

He nodded and handed it over. The cup was warm against my palm and the steam rising up around it smelled divine.

"The first shop I went to didn't have almond milk," he said. The morning light played up his hazel eyes and for a moment I was caught in his allure. The dark brows, the dark hair, the tan skin. A weaker woman would have thrown herself at him a long time ago. Me? I had goals. Goals that didn't include seducing Julian Lefray, my one and only friend in New York City.

"That's okay, I drink it black sometimes," I said before taking my first sip. I'd prepared myself for the bitter taste, but was surprised to find the coffee slightly sweetened.

"I found it somewhere else," he clarified with a little

smile.

Warmth spread from my belly, up around my chest, holding my heart in a tight grip. He'd gone to that much trouble for me?

"Is this the building?" he asked, peering over my shoulder.

"Yes! Just look at it!" I exclaimed, waving my hand toward the storefront.

He stepped closer, peering through the glass and studying the square footage just as I'd done a few minutes earlier. The tree-lined sidewalk was already getting busier as the rest of the city woke up. People were trickling out of their apartments, heading out for breakfast. I knew that by midmorning, it'd be a lively street. Perfect for a clothing shop.

"The location is great," Julian nodded, pulling his face away from the glass.

I nodded.

"We could build out the front of the space for Lorena's shop and then keep that entire back section open for offices," I said, pointing toward the rear. Without the lights on, it was hard to see into the distance, but it seemed like there was plenty of space.

"I like it a lot," he affirmed. "How'd you find it?"

"I was on a morning jog and I happened to wander by."

Julian arched a brow. "You've never mentioned you're a runner."

I smiled. "'Runner' is a strong word. On occasion, I've been known to move slightly faster than a walking pace, but it's not very often."

The side of his mouth hitched up. "I usually run over at Central Park. Have you ever done that trail?"

I laughed. "You'd have to carry me for most of that."

83

He smiled. "Nah, you could do it. We could walk for parts of it. Think of it as a team building exercise."

Was I willing to run just to spend time with him? I chose not to read into that fact.

He nodded toward the subway entrance a few yards away. "C'mon, let's head over there before breakfast."

My face fell. "What about the property?"

"I'll have my agent set up a time to view it," he promised, walking backward toward the subway entrance.

When I didn't immediately follow him, he paused.

"That's it? I feel bad for waking you up," I said, moving to join him. "Your response wasn't as awesome as I'd hoped it would be."

"I like it," he said with a reassuring nod.

"That doesn't sound very convincing."

He laughed and came to stand in front of me. "Jo, I love it. Thanks for waking me up at the ass-crack of dawn to see it. I don't know what I would do without an employee as dedicated as you are."

The bastard was patronizing me.

"I hate you," I said, hitting his shoulder playfully.

"No." He smiled, pretending to massage where I'd just hit him. "You can't hate your only friend in New York."

I narrowed my eyes. "Pfft. I have way more friends than you."

He arched a brow; he clearly didn't believe me.

"Like Dean," I said with a triumphant smile. I'd only met him last night but that didn't mean we weren't friends.

He rolled his eyes. "Right."

"He's pretty cute."

I'd said it as a joke—partly—but Julian obviously didn't take it as one. His laughter died and his gaze sliced over to me.

"Dean has a new girlfriend every week. He's not the settling down type."

I held up my free hand. "Whoa. It's not like I want to date him."

He didn't seem convinced, so I pushed further. "Besides, I don't date. Ever."

There. Julian had the truth and he could do with it what he wanted.

I brushed past him and headed toward the subway entrance, ignoring my flaming cheeks. He jogged to catch up with me and I could feel him studying me, clearly struggling with what he wanted to say. We walked down the stairs in silence. I swiped my subway card, pushed through the metal barrier, and headed toward the blue line track, all the while keenly aware of Julian's presence beside me.

"Why not?" he finally asked as we took our seats beside each other on the subway.

I tilted my head. "Why not what?"

"Why don't you date?"

His voice was gentle, and where I'd assumed there would be hints of judgment, there was only curiosity.

"Do I need an excuse?" I laughed.

He chuckled. "You make it sound like it's worse than pulling teeth."

For me, it was.

"The last time I went on a good date, I was in the seventh grade and Hunter Buchanan invited me over to play Mario Kart with him for three hours."

Julian started to crack up. "You're kidding me."

I shrugged. "I wish."

"Are you a virgin?" he asked. Just like that. Point blank.

I gaped so wide my jaw practically came unhinged.

Jesus. Good thing the subway car was fairly empty.

"No!" I said, glaring over at him. "I'm not a freaking virgin. How lame do you think I am?"

He held up his hands in defense.

"What? You made it seem like that was the case. I thought I was going to have to do you a favor."

My cheeks were on fire. I knew I was blushing so hard that the astronauts on the space station would be able to detect it.

"By deflowering me?! Oh my god, Julian, you're verging on asshole territory right now."

"No! No," he said, reaching for my arm so that I couldn't move away from him. "That's not what I meant."

He tried to catch my eye, but I held my gaze steady at the top of the subway car. There was an ad about an apartment finder service stretched across the edge of the ceiling; I focused on it like my life depended on it. I knew he was kidding, but the whole conversation was beyond embarrassing. My self-confidence was lying in a pool on the ground, and my ego was mixed in there with it. I didn't need Julian to make it any worse.

"Jo—"

I shook my head. This conversation needed to end. Now.

"You know what? None of this even matters anyway because I have a date." I forced myself to look at him as I continued, "Tomorrow night in fact."

His grip loosened on my arm until he let it slide completely away.

"Really?"

His brows were drawn together, but I did nothing to relieve his confusion.

"Really." I nodded as an elaborate lie started to play out

in my mind. "A friend of Dean's asked me to get drinks during the restaurant opening and I told him I'd think about it."

Hmm, that seems fairly logical. Even if I'd been with Julian most of last night, that didn't mean I hadn't had a few moments to myself, a few minutes for someone to hypothetically hit on me.

"And you're going to go?" he asked with a sharp tone.

I nodded, smug and annoyed by his line of questioning. "Yup. I think it's time to finally push myself out of my comfort zone, make some other friends in New York besides you."

Chapter Thirteen

Josephine

Did I have a date the following night? *Sure.*

Was it with a real person? *Technically, no. (Unless ghosts of relationships past count.)*

Would I be dressing to the nines, going to a bar, and sitting alone? *Yes.*

Why? *Because stupid Julian with his stupid good looks could suck it.*

In truth, I hadn't thought much about my love life in the recent years. When you go to an all-girls high school and then enroll in a fashion program for college, your odds of running into cute, eligible, interested men are just about zero. I'd dated off and on in Texas, but there'd been nothing serious and no one worth remembering.

I'd secretly hoped that moving to New York would change that, but it's not like I'd had much time to spread my wings (*or my legs*). So far I'd spent nearly all of my time working with Julian, hanging out with Julian, or texting Julian, which is why I was taking a night off from him, or at least a few hours.

I'd looked up good bars around my apartment. I knew that I could sign up for a dating site or download one of those "hookup" apps, but I wanted to do it the old school way. Surely there was still hope for people like me.

I'd decided to go to an intimate cocktail bar near my tenth-floor walkup. (Yet another reason I didn't need to exercise. Ten sets of stairs is the work of the devil.) It was called The Merchant and it catered to a young professional crowd. At 5:45 PM, it was already packed and I had to slither past groups of friends to find the bar toward the back.

My skin crawled with nerves as I made my way through the crowd. It seemed like everyone else was sitting with at least one other person, but I was hoping I wouldn't stick out like a sore thumb if I sat at the bar by myself. The music was loud and the conversations were flowing around me. I kept waiting for someone to notice me, but no one even batted an eyelash as I pulled back one of the bar stools and reached for the drink menu. In some ways it felt like New York was a city for the lonely.

"What can I get you?" the bartender asked with a heavy New York tongue. His blond hair was buzzed short and he had a five o'clock shadow that was working wonders for his otherwise baby face. I smiled and then motioned to the drink menu.

"Could I have just one more second?"

He nodded. "Take your time."

There were all sorts of fancy cocktails with ingredients I couldn't pronounce, but I didn't have much to spend, not if I wanted to stay within the strict budget I'd set for myself.

"Do you have any sauvignon blanc?" I asked the bartender with a friendly smile. A glass of wine couldn't cost that much.

He furrowed his brow. "Let me check."

He walked to the other end of the bar and I turned to inspect the patrons around me. I was smack-dab between two couples. The two on my left had thick foreign accents and were using boisterous hand gestures as they chatted loudly. They didn't even notice me watching them as they continued their conversation at lightning speed. Even if I'd understood what they were saying I couldn't imagine keeping up.

"Here you go," the bartender said, sliding a glass of wine across the bar.

I met his eye and smiled.

"Although between you and me, you shouldn't come to a bar and order wine," he said with a flirty smile.

"Oh really?" I asked, quirking a brow as I took a sip. "Tastes pretty good to me."

He laughed and wiped down the section of the bar in front of me. Maybe he was actually cleaning, or maybe he was stalling so we could keep talking.

"It's a waste of my talents as a mixologist. Unless I'm using the shaker, I'm basically a glorified bottle opener," he said with a wink.

I cracked up. "Oh really? Well, what's your favorite drink to make?"

He dropped his right brow as if I'd just issued a

challenge.

"How about I make it for you?" he asked, already reaching for the shaker and a bottle of Tito's Vodka. "On the house, of course."

I smiled. We were flirting. This was flirting 101 and I was doing a fairly good job of it. *At least I think I am.*

I opened my mouth to reply just as someone spoke up behind me.

"Owen, we'll never turn a profit if you offer every beautiful woman a drink."

I thought I recognized the voice. Dark, deep, and confident. I spun around in my chair and grinned when I saw Dean standing there, hands tucked into his tailored suit pockets and a wicked smile lighting up his devilish glare.

"Dean! What are you doing here?" I asked, leaning forward and accepting his kiss on the cheek. His five o'clock shadow rubbed against my cheek as he pulled away and I realized that I hadn't been 100% honest with Julian earlier. Dean was definitely a catch, and were he not Julian's friend, I'd have a really hard time staying away from him.

"This is actually my bar," he admitted somewhat sheepishly. "What brings you here? Out with friends?"

Dean waved to Owen, the bartender, as the hostess greeted the couple beside me. Their table was ready in the lounge, which meant Dean could nab the open seat beside me before someone else swooped in. He slid into the vacant seat and turned his full attention my way.

"No. I'm here by myself." I held up my glass. "A girl needs a glass of wine every now and then."

He laughed.

"This is actually the first bar I've been to in New York," I admitted.

His eyes widened and he held his hand to his heart as if he were wounded. "Then you have not had the proper New York City tour guide."

Is that true? I thought back to the day before, when Julian and I had explored Central Park and then eaten breakfast on the steps of the Natural History Museum. After we were sufficiently stuffed, I'd forced him to help me grocery shop and we'd stolen every free sample inside the Whole Foods bakery department until a customer service employee had politely asked us to purchase something or leave. All in all, it was an awesome day.

"Is Julian keeping you at work until all hours of the night? Is that why you haven't gone out much?"

I shook my head. "No. Not at all. I'm just a homebody by nature. This city can be a little intimidating."

He turned to the bar as Owen passed him a drink. I smiled at him, but the flirty man who'd been there a few moments ago was gone, probably too intimidated by the fact that his boss was watching now.

"To friends," Dean said, holding his glass up toward mine.

"To friends," I repeated, clinking my glass with his.

"Now tell me how you like working for Julian."

Julian, Julian, Julian. Even when I wasn't with him, he seemed to find a way to become the topic of my thoughts and my conversations.

"It's fun," I answered. I knew I was being vague, but I wasn't sure how much I wanted to divulge.

"Have you two found a workplace yet?"

I shook my head.

"So do you just work from coffee shops or something?"

I glanced down at my drink. "Uh, no. We usually just work from his hotel room."

He grunted in disbelief. "Guess that explains your relationship with him."

"Our relationship?"

He nodded.

"It's strictly professional between us," I began to clarify before backpedaling. "Well, I mean we hang out and talk outside of work, but it's strictly…"

"Professional?" Dean asked, the dark look in his eyes challenging me to be honest.

I nodded.

"Well since you two are so friendly, you should come out with us on the boat this weekend."

My brows rose in surprise. "You have a boat?"

He nodded and rolled his glass between his hands. "It'll be the first warm weekend of the year and a few of my friends and I are going to celebrate out on the water."

He must have sensed my excitement.

"I'm sure Julian could swing by and pick you up on his way to the marina."

Why did it feel like Dean was trying to play matchmaker?

Would Julian want me to tag along on the boat or would I cramp his style? I was sure Dean would have girls on the boat, girls that Julian would want to talk to.

"Earth to Josephine? How about it?" he asked, offering me a persuasive smile.

Well, when you put it that way…

"I'm in," I smiled.

Chapter Fourteen

Julian

I fell back against the grass and splayed my legs out in front of me, shaking them out like noodles. My legs protested the stretch, but I pushed through the initial shock, knowing they'd thank me later. Dean and I had just finished up a twenty-five mile loop on our bikes, ending at a small park in Brooklyn. The sun was shining overhead and I could hear kids playing on the jungle gym a few yards away. I tossed my bike helmet beside me and leaned back against my palms so I could start to catch my breath.

"I had quite an interesting conversation with Josephine last night," Dean said, tossing a water bottle at me. I thought fast to catch it before it collided with my chest and then pulled the cap off with one twist. It was ice cold and I guzzled nearly half of it down with one gulp.

After I swallowed, I finally registered what Dean had just told me.

"Conversation with who?" I asked, squinting to make him out in the glare of the sun.

"Josephine," he answered simply.

"When was that?" I asked, annoyed by my inability to sound casual. Sure, my lungs were still burning from the bike ride, but the thought of Dean and Josephine together burned far worse.

Dean glared over at me and I knew he'd caught my strained voice too.

"Last night. She was at my bar," he said with a shrug. The message was clear: don't kill the messenger, asshole.

"Provisions?"

He shook his head as he rotated his bike tire, checking for any damage from the ride.

"No. Merch."

Josephine was supposed to have been on a date the night before; had Dean seen the guy she was with?

"What—"

"And before you ask," he interrupted. "She was alone."

I frowned. "What do you mean? She was supposed to be on a date."

Dean pulled his foot up behind his leg, stretching out his quad.

"I don't know, man. When I saw her, she was sitting at the bar alone. I kept her company for a few minutes and then I had to get back to work."

Interesting.

"And I invited her out on the boat with us this

R.S. GREY

weekend."

My gaze shot back up to him. The asshole. "I was supposed to check out some properties with my agent on Saturday."

He smiled like the cat that caught the canary. "Guess you'd better reschedule. That is, unless you don't mind if I take Josephine out without you?"

I knew what he was doing. He knew what he was doing. Dean wasn't interested in Jo. He was interested in calling my fucking bluff.

"I'll see what I can do," I said, already reaching for my phone so that I could text my agent. "But I gotta run."

"Heading to visit your sister?" he asked.

I nodded. "Yeah, she's a few weeks into her program and she's bored as hell. I try to stop by as much as I can."

He dropped his leg and stretched out his other quad.

"The tabloids haven't been hounding her, have they?"

"Thankfully, no."

He shook his head. "I'm sure your mom has that all under control."

Dean and I had been friends for years, so he knew how our family operated.

I arched a brow. "Lucy Lefray? Of course she does, and there's already a contingency plan in place in case the media does find out."

"Are you serious?" he asked.

"We're supposed to say she's seeking treatment for exhaustion." The vague lie reeked of Lucy Lefray. "But Lorena wouldn't care if anyone found out she was seeking treatment for a drug problem. If anything, she'd be more embarrassed to admit exhaustion than drug use. Unfortunately, my mom doesn't agree."

"Guess that's the price you pay when you come from

blue blood."

• • •

The next day, Josephine and I were working in my hotel room, quietly typing away on our separate assignments. She was on the couch across from me and I found myself continuously trying to surreptitiously study her.

Our morning had followed the same routine it had for the last three weeks: I ordered us breakfast, she fixed our coffee while I spread butter on our toast, then as soon as we were ready to work, she slipped off her high heels and tucked her feet up under her on the couch. It wasn't the best working situation, but she'd been a trooper about it.

"I promise I'll find us an actual office soon," I said as she readjusted on her seat for the hundredth time that morning. She glanced up from her laptop and smiled.

"This is fine, I swear." For a second it looked like she wanted to elaborate and then I caught a mischievous glint in her eyes. "Other than the day I found you in your skivvies, it actually hasn't been that weird."

I laughed. "Yeah, I'm still expecting a lawsuit for that."

Since that first morning, I'd made it a point to always have my slacks, shirt, and tie on well before she arrived. One time could be written off as a mistake. Twice and she'd write me off as a weird-ass creeper.

"Don't worry, I didn't report you to HR or anything," she joked.

I smiled. "Should we hire an HR person next?"

She scrunched her nose in distaste and shook her head. "How about we hire a personal chef instead?"

"I like your moxie. You're hired. Now go make us some manicotti."

She playfully dusted her nails on her blouse. "You couldn't afford me."

I laughed and she bent forward to grab her coffee cup off the table. Another few inches of blouse spilled over the top of her computer screen. It was a cream silk top that brought out her recent tan. For just a moment, I let my gaze follow the elegant curve of her neck, down over her collarbone, and then lower. The top button of her blouse was open and the few inches of exposed skin there made it perfectly clear why Josephine was quickly becoming my favorite fantasy.

I'd just pulled my gaze away when her phone vibrated on the table beside mine. I glanced down and read the caller's name as it flashed across the screen before she snatched it up: Forest Financial.

"Feel free to take it," I offered.

She shook her head and dropped her phone a few feet away from her on the couch, well out of her reach.

"It's okay. I'm right in the middle of setting up a Facebook page for the brand and I want to get it finished before lunch."

"I thought Lorena already had one," I protested.

Josephine turned her computer so I could see the screen. "She did, it's just that she never finished setting it up and she hardly ever posted. No one even knew that it existed. I want to revamp it and then post some promotional content so we can start to build her presence there. I redid the top banner and added professional photos of her last line. We should be posting everyday so that everyone can stay up to date with the brand."

I mentally high-fived my past self for hiring Jo. Sure,

she was funny and interesting and gorgeous, but also in just three weeks she'd managed to completely overhaul Lorena's online presence. I knew the business side of things, but the creative end of the company was beyond my scope. We needed to hire a full marketing team, but for now Jo would work just fine. Besides, I kind of liked it being just the two of us.

"What do you think?" she asked, hope brimming in her eyes.

"It looks great," I said, truly meaning it. The old version versus the new version was like night and day. The new version actually looked like a real brand. "Do you do the graphics for your blog as well?"

She smiled wide and then glanced down to her computer. "Yeah. I took classes for it in college. I'm not a graphic designer or anything, but I know enough to get by."

I nodded. "I can tell. Your blog looks really professional."

She flicked her gaze up to me and then offered up a crooked smile. It was the sort of smile I gave my mom when I was about to beg for something.

"What's up?" I asked.

"I have a favor to ask of you."

I tilted my head, interested in what she was about to ask for. The last time I'd mentioned a "favor" around her, it hadn't gone so well. This time I was going to wait for her to speak first.

"Would you mind helping me take a few photos for my blog? I want to do a few photos in Central Park."

Oh.

That's it?

I opened my mouth to agree, but she spoke up quicker.

"I promise if you help me then I'll get you another one

of those ice cream cones from the stand near the subway station."

Her pale green eyes looked so earnest. I'd have been a fool to say no.

"Of course."

She smiled.

"Really? That'd be so helpful—"

She'd barely uttered the words before her phone started vibrating on the couch beside her. I wondered if it was Forest Financial again, but I was too far away to read the caller ID. She cursed under her breath, tossed her laptop aside, and stood to retrieve it.

"I guess I should take this," she said, shaking her head as she headed into my room.

The door closed behind her and I went through a mental checklist of the embarrassing things she could find in there. I thought I'd picked up my dirty clothes that morning, but I couldn't recall. Not to mention, there was about a fifty-fifty chance that I had a box of unused condoms sitting out on my nightstand. Yeah, that's right. Unused. Fuck. I couldn't recall the last time I'd had a dry spell last this long.

Back in Boston, this never would have happened. My "Little Black Book"—aka my iPhone—was jam packed with women that would have been enough for one night. Now? Now I had Josephine hijacking my every thought so that there wasn't room for any other woman.

I heard Josephine's voice drift through the bedroom walls and I did my best to ignore it. She deserved some semblance of privacy.

"Hi Ms. Buchanan—Yes, I did receive your message."

La la la, not listening.

"No. No. I'm getting paid in two days and I will put all of that money toward this month's payment. That's the best

I can do right now—"

I paused my typing, too curious to pretend I wasn't listening at that point. Was Josephine in some kind of money trouble? I tried to hear the remainder of her conversation, to decipher if she was talking to her landlord or someone else, but she must have moved away from the door.

It didn't matter. I'd heard enough.

When she walked out a few minutes later, her paycheck was sitting inside an envelope next to her purse. She'd find it when she packed up for the day and I'd offer some excuse about needing to pay her early.

She closed the door and puffed out a breath of air as if trying to calm herself down. Even still, she looked frazzled. She brushed her hair back away from her face and then tucked her phone into her back pocket with a touch too much force.

"Everything okay?" I asked, doing my best to sound unbiased by what I'd just heard. A part of me wanted to ask her point blank if she was having money problems. I wanted to help her if she needed it, but I didn't want to offend her either.

"Yup," she replied with a thin, fake smile. "Fine."

I was about to question her answer when she glanced up and met my eye. The emotion there warned me not to push the subject.

"About this weekend," she began.

"What about it?" I asked.

She rounded the back of the couch as a smile crept onto her face.

"Does Dean have a margarita machine on that crazy-ass boat of his or are we going to have to stop and rent one on the way?"

I burst out laughing. Even in the middle of a stressful morning, Jo had a way of surprising me.

"Libations aplenty." I grinned. "I promise."

Chapter Fifteen

What Jo Wore

Post #1257: A little help from my friends...
Comments: 120   Likes: 1130

Today's post is a little different. I won't be sharing any outfits or accessories with you guys. Instead, it's confession time.

My move to New York has been really hard. My parents weren't thrilled with my decision to leave Texas (to put it lightly), and because of it, my mom and I haven't talked in weeks.

That's never happened before.

It's hard not to think that maybe I've made the

wrong decision in coming here, especially since I know how nervous they are about it. I'll be honest, this city is NOT all sunshine and daisies. It's stressful and intimidating. It'd be a lot easier if I had some family here, but I don't. They're all a billion miles away.

New York was my dream and it still is. I'm not ready to give up on it yet.

In the meantime, do you guys have any advice on how I should convince my parents that I'm doing the right thing? That just maybe I know what I'm doing?

Let me know what you think.

Until tomorrow,
XOJO

• • •

Josephine

On top of my have-to-do-something-soon-or-I'll-be-homeless money problems, there was another issue weighing on my mind since I'd moved to New York: I hadn't talked to my mom in weeks. Not once. She refused to accept my decision to move to New York and I knew if I called her, she'd try to convince me that I'd made a huge mistake by moving away from Texas.

I'd assumed that she or my dad would have made more of an effort to keep in touch. I guess they thought I'd made my bed and now I had to lie in it. Well I'd be damned if I told them that my current bed was a used futon with a lumpy rock trying to pass itself off as a mattress. Every night I drifted off to the gentle sounds of my upstairs neighbors tromping around like a herd of elephants.

It wasn't perfect, but I was in New York and it'd take a lot more than a crappy bed to convince me to move back home. Like, oh, I don't know…my mountain of student debt. I pushed the thought away as I started to get ready for a day out on the boat. There was no point in dwelling on it. I'd be okay for a little longer. Julian had paid me early and I'd put most of it toward my outstanding loan.

I'd already started to look for another job, something I could do in the evenings. The night before, after a glass of $5 wine, I'd perused the pages of Craigslist, trying to stay away from the call girl ads in favor of something more suited to my degree.

I'd had a hard enough time finding the position with Julian. The chances of finding another job that would allow me the flexibility to continue full time at Lorena Lefray were slim to none. Still, I'd made a mental note to search around for jobs when I got home that night. Dreams were fun and all, but I didn't have the luxury of living in New York and pursuing mine scot-free. When I'd packed my bags and left for greener pastures, I'd known that my decision had come with strings attached. Unfortunately, it now looked like those strings were more like chains.

Chapter Sixteen

Josephine

The moment we arrived at the marina, I realized I'd made a huge mistake. Julian punched in the private access code and two wrought iron gates stirred to life. A brick-paved drive lined with rose bushes led us toward the guest parking lot. Attendants in white oxfords and starched slacks zipped around on golf carts, helping guests at the marina and ensuring that everything was running as it should be.

I stared out the window as I unclicked my seatbelt. Dread was already swimming in my stomach.

"Uhhh, I thought we were going boating," I said, focused on a group of gorgeous girls stepping out of a

Mercedes SUV a few yards away from us. They might as well have been in ball gowns compared to my outfit.

Julian peered over my shoulder and I turned to meet his eye. Whereas I probably looked like I'd just seen a ghost, Julian looked calm and collected.

"We are," he said.

"*No*. We're going yachting," I said, pointing toward the rows of massive sailboats that lined the front of the marina. "Those girls are wearing designer dresses and high heels."

I was wearing a colorful, short cover-up over a royal blue bikini. I had on gold strappy sandals and I looked cute-as-fuck. Did I, however, look like I was about to go yachting with New York City's upper elite? No. I probably would have fit in better at the Jersey Shore between Snooki and JWoww.

Julian's gaze drifted down, taking me in inch by inch, and then he smiled as he met my eyes once again.

"I think you look great."

I rolled my eyes. "Oh please."

From our vantage point, I could see the guests who'd arrived before me. The women were definitely the ones from the SUV beside ours, and I could already see their layers of jewelry and vintage scarves from yards away. Gag me. I hadn't realized I was spending the morning with the future Queens of England.

"Normally in Texas, boating means taking a shitty boat out on the water and then docking it as soon as possible so that you can float around in the water and drink beer."

Julian smiled. "Ah, I see. I guess I should have mentioned that Dean has a yacht."

"Yes. I see that now, obviously. I look so out of place in this outfit. Apparently I should have put on some starched khakis."

Julian cracked up. "You look amazing. I promise."

"We both know why you're saying that," I offered with a pointed stare.

I wasn't an idiot. I'd been well-endowed since the age of thirteen. My chest had a way of making even the most self-respecting men babble every now and then.

He nibbled on his bottom lip for a second and then reached for the hem of his shirt. "All right, let's swap outfits."

I squeezed my eyes shut as laughter overtook me.

"I'm fairly certain you'd look hideous in this bikini, but thanks for the offer."

I held up my hand, pleading with him to stop. The guests on the sailboat had surely seen us by now. We probably looked like weirdos just sitting in the car.

I took a deep breath and pushed my insecurities aside. "It's fine. I mean you're wearing swim trunks, so it can't be that bad that I'm in a bikini."

Julian nodded and hopped out of the car so he could get my door. He offered me a reassuring smile before grabbing the bag from my shoulder. I'd stuffed in a towel and some snacks in case Dean wasn't one to provide food. There was no way I'd last all day out on a boat without some Cheez-Its to hold me over.

We continued on toward Dean's boat. The closer we got, the more I realized just how large it was. A family of ten could have easily lived on the damn thing and I bet Dean took it out maybe five times a year, tops. Jeez.

Julian ushered me toward the bridge that connected the dock to the yacht, but before I could step forward, he reached out for my elbow to stop me. I stared down at his hand and then looked up to see him concealing a devious smile.

"I'll be honest," he said with a smirk. "I knew you'd be underdressed as soon as I picked you up."

I narrowed my eyes.

"And you didn't tell me to change?" I asked.

"I decided I'd rather be selfish," he answered, finally releasing the mischievous grin he'd been doing his best to hide. Julian wanted to see me in a bikini. What a stupid turd.

"You suck, Julian," I said, turning so quickly I almost ran directly into Dean's chest.

I hadn't even realized he was so close.

"Here here," Dean said, holding his beer in the air to show his agreement.

Julian laughed and kept hold of my elbow as I stepped forward onto the boat. Once I was sure of myself, I stepped out of his grasp and took in Dean, instantly feeling better about my outfit.

The girls I'd seen might have been dressed to the nines, but Dean was ready to party. He was wearing a captain's hat, a loose Hawaiian shirt, and black swimming trunks. He looked silly and yet still devastatingly handsome. His Hawaiian shirt was unbuttoned and his tan chest was on full display. Clearly, opening and running multiple restaurants still allowed plenty of time for the gym.

"Finally a girl who knows how to dress for a day on the water!" Dean said, reaching for my hand and forcing me to spin around in a circle. I played along and laughed. Normally I would have shied away from a display like that, but I wanted to tease Julian any chance I could get.

"Easy," Julian warned from behind me, his tone suddenly harsher than it'd been a second before.

I frowned and turned back, ready to argue, but Julian was staring out over the side of the boat as if he hadn't just acted like a jealous boyfriend. Dean dropped my hand and took a step back.

"Well then," Dean said, holding out his arm to usher us farther onto his boat. "Let the festivities begin."

Chapter Seventeen

Josephine

Dean's choice of booze? Epic. Dean's choice of party music? Awesome. Dean's choice of female friends? Lackluster.

The girls onboard the yacht were just as snooty and stuck-up as I'd feared they would be. The fact that my bikini came from Target would have probably sent them all into conniption fits. They were each decked out in name brands that even the most fashionably inept person would recognize: Berkin bags (because, duh, that's a good choice for sailing), Michael Kors wedges, Chloé sunglasses, Chanel scarves, and dresses that cost four times my rent.

111

Y'know, just casual outfits for the high seas…

They weren't all bad, though. There was a tall, gorgeous black girl named Nadine. She and her friend, Kelly, both worked for a PR firm in the city. I got a good vibe from the two of them. *I'll be honest though, it's mostly because they complimented my cover-up.* Then there was Kensington Beatrice Waldorf III. (How's that for a name?) When I joked with her about a nickname, she reluctantly offered up Kenzie. She was an accessories editor at Wardrobe Magazine and actively sneered when I mentioned I was from Texas.

"So you rode horses to school and all that?" she asked with a look of horror.

For two seconds, I couldn't tell if she was being serious.

"Longhorns, actually," Julian offered from where he stood a few feet away. He and Dean were busy popping the lids off beers so they could pass them out around the group.

Nadine and Kelly cracked up, but Kenzie shrugged and stared down at her phone, clearly bored.

Alrighty then…

After I had a cold beer in hand, I took a moment to explore the deck. I'd been on plenty of boats in my life, but none of them compared to the behemoth Dean owned. I had to squint to make out the top of the main sail; it was that tall. The deck was covered in polished teak and lined with clean, white cushions for lounging.

At the front of the yacht was a u-shaped seating area surrounding a built-in cooler, currently overflowing with wine and beer. A shallow walkway led around the u-shaped couch so that people could sunbathe near the bow of the boat. Something told me these New York girls weren't about to ruin their flawless skin with a day in the sun and I'd likely have the entire lounge area to myself later.

"Josephine!" Dean called from the back of the boat where he was gathered with Julian and a few new people. I guessed they must have boarded when I was checking out the sunbathing spot.

"What's up?" I asked as I ventured back toward them.

"Julian told me you've been craving a margarita."

I felt my cheeks redden as my gaze slid to Julian. I had enough southern etiquette engrained in me to know that it was rude to start making drink demands at a party.

"No, no. I already have a beer and it's more than perfect," I assured him, even holding up the bottle to prove it.

Dean smiled. "Too late. George already turned on the margarita machine downstairs and now I'm craving one too." He waggled his brows playfully. "Besides, I'm all about satisfying needs."

I opened my mouth to protest, but Dean was already talking to another guest and I didn't want to be even more rude. Julian came to stand beside me and took the beer out of my hand. I glared over at him.

"You weren't supposed to say anything," I hissed under my breath.

"You deserve a margarita," Julian said with a shrug.

"I just don't want to be rude," I said, watching him bring my beer to his lips and swallow back nearly half of it. I guess he assumed I didn't need it anymore since I was about to get a much-deserved margarita.

"You couldn't be rude if you tried," he argued with a knowing smile. "Now what should we do? We have another fifteen minutes until we set sail."

I scanned the boat. The girls were standing in a group near the bow, rifling through the wine options. Near the back, new guests were piling in, greeting Dean like an old friend. There were already ten or fifteen people on the boat and I only knew two of them. I felt like a fish out of water.

"Do you know many of these people?" I asked.

Julian scanned the crowd. "I recognize a few faces, but I've been out of New York too long."

"Looks like it's you and me then," I said, catching his eye.

He smiled and I took a moment to study him there. He'd put on a ball cap once we'd stepped onto the boat. The shadow beneath the brim did its best to hide his hazel eyes, but they persisted, as bright and alluring as ever.

"Want me to take a few photos for your blog? Are you going to do a post about this?"

"Are you serious? Yes!"

I'd wanted to take photos the second we'd stepped onto the boat. I knew my readers would die over Dean's yacht, but I'd been too embarrassed to broach the subject myself. I didn't want Julian to think I was a dweeb.

"I didn't bring my camera though," I lamented, opening up my bag to confirm what I already knew to be true. I hadn't wanted to take the chance that it would get wet. If it got damaged, it'd take me months to replace it.

Julian held up his iPhone. "I'll just use my phone. They won't be perfect, but I'm sure you can tweak them once you get home."

I nodded and dropped my bag onto one of the lounge chairs nearby. If I stood against the railing, most of the marina would be hidden off to the left. The water and the sky would make for a perfect backdrop for the first few photos.

"Who usually takes your photos?" Julian asked as I tried to strike a pose that wouldn't be too obnoxious. I usually took photos when no one was around; I didn't really need Dean's girlfriends as an audience.

"Other than the day I helped you," he clarified.

"My landlady," I admitted with a sheepish smile.

He snapped two photos and then I tried a different pose. I stretched my arms out against the railing and smiled at the camera. I'd realized early on that my blog photos turned out best when I didn't pretend to know how to model. There were a few standard poses: up close shot of the outfit accessories, subtle glance over the shoulder, active interest in something on the ground, and then a subtle smile that looked mysterious on other bloggers, but only ever made me look constipated.

"But I almost put an ad up on Craigslist the other day," I mentioned.

"For a photographer?" he asked, clearly unimpressed. He lowered his iPhone as he waited for my reply.

"Yes," I shrugged, "but then I realized that I'd probably end up on some fetish porn site or something."

Julian laughed and shook his head.

"Uh, yeah, Jo, don't hire a photographer off Craigslist."

Clearly he didn't understand how hard it was to find a photographer who would take photos for free.

"I just need to find someone better than my landlady. She takes the blurriest photos and I basically have to bribe her into taking them. Last week she made me listen to like two hours of her stories 'from the homeland' before she finally agreed. After thirty minutes, I ended up with three photos of my blurry face and about thirty photos of her thumb covering the lens."

Julian laughed, his deep dimples driving me as insane as ever. He snapped a few more photos while I tried to focus on anything but his appearance. His face was already hard to behold, but somehow the baseball cap brought out a new layer of appeal.

"I can always help you, y'know," he offered as he held his phone up for me to inspect the photos he'd just taken. I stepped closer and watched him scroll through them, ignoring the exhilarating feeling of being close to him.

"You say that now," I joked, "but you'll realize soon that this volunteer job has very few benefits. You just have to follow me around and snap as many photos as you can."

"I can think of a few benefits," he offered, with unmistakable lust in his tone.

I stared at his mouth, at the lips that had just formed those seductive words. They were right there, so close that I could reach out and steal a kiss. I inhaled once, slowly, and then convinced myself I'd read too much into his statement.

"Julian, less play-flirting. More snapping," I said, helpless to prevent the smile spreading across my face as I stepped back toward the railing.

I peered over at him from beneath my lashes and waited for him to start taking photos. He didn't. He stared straight at me with his eyes full of questions and his lips full of unspoken desire.

"Who said anything about play?" he finally asked.

It was his dark brow, subtly raised beneath the brim of his baseball cap that made my stomach dip low.

We were entering dangerous territory.

Chapter Eighteen

Julian

For the past few weeks, I'd done my best to give Josephine her space. Every urge that wasn't strictly wholesome, I'd ignored. Mostly. We danced around each other, flirting and teasing, assuming it was all in good fun. Now, as I watched her accept a margarita from Dean and laugh at whatever babble he was throwing her way, I fought the desire to walk closer and slip my hand beneath her cover-up. I'd run my hand along the curve of her ass and up over her hip. The bikini offered up no shortage of soft skin, ready for exploration.

Once she had her drink, she glanced over her shoulder

and found me sitting against the edge of the boat. I didn't look away and she tilted her head in question. I held my beer up and smiled. She laughed and followed suit, holding her margarita up in a long-distance salute.

My gaze traveled over her as she took the first sip of her drink. The sun shined through the thin cotton and for once I was graced with every inch of her hourglass figure. Had she worn that outfit knowing full well it would drive me insane? Had she tied that string around her neck considering the fact that I'd be the one untying it at the end of the day?

I gulped down another sip of her beer and stared out at the horizon, trying to subdue the caveman part of my brain. The beer did little to soothe the ache caused by Josephine.

Fuck.

As much as I wanted Josephine, I had to remember that she was my employee.

I needed to get laid. I needed one night with someone less vulnerable, less *employed* by me. Josephine had moved to New York a month ago. She had no friends, no connections. If something happened, I'd most likely be her emergency contact. That knowledge came with certain responsibilities. Sinking my dick into her would be an amateur move, something I would have gladly done in my twenties, too preoccupied with the ache in my pants to worry about the consequences of my actions. I could only imagine the conversation she'd have with her parents. *"Yeah, my job is good. My boss tried to fuck me on a boat yesterday."*

"How ya holdin' up, champ? You look like you're about to crush that beer bottle in your hand," Dean said, patting my shoulder as he took the seat beside me.

"Great," I muttered, squinting out toward the ocean.

"Are you pissed I invited Jo?" he asked, leaning back against the cushion.

I thought of how to answer and then I caught the tail end of her laugh. Fuck me. Fuck me.

"I think I'm in trouble with that situation," I offered, not bothering to turn his way.

Dean was the gloating type. There was no need to feed his ego.

He laughed and hung his head. "Took you three weeks to realize something I saw the first five minutes I was around you two."

"Maybe you're a fucking psychic," I muttered sarcastically, angry at the wrong person.

He patted my shoulder.

"You need to relax. We're on a boat, my friend. Not to mention, we have a dozen ladies onboard who would be more than willing to deal with that little problem Jo has caused in your pants."

"What did I cause?" Jo asked, a few feet back.

I squeezed my eyes closed and willed her to walk away.

"Julian?" she asked.

I ignored her.

Dean shook his head and moved away. "C'mon, Jo. I'll make you another margarita. Julian is having a little temper tantrum."

I gripped my beer and stared down at the label with every ounce of willpower I had.

"Why?" she asked as Dean wrapped his arm around her shoulders and dragged her away.

Thank god Josephine had the sense to follow him.

I stayed right where I was and finished off the beer I stole from Josephine with a sense of determination. As soon as I was done, I popped the cap off another one.

Drinking away my problems was a new endeavor for me, one that I knew would never work in the long run. For now, I was only concerned with the next six hours (i.e. being stuck on a fucking boat with Josephine while my hormones raged inside me like a fourteen-year-old).

My plan was to drink beer until my vision blurred and my limbs went numb. That way I wouldn't be in any danger of doing something stupid with Jo. I'd fully committed to my drinking-induced-coma plan when one of Dean's friends, Kiki or Kenzie or something, sidled up beside me on the edge of the deck.

"Is that one for me?" she cooed, glancing down at the beer beside my foot. I glanced at her, back down to the drink, and then I shrugged. I wanted to tell her to go find her own drink. I had no clue how long we were sailing and there was a finite amount of liquor, but if she wanted to steal my beer, then so be it. I wasn't an asshole.

"All right then," she said with a laugh, like I was being funny.

I wasn't.

"Are you usually this quiet?" she asked, turning toward me so that her knee bumped against mine. I studied the contact, wondering if there would have been a spark between us before Josephine had weaseled her way into my life, cause there sure as shit wasn't one now.

I took a deep breath and cut her some slack.

"No. I'm in a quiet mood today," I muttered.

"Strong and silent type, eh?"

I ignored the urge to turn around and find Josephine, to see if she was hanging out with Dean or if she'd found a different guy to spend time with. There were plenty of guys on the boat. Plenty of them who were smart enough to realize Josephine was the best option, *the only option*, to spend time with during our voyage out into the…

Where?

The New York harbor?

"Where the hell are we even going?"

The girl beside me giggled again. "Out into the open-ocean! Like real sailors!"

I scanned over her. Sailors don't wear high heels, but I decided not to point that out to her.

"You know what? On second thought, I think I'm going to need that beer back."

She scrunched her brows in confusion.

I pointed to the drink in her hand.

"Are you fucking kidding me?"

That pretty much sealed my fate. She muttered something about me being a brooding asshole as I walked away, but I just tipped my bottle to her and swallowed down another mouthful of now-lukewarm beer.

Cheers, assholes.

After my fifth beer, I knew I'd made a mistake. I needed to slow down. We were in open ocean, out far enough that if I decided I'd had enough and wanted to jump ship, I'd only manage to swim back about halfway before getting eaten by sharks. I cringed at the thought. As terrible as that experience sounded, at least I'd be done with the charade I was playing. I'd be far away from Josephine and her siren call.

"What's your plan here, Julian? To drink up all of my good beer until we're left with the girly shit?" Dean asked, leaning against the rail next to me.

I ignored his line of questioning and peered over my shoulder to see if Josephine was still chatting with some guy near the bow of the ship.

"Who's that she's talking to?" I asked, lacking my usual

knack for subtlety.

"That's Eric, one of my managers at The Merchant."

He was looking at Jo like she was water in the desert.

"Is he into women?" I asked.

Dean choked on his beer.

"I'm not sure. Want me to ask if he's interested in you?"

I resisted the urge to punch him in the face.

"Why don't you go tell him that if he keeps talking to Jo, we're going to have a big problem."

Even to my drunk ears, I knew I sounded like a douchebag, and not even an intimidating douchebag at that.

"Wow. You want me to tell him you'll be waiting for him by the flagpole at recess?"

Dean was laughing, but I couldn't find the humor in the situation. I was frustrated beyond my boiling point. Something was about to happen and if I wasn't careful, I'd do something that could ruin my relationship with Jo.

"Well, if you don't like them talking, I wouldn't turn around now," he said.

Of course, like a fucking idiot, I turned to look over my shoulder and saw Eric rubbing sunscreen on Josephine. She'd pulled her cover-up down to expose her shoulders and back, and Eric looked like a man finding a bag of treasure at the end of a rainbow.

"You've got to be fucking kidding me."

Dean shook his head. "It's nothing, man. They aren't fucking, dude."

"Yet!" I said, throwing my empty beer bottle into the bin a few feet away. The glass slammed against the other bottles as I pushed off the railing.

"Where are you going?" Dean asked as I walked away, toward my demise.

"To get Josephine."

He laughed. "Try not to get any blood on my boat in the process."

I wasn't going to make any promises.

Chapter Nineteen

Josephine

The name of the game was avoidance. I was avoiding Julian's stare as he watched me from afar the entire morning. I was avoiding my desire to glance his way, to confirm that the girls were leaving him alone. He kept his distance, but his gaze had a way of constantly reminding me that he was there, on the boat, just as sexy and unattainable as he'd ever been.

After he'd finished taking my photos, I'd tried to keep myself as far away from him as possible. It seemed easier to keep my composure with him on the opposite side of the boat. Unfortunately, none of the girls on the boat were volunteering to be my friend (*shocker*), which meant I was at the mercy of Dean's guy friends if I didn't want to be a loner. One of them in particular had taken a quick liking to me.

Eric was a manager at one of Dean's restaurants, and while his beefy look wasn't my usual M.O., beggars can't be choosers. He was nice and didn't set off my standard "BACK UP THIS GUY IS A CREEP" alarm.

"I think we need another drink," Eric said, waggling his eyebrows playfully.

"More drinks?" I asked, trying to gauge how drunk I was. We still had a few hours on the boat and if I didn't pace myself, I knew I'd be in trouble. I'd already had three margaritas, which was more alcohol than I'd had in a few months. Another drink and I'd be three sheets to the wind.

"Just a shot," Eric said. "C'mon."

There was loud music blaring over the speakers of Dean's boat so that I could hardly hear myself think, much less listen to my logic. Why couldn't I have a shot? It was free, and I was on a freaking boat.

"Yeah, Jo, why don't you take a shot with Eric," Julian said from right behind me. I'd never heard him so angry.

I braced myself before turning around, but it didn't help. My stomach dropped when I spun to take him in. He was right there, less than a foot away after a morning of staying away from me. I held my breath as he leaned in close, his breath hitting my cheek as he tried to whisper in my ear.

"He wants you drunk so he can fuck you."

His whisper was loud. Loud enough that I knew Eric had heard.

"Julian!" I leaned back and narrowed my eyes, annoyed with him for acting like a drunk asshole.

I cringed and mouthed "sorry" at Eric. He shrugged and smiled, not even denying the accusation. *Well then...*

"You're such a tease. Such a fucking tease," Julian said, swaying slightly as he spoke.

He reached out to steady himself on my arm, gripping tighter than necessary.

Eric stepped forward, but I shook my head.

"It's fine. He's a friend," I said to Eric, trying to keep the situation from getting any worse.

"A friend?! Ha!" Julian laughed as if I'd just said the funniest thing in the world.

"Er, I'm going to go grab those shots," Eric mumbled, backing up as if realizing he didn't want to mess with any of my craziness.

"Grab us all one, Eric. C'mon, we'll all take a shot. You, me, and Jo. Oh, I'm sorry, you probably don't know that's her name. Josephine. J-O-S-E-P-H-I-N-E."

"Julian," I whispered, reaching out to grip his arm to hold him steady. "You're being ridiculous."

He stared down at where I was touching him as if mesmerized by the connection.

"What the hell has gotten into you? You're being an asshole," I hissed, dipping my head down so no one else could hear me.

"What's gotten into me, Jo?" he asked with an incredulous tone.

He took a step closer to me, pulling my body flush with his. His hands gripped my upper arms and his mouth met my hair, just above my ear. His chest pressed against mine so that I could feel his wild heartbeat hammering a crazy rhythm.

"You," he bit out.

I'd never heard the word uttered with so much anger.

I leaned back, trying to catch his eye to see if he was serious, but he moved at the same time, jostling the beer bottle from his hand. It slipped between us, landing with a thud in the center of my big toe.

SHIT.

"Ow! Fuck, Julian," I groaned, angry that the damn thing had landed on my foot and not his. I picked up my foot to relieve the ache, but it didn't do any good. When I glanced down, I saw a trickle of blood dripping onto the deck from where the glass had cut my skin. I could tell the cut wasn't deep, but I still squeezed my eyes shut, trying to calm down. I hated the sight of blood.

"Jo, are you okay?" he asked, bending down to touch my foot. "We need to get a bandaid for this."

I shook my head, too annoyed to listen to him. I pulled out of his grasp and headed for the door to the cabin, praying Dean would have some kind of first aid kit stored away down there. Even just rinsing it with water would be better than nothing.

I limped to the stairs, thankful that no one seemed to be privy to our little argument. The cut was bad enough, I didn't need embarrassment piled on as well. I unlocked the door and slipped down the stairs, careful not to drip blood anywhere.

Thankfully the cabin was empty and I was able to find the bathroom just off the main room to the left. It was small, but functional. Dark cabinets hid toiletries and towels. Beneath that, I found a small first aid sack.

I reached to unzip it just as a hand wrapped around mine, halting my movements. I jerked around to see Julian hovering over me with clear intent.

"I've got it. I don't need your help."

"Stop," he said.

I narrowed my eyes.

"You're being ridiculous. Take a seat on the sink and let me help you," he said, jerking the first aid kit out of my hand before I could protest. My blood was still boiling. Who did he think he was? He'd caused the damn cut and now he had the audacity to boss me around like a child?

I opened my mouth, ready to argue, but something in his stare warned me against it. I took a deep breath, in through my nose and out through my mouth, and then I pushed up onto the sink and crossed my arms.

I'd let him clean my cut and then I'd get the hell out of there. I'd rather sit up on the sundeck by myself than deal with his brooding crap.

He knelt down on the floor and slid my foot out of my sandal. I stared at the wall behind his head as he cleaned the wound and rifled through the first aid kit.

"It doesn't look too bad," he said as he tore open a Band-Aid.

I tightened my arms across my chest and ignored him. Instead, my mind ran through what had just happened a few minutes earlier.

"What's gotten into me? You."

You.

The tight ball of tension in my stomach uncoiled and then wound into something darker, sexier, needier. Julian wanted me. He'd just admitted it.

I nibbled on my bottom lip as he wound the Band-Aid around my toe. He tossed the wrapper into the garbage, zipped up the first aid kit, and tossed it into the sink beside me.

When he finally stood, he interrupted my view of the wall so that I was instead forced to stare at his chest. It rose and fell with that same wild rhythm as before.

My mouth opened, but no words slipped out.

It was a matter of seconds, milliseconds, nothing-seconds before he slammed the door, confining us both in the small space. There had hardly been room to move before he'd stepped inside, and now I was stuck. Stuck sitting on the sink as Julian blocked my only escape route.

I fought to breathe, fought to see past the next few moments. It was impossible; I couldn't see beyond those four walls. I couldn't see beyond that eight square feet of space.

I turned to reach for the door handle, to push it open and get some fresh air, but Julian was faster. He caught my hand in his and held it down against the sink. I couldn't move my fingers beneath the weight of his grip.

"Julian—"

You're drunk.

You're my boss.

You're too sexy, too old, too *everything*.

Every possible ending to my sentence fell short as I met his eyes and found a look of such burning desire that I was rendered speechless.

"Tell me to leave, Jo," he insisted.

I couldn't.

"I'll leave and then you can go right back to flirting with those guys upstairs," he said, leaning forward and gripping my waist.

"They all think you're so sexy. They think they could be the one to have you."

His fingers tightened around my waist and I clenched my teeth together. There was a tipping scale inside of me. On one side, my anger boiled over, so ready to snap at him for acting like he owned me. On the other side—the side that I knew was about to tip—was my desire to finally know what it felt like to succumb to Julian.

One second we were two people with separate lives and separate desires, and the next we were together, so achingly in need of one another that I thought I'd scream until my voice gave way. He picked me up off the bathroom sink and we collided into the bathroom wall. I gasped, scared that every single person above could hear the ruckus we were making.

His fingers dug into my hip, scraping my skin and making me cry out.

"You're being an asshole," I hissed.

He kneed my legs apart and I wound a leg around his hip, pulling him closer.

"You look so fucking good. It's driving me *insane*."

I yanked his hair. Hard. He reared back and stared up into my eyes. Those hazel irises were clouded with lust, so dark and tempting that I feared what they could do to me if I only let them.

The challenge was there, written in our body language. He ground himself against me and I tightened my leg around his waist. His fingers slipped beneath the material of my bikini bottom and I let my fingers slide down the back of his neck.

"Do it," I told him, staring straight into his eyes. "Just do it so we'll know."

I watched his chest rise and fall. Once. Twice. And then his lips were on mine, crushing me back against the wall. It fucking hurt to be slammed into the side of the boat. I fisted his hair and tilted my head, trying so hard to keep up, knowing full well that I never could.

The match was lit and the blaze that grew between us was spreading beyond our control. My skin burned with it as he untied the knot behind my neck. The thin material of my bikini top slid away and just like that, I was completely bared for him. So exposed that I wanted to squirm away from his gaze. It was too much. I knew he'd be too much.

The deep groan that followed as he cupped my breasts spread the burn through my body. His mouth dipped to taste my skin, kissing down the very center of my chest, over the swell of each breast.

I gripped his shoulders and let my head tip back, too weak to carry the burden any longer. He propped me up onto the sink and I wound my legs around him.

I ripped the hem of his shirt as I tried to pry it over his head. He resisted, not wanting to let go of me for even a second.

"Julian," I groaned, frustrated that he wasn't giving me the access to him that I craved.

He growled and ripped the shirt off his head, practically splitting the fabric down the middle.

I untied the string of his swim trunks and the material sagged down. The dark hair that was sprinkled across his chest led down the center of his pants, down to what I craved most. He didn't even seem to notice. He was enamored by me, spreading his touch over every inch of skin he could reach.

I was so ready, almost angry with how ready I was for him.

The continuous tease of having to be around him the last few weeks had built up the desire in my veins. Each day the passion had built with no outlet for escape.

Now, we finally had the chance to do something about it—in this fucking bathroom. I knew I could finally alleviate the ache. I slid my hand past the waist of his swim trunks and gripped him in my palm.

"Fuck," he moaned, leaning his head against the glass

over my shoulder.

I slid my palm up and down slowly, feeling the length of him. He'd fill me up, sate my desire, and leave me with a feeling of utter completion. I knew that…now I wanted to *feel* it firsthand.

"Julian—" I breathed, prepared to beg him at that point.

Just then, a fist pounded against the bathroom door, practically shaking it off its hinges.

"Excuse me! Some of us need to use the freaking bathroom!"

I jumped a mile in the air, scrambling to pull my hand out of Julian's swim trunks and cover myself lest the person actually pried the door open like they were threatening to do.

"Seriously. I need to pee!" the girl yelled again, just as pissy as before.

She kept pounding her fist against the door, rattling the wood on its hinges.

"Shit," Julian groaned, shoving his hand through his hair and taking a step back.

I was sitting there with my legs splayed open and my breasts poorly hidden behind my arm. I knew how I looked. I knew why he couldn't look away.

His gaze slid over me and his nostrils flared.

"Hand me my cover-up, you jackass," I said, pointing to where it lay in a puddle on the floor.

He raked his hands through his hair and then bent down to retrieve it.

I took a deep breath and tried to settle my nerves.

Another round of pounding started on the door, louder and longer this time.

"Stop fucking pounding. We're coming," Julian yelled.

"Julian—

He shook his head and looked away. "If you had any idea how much I'm restraining myself right now, you'd tie that bikini back up and put your dress back on." His hazel eyes swept across me. "I'm two seconds away from fucking you while she listens outside."

My mouth dropped.

"It's your call."

Chapter Twenty

Julian

Can someone die from a case of blue balls? Would I be the first?

I was due to visit Lorena on Sunday afternoon. We had an entire sheet of topics to cover that she'd emailed to me the night before. (Apparently you have a lot of time to create Excel spreadsheets in rehab.) I needed to get my head in the game but I'd hardly managed to sleep off my hangover from the day before. Every time I took a step, it felt like a donkey was dropkicking the back of my head, and I was still carrying around the weight of what could have been, thanks to the boat-ride-from-hell the day before.

The next time Dean invited me on his boat, I was going to come prepared with a box of condoms, a padlock, and a port-a-potty for the top deck. For fuck's sake, I'd been two seconds away from reaching the pinnacle of nirvana, and White Wine Wendy couldn't hold her pee for a minute longer.

WE WERE ON A BOAT. Pee off the side dammit.

"Julian! My beautiful, annoying big brother," Lorena sang as I pushed through the door to her room. She was sitting at her kitchen table with papers spread out around her, clearly ready to conduct business. Me? I was ready to stick my head between my knees and pray for the apocalypse. The fiery pits of hell had nothing on the pounding headache positioned right behind my eyes.

"C'mon. You're walking like a snail. We have a lot to get done and I have a rebirthing ceremony at noon."

I arched a brow. "Rebirthing ceremony?"

She shrugged. "They give you cookies. It's the only time they give you actual sugar in this place. It makes no sense. I was addicted to cocaine, not sweets. Why do I have to pretend to be 'born anew' to have some freaking candy?"

"I'll sneak you in some the next time I visit," I promised, pulling out the chair across from her. The sound of the metal legs scraping against the floor felt like daggers stabbing my head.

I leaned against the seat and waited for the room to stop spinning. When it did, I was met with a smiling Lorena, clearly pleased to see how shitty I felt.

She looked more like her old self than she had in years. Gold bracelets encased her right wrist, jingling every time she moved. She was wearing bright green glasses and her hair was braided across the crown of her head. Her shirt read, "Black is the new black," which I found funny even in my present state. She looked like the Lorena I'd grown up with, the creative genius that no one really understood.

"Do you have any new spaces for me to look at?" she asked, drawing the topic back to work.

I groaned and forced myself to get it together. I'd promised Lorena I'd take care of her business while she was in rehab, and I didn't want to let her down.

Josephine and I had narrowed down our top three picks for her store. I passed Lorena a folder with photos and floor plans of the three spaces. She vetoed the first two right away, cursing their uppity locations. The third one—the location Jo had found during her morning walk—Lorena loved.

"And it's within our price range?" she asked, scanning through the photos I'd brought along with me.

"It's at the top, but the foot traffic would ensure that the storefront would pay for itself. We'd convert the back space to offices. I think people will like the idea of shopping at your store, knowing there's a chance that they'll get to meet you while they're there."

She nodded, enamored with the photos. "I completely agree. I can't compete with Michael Kors, but there's something about a designer you get to know. Everyone wants to brag to their friends that they bought a dress that the designer handpicked for them."

"Exactly."

"When can we move in?" she asked, glancing up at me with her bright hazel eyes.

I smiled. "Next week if we incentivize the landlord. It'll take a few months to renovate, so the sooner we're in, the better," I said.

"Let's do it then." She dropped the folder and stared up at me, her features infused with excitement for the first time in months. "Next topic."

I nearly slept with your one and only employee and now I'm worried she's going to quit and leave us high and dry.

"Julian?" Lorena asked, eyeing me with suspicion.

"Oh, um," I scanned down our itinerary, unable to focus on a single line.

"Did you talk to Mom? Is that why you're off?"

My gaze shot back up to her. "No?"

"You still haven't seen her since you've been in town?" She seemed surprised.

"Why would I see Mom?"

Lorena flattened her hands across the edge of the table, collecting her thoughts. I settled into my chair, prepared for a lecture. When she pushed her glasses up onto the top of her head, I knew I was really in for it.

"I am the first person to throw Mom under the bus. Believe me, I barely like her at this point."

For good reason. Lucy Lefray was from New York royalty. She'd grown up around the Vanderbilts and the Rockefellers in the upper echelon of wealth, lived the life reserved for the top one percent of the one percent. From a young age, she'd groomed me to run a Fortune 500 company and marry some suitable socialite by the age of twenty-five. *Lorena?* My mother could hardly look at her. *A fashion designer?* Lorena might as well have been a prostitute for the way my mom sneered at her. I can still remember the day Lorena dyed her hair for the first time. My mother didn't leave her room for a week. She acted as if Lorena had killed the family pet. Lorena had added blonde highlights to her brown hair. *The horror.*

"So if we both don't like her then it's settled." I smiled and scanned down the list of items left to discuss.

Lorena cleared her throat until I finally looked up and

met her eye. "She's older now, Julian. Her edges are starting to soften and I think it would mean a lot if you stopped by to see her, or at the very least, let her know you're back in town. It'd break her heart to realize that you're in New York and you don't even care to see her."

"I'll shoot her a text message."

"Julian," Lorena chastised.

I held up my hands. "Fine. I'll think about it, Lorena. I have a lot on my mind, least of which is whether or not I should try to schedule a tea time with Mom."

Lorena smiled and picked up her itinerary.

"Perfect. Okay, on to topic number two. I think it's about time for me to meet our Employee of the Month!"

Jesus Christ. Someone get me a beer.

Chapter Twenty~One

Josephine

It was the Monday after the "boating incident" where I'd almost let Julian ravish me below the deck—no pun intended—and I was not prepared to go into work. I had the same kind of dread in my stomach that built up right before I had to wax my hoohah before swim season.

I took my time applying my makeup, trying to relax myself. I'd called Lily the night before to get her opinion on the matter, but she'd only made me feel worse.

I think a part of her was shocked that I'd let it go that far.

"The plan was for you to move to New York so you

could get a job and an apartment before I move up there in a few months. This plan did not include sleeping with your boss. Don't you see how that could not only jeopardize your career at Lorena Lefray Designs but also EVERYWHERE else in the entire city? Seriously, Jo, is his penis made of pure gold? Ivory? Does it sparkle? Because sleeping with him cannot be worth more than your career in fashion. Think about it."

"I know that! You don't have to tell me that," I huffed into the phone. "Don't you think I'm already panicking enough as is? He was drunk and I almost took full advantage of him!"

Lily didn't believe that for a second.

"You two have been circling around each other like a couple of bloodthirsty sharks. You did not take advantage of him."

I groaned.

"Just focus on what's important, Jo. I'll be moving up in a month and then you won't have to hang out with Julian anymore. You'll have me."

Just hearing her reassure me that she was headed to New York melted away most of my anxiety. I needed her in New York. I needed reinforcements. If Lily had been with me on that boat, I never would have let it go that far with Julian.

"Once I have the money saved for a bus ticket and first month's rent, I'm there," Lily said.

I made her swear to that promise.

After we'd hung up, I'd made a promise with myself not to screw up the opportunity that had fallen into my lap. There were any number of outcomes that could happen if Julian and I decided to pursue some kind of relationship. All but one of them ended in a break-up and my inevitable termination from the company. Truthfully, I knew I only had one option: I would continue on as Julian's employee and his friend, nothing more. We'd be cordial, I'd get my job done, impress him, and move my way up in the world.

I couldn't let this job slip through my fingers. I had debt collectors at my door, next month's rent to worry about, and Lily couldn't move to New York if I was unemployed. I owed it to her to commit to the position I'd been given, even if that included putting my love life on the backburner for the time being. This conclusion meant that I had to be upfront with Julian.

I huffed out a breath of air and pushed off the counter to pick out the most conservative outfit I could find. I settled on a loose pair of slacks and a boring, gray blouse that completely hid away every ounce of cleavage. I pulled my hair into a low bun and slipped on a pair of flats. Hopefully the message I was trying to send would come across loud and clear. Me = employee. You = boss. Even a caveman could understand that.

By the time I started my trek to work, I was still trying to push aside stray memories from the boat. One particularly vivid image—Julian gripping my hands in place above my head—had just played out in my mind when my phone vibrated in my pocket. My hand shook as I reached in my purse, assuming it would be Julian calling.

It wasn't.

My mother's face lit up my small screen and my stomach dropped. I hadn't talked to her in weeks and this was the precise moment she chose to call me? I veered off to the side of the sidewalk and leaned against the side of a building to try to drown out a bit of the street noise.

"Hello?" I asked after the call connected.

"Josie. It's Mom. Is this a good time to talk?"

I stared out across the sidewalk. Technically, I had ten minutes until I was supposed to be at work and I was already a block away from Julian's hotel. I had no excuse.

"Yes. Yeah, can you hear me all right?"

The morning streets were full of honking taxis and bustling pedestrians scurrying to work as quickly as possible. Chances were it sounded like I was in the middle of a circus.

"Yes. I have you on speakerphone over here so your dad can hear too."

I smiled. "Hi Dad."

"Hi Jos," he chimed in.

I hadn't heard from either of them in a month and now they were calling me together? Something was up.

"How are you getting on in New York?" she asked.

"Good," I replied, treading lightly.

"We read up on the news every day. Looks like someone gets mugged or killed every night of the week up there."

And yet they didn't think it was necessary to check up on me until now…

"Yeah, but I don't walk around at night and I always have pepper spray on me."

"You know you wouldn't need that pepper spray back home…" my mother mumbled.

You're right, 'cause I'd hurl myself off a bridge from sheer boredom before I ever got the chance to use it.

"How are things at the shop, Dad?" I asked, ignoring my mom's little dig.

"Oh, same as always. Slow, but steady."

"Slow but steady" could have been the motto of my entire hometown. Seriously.

"Well we just wanted to check up on you. I know

you're busy with all of those New York dreams of yours… will you be making it home anytime soon? Maybe for your dad's sixtieth next month?"

Guilt clawed its way up my vocal cords until I had to clear my throat just to be sure I could still talk.

"I'll try. Really."

I knew I was making false promises, but I couldn't tell them the truth. I had so many people watching and waiting for me to fail. I'm sure every single person in my hometown had placed a bet on how long I'd manage to stay in New York before crawling my way back home. They'd all taken it as almost a personal insult that I'd wanted to leave and make something of my life. They'd sleep a little better at night knowing that I'd gone out to fulfill my dreams and landed face first in the dirt.

Why?

Because it meant that every time they got the urge to reach for more, to dream a little bit bigger, they could rest easy in their ranch-style house, with their .2 acres of land and their 2.5 children, knowing they'd made the right decision—the proper decision—while "that ol' Josephine Keller wasted her youth on foolish dreams."

I'd be damned if I let them see me fail.

"Listen Mom, I gotta go. I need to get to work. I'll let you know if I'll be able to come home next month."

Before she could reply, I hung up and shoved my phone back into my purse. Fierce determination coursed through my veins. All memories of the boat ride were packed away and shoved below. For now, I needed to focus on myself.

Chapter Twenty-Two

Josephine

Open laptop, read emails, order breakfast, pour coffee, avoid eye contact, stay at least two feet away from Julian, and for god sake's stop remembering what it felt like when he kissed you.

I'd been working at Julian's hotel for fifteen minutes and my resolve was already slipping. I'd felt confident when I'd stood outside his door and knocked twice. My shoulders were pushed back and my head was held high. Then, Julian had opened the hotel room door and sucked the confidence right out of me with no effort at all. He was wearing a fitted navy suit, brown belt, and sleek brown shoes. The top button of his white shirt was undone and his midnight black hair was still slightly damp, like he'd just stepped out of the shower minutes earlier.

He'd ushered me inside and I'd mumbled a greeting, averting my eyes so that I could keep hold of what little resolve I had left.

For the first fifteen minutes of my being there, neither one of us had said a word.

"More coffee?" he asked, breaking the silence with an offer I couldn't refuse.

I nodded and he rounded the couch to pour more medium roast into my mug as I held it up for him. His shoes hit the hardwood floor and with every step, I felt my nerves ratchet up another notch.

I stared at my computer screen, all the while trying to concentrate on where he was in proximity to me. He was busying himself with something behind me and I tried to think of what our normal working life was like. Normally, I'd have turned around and asked him about his weekend, how his Sunday had gone, but there was no way I'd open up that line of discussion.

"You're quiet this morning," he said as he stepped back around the couch and took a seat across from me.

My stomach fluttered.

"Am I?" I asked, not meeting his eye.

I could see him smirk out of the corner of my eye.

"I'm just thinking about work things," I muttered.

He nodded, studying me in a way that made chills creep down my spine.

"So are we going to talk about—"

"Julian." I held up my hand to cut him off before he could utter another word. "Let's just concentrate on work and we can talk about this another time, maybe when I'm not on the clock."

His smirk slipped away. Clearly, he hadn't expected that response.

"So even though you and I almost—"

I clenched my jaw and gripped the edges of my laptop. "Julian, please. It's complicated."

His calm eyes, the eyes that had greeted me at the door fifteen minutes earlier were gone, replaced with a brewing storm behind dark brows.

I thought he'd push the subject, draw up memories that I was intent on pushing aside for the next eight hours, but he didn't. He opened his laptop in silence and we got to work. For hours, we fired off emails and read through contracts for the space we wanted to rent. I began calling architecture firms around town, explaining our project and scheduling initial design meetings.

We didn't utter a word to each other unless it was directly work related. His tone was distant and cold. I could hardly meet his eye, even if he was only firing off the names of firms he wanted me to get in contact with. I hated every minute of it, but it was the way it had to be.

After lunch, I settled back into my seat and pulled up the email I'd started to draft before running down for a sandwich.

"The other night, I went to this ice cream shop down the street from my hotel," Julian began, pulling my attention from my computer.

"What?" I asked, confused.

"Do you ever really crave ice cream?" he asked, a hint of a smile covering his lips.

What the hell is he talking about?

"Uh, sure, I guess."

"Well, I really wanted some the other night, so I went down to this shop and stood in line. It took forever to get to the front to order. It almost felt like I'd been waiting there for weeks."

I arched a brow. "Sounds like you should have just picked up some ice cream from 7-Eleven."

He smiled. "I couldn't. It had to be *this* ice cream."

I narrowed my eyes in confusion but held my tongue.

"So anyway," he continued, "I got to the front of the line and I asked to sample the flavor I'd been eyeing—y'know, just to get a little taste."

"Mmm," I hummed. "You're going into way too much detail about ice cream."

He ignored me.

"And after I'd had that tiny sample, I knew I wanted more. It tasted amazing, just like I'd known it would. So I asked for two perfectly round scoops in a waffle cone."

"Okay. That's the weirdest way I've ever heard someone describe—"

"But you know what happened right after I paid and walked out of the shop?"

"You realized you were being really weird about ice cream?" I joked.

He laughed. "No. I leaned in to take my first bite, tripped, and the entire ice cream cone fell to the ground. Can you believe that? Right before I really got to enjoy it."

I stared at him, mouth in a thin line, annoyance building within me.

"I know what you're doing," I said.

"Has that ever happened to you before?" His gaze held mine as he teased me. "Have you ever been so close to getting something you've been craving, only to have it ripped right out from under you before you can really savor it?"

I stood up and carried my laptop toward the bathroom. "I asked you not to talk about it, Julian. Not during work. I have to take this job seriously. Do you?"

"Jo—"

"This job means everything to me. Can't you see that?"

Before he could answer, I continued.

"I can't blame you for being confused about my priorities. We've both crossed the line from the very beginning. I assumed I could have my cake and eat it too, but now that the choices are right in front of me, I know I have to choose my job over you. I can't afford to be fired."

The image of moving home and working at the town Dairy Queen was enough of a reality check to set me straight. No more fooling around.

He stood and held up his hands. "You're right. I'm sorry. Okay? I'm sorry. I've got to run some errands anyway, so don't stuff yourself in the bathroom. You can stay right where you are. I promise that when I get back I'll be on my best behavior."

He stepped closer and bent to find my eyes.

"Okay?" he asked.

I hated that I could smell his body wash. I hated that I had to tell him lies, when inside, deep down, I wanted to continue right where we'd left off on the boat.

Being an adult sucks.

I stayed right where I was as he walked out of the room, letting the door fall closed behind him with a heavy thud. When he was gone and I had the entire hotel room to myself, I finally felt like I could breathe again. I pulled up my work calendar and started hammering away at each item. From then on, I was going to impress Julian with my work ethic, not my bra size.

Julian was still out running errands when his hotel phone rang late in the afternoon. I'd attached his phone number to a few of the emails I'd sent out to architecture firms, so I didn't hesitate to answer the phone. If they were already getting back to us, it was a good sign that they were in need of work.

"Hello, this is Josephine Keller," I answered, poised with a pen, ready to take notes.

"Josephine?" a shrewd voice asked on the other end of the line. "Who are you? My son's girlfriend?"

I nearly dropped the phone. The feminine voice was crystal clear and confident, with an air of aristocracy laced through every syllable.

Holy shit. *It's Julian's mother...*

"Oh, no. No," I clarified. "I'm his personal assistant."

She cleared her throat, clearly annoyed.

"And yet you're in his hotel room, answering his phone?" Her tone said it all.

I fidgeted in my seat as if she were there, staring me down. "Oh, yes, it's just that we... he and I have been working from his hotel room while we try to find an office space."

Nothing about the situation was suspicious and yet I sounded guilty even to my own ears.

"Of course. How very...orthodox."

I wiped my sweaty palm on my pants before switching the phone to my other ear. Where the fuck was Julian?

"Would you like me to connect you with your son? He actually just stepped out but I could have him call you back—"

She didn't let me finish.

"Actually, don't bother. This will work out better. I have a few things to discuss with him and it's better if he can't argue with my requests."

I rubbed the back of my neck as I worked out her words. "So you'd like me to take a message?"

She took a deep breath as if trying to calm herself. "I'm confused. Are you not his assistant? Is this not in your job description? Perhaps he has you employed for different reasons?"

Had she just implied that that I was Julian's hired sex girl? Jesus. I could feel the heat rising to my cheeks.

"Of course I can take a message, ma'am," I replied with a honey-dipped tone. "Let me just grab my pen." I'd be damned before I let her know she was winning.

I scrambled to find a clean page in my notebook, but she didn't wait. She rattled off details as I ripped pages away.

"I have a fundraiser at the Four Seasons hotel at 8:00 PM Wednesday night. Since my son is back in New York City, I've arranged a date for him. Her name is Priscilla Kinkaid and I'm dear friends with her mother. I'd appreciate it if he would have his driver pick her up so that they may arrive together. It would be very rude to have her drive separately."

I stopped writing.

"Priscilla Kinkaid?" I asked.

Everyone with a computer and a half-decent internet connection knew who Priscilla Kinkaid was. She was this decade's Paris Hilton, except without the sex tape and the tiny dog. She was all over the fashion world, and as a fashion blogger, I knew just how stylish and ungodly beautiful she was.

Julian's mother sighed. "Yes. Please pay attention. I haven't got all day."

I stared down at my notepad.

"Go ahead," I muttered with a cold tone.

"I'm going to email you the details and Priscilla's address. I need you to convey to Julian that this event is of the utmost importance to me, especially with how *ill* his sister is right now."

Julian had revealed to me weeks ago that Lorena wasn't actually staying in the hospital, that she was seeking treatment for something in rehab. Still, the way Mrs. Lefray spoke about her only daughter sent a chill down my spine.

"Okay," I replied before rattling off my email address for her. "You can send all the details to that address."

She jotted down my email address and I wondered if Julian would actually go through with something like this. Did he still let his mother boss him around like he was a child?

"Could you also draft an email from Julian explaining how excited he is to escort Priscilla to the fundraiser? It doesn't have to be long, but I'd like him to send her something."

My mouth dropped.

"I can't hack into his email account," I argued.

"Don't be ridiculous," she replied, as if offended that I would even assume that's what she wanted. "You just need to draft it and then he will send it off himself."

Before I could offer a response, she continued. "Anyway, I've got to run, but I need you to get all of this done today."

I'm sorry, I didn't realize I worked for all three Lefrays...

The line went dead and I pulled the phone away from my face to stare down at it. Lying beside the receiver, on the front of my notepad, was a chicken-scratch list of things she'd just ordered me to do. Every item written there made my stomach churn in disgust. Not only did I have to ignore my feelings for Julian, I now had to actively set up his date with another woman? I wanted to shred the note into little pieces and flush it down the toilet. I wanted to delete the email his mother was undoubtedly drafting at that very moment, listing every detail about his hot date. I wanted to feign amnesia about the whole topic.

I hadn't yet decided what I would do about it by the time the hotel door opened and Julian stepped in. I was sitting on the couch with the list beside me and his mother's email open on my laptop. I didn't look up when he rounded the back of the couch, but I listened to the sound of his shoes hitting the hardwood floor and I picked up the scent of his spiced aftershave as soon as he stepped close.

"Italian cream cake," he said, holding out a clear plastic takeout box in front of my line of sight. "As a peace offering."

For two seconds, I couldn't reply, too choked up with the weight of indecision. Why did his mother have to call when he was out? Why did I have to know just how gorgeous Priscilla was? Could she not have picked someone a little less easy on the eyes?

"Jo? Are you still mad at me?"

I blinked up at him, catching sight of his earnest eyes. I smiled and shook my head, too caught up in his sweet gesture to ignore him.

I reached out for the cake and laughed. In the corner of the box, there was a little dollop of icing.

"You got me extra icing?"

He smiled. "You mentioned that you preferred it that way. I figured it wouldn't be much of a peace offering without it."

He tucked his hands into his suit pockets and took a step back as I set the cake down on the table in front of me.

God dammit, did he have to act like my perfect soul mate at this very moment? I held the name of his very hot, very single, very blonde date in my hands and he was bringing me cake.

"What did I miss while I was gone?" he asked, unbuttoning his suit jacket and taking a seat on the couch across from me.

The shredder was only a few feet away. I could just reach over and drop the notes right into…

"Jo?"

I sighed. The truth. I had to tell him the truth. "Your mom called."

His eyes widened. "Did you speak with her?"

"No. I told her I'm not allowed to talk to strangers."

He looked truly horrified. "Seriously, what did she want?"

I held out the sheet of notebook paper and watched his long fingers wrap around the edge and pull it away from me.

"She wanted me to deliver that message to you," I said.

His brows furrowed as he read my chicken scratch and then his jaw tightened. I watched the muscle shift beneath his sculpted cheek and then I turned to stare out the hotel window, wishing I'd never answered that damn phone call.

"You took this message?" he asked, staring back up at me with clear confusion.

"Every word," I said with a flat smile, finally turning back to look at him. "Looks like you have a hot date on Wednesday."

Chapter Twenty-Three

Julian

I pulled my tuxedo jacket off the hanger and slipped each of my arms inside. I straightened the lapels on my jacket so that they lay flat against my chest and then reached to pull my cufflinks out of a small leather box. My father had passed them down to me on my fourteenth birthday and each one was inscribed with a cursive L. Once they were in place, I paused and stared up at my reflection in my hotel mirror. My black tie hung loosely around my neck, waiting to be fastened into a bow. My hair still stuck up in every direction from my shower. I'd need to tame it before I left for my mother's fundraiser, but I was taking my time, dragging my feet to get ready.

Truthfully, I hadn't wanted to go to the fundraiser, especially not with a date handpicked by my mother. In the beginning, I'd set my heels in about the event, but then I spoke with Lorena and she planted the first seed of guilt in my mind.

I hadn't seen or spoken to my mother in months. I'd moved back to the city without even telling her and now she knew I was here and didn't care enough to see her. My mother had a nasty streak to her, but it didn't make me sleep any better at night, knowing there were ways I could have tried harder.

So, I leaned forward and tied my bow tie, resolved to attend her fundraiser for at least a few minutes. It wouldn't kill me.

By the time I left the hotel, my mood hadn't shifted in the slightest. I was annoyed to have to spend a night schmoozing with fundraiser guests I didn't care about, all the while knowing Josephine wouldn't be present.

Given the choice, I would have invited her as my date for the event, but I knew it wasn't a good idea. I wasn't out to piss my mother off just for the sake of it, and I owed it to Josephine to give her some space.

In the span of a few weeks we'd gone from strangers, to coworkers, to friends, and then I'd gone and pushed too far, too fast and fucked it up.

What happened on Dean's boat was the result of every repressed thought I'd had for the last few weeks, every time I caught myself watching Jo work, every time I thought of what she'd look like splayed out across my bed.

I'd been selfish to kiss her when I was drunk. To Josephine, it seemed like I was playing with her life, like it was all a game. I hadn't kissed her for my amusement. I'd kissed her because I damn well wanted to and now I had to consider the real implications of falling for my employee.

I laced up my shoes, pulling the strings tight as I tried to decide how best to handle the situation with Josephine. My phone buzzed on my desk in the other room, but I didn't bother checking it until I was walking out the door a few minutes later.

I called for the elevator and swiped my finger across the screen, surprised to find a text from Josephine.

Josephine: I forgot to tell you that I ordered flowers for Priscilla.

I bristled at the thought. Why the fuck had she done that?

Julian: You didn't have to do that.

The elevator arrived and the doors swept open as my phone vibrated again in my hand.

Josephine: Your mom asked me to...I didn't want you to get in trouble.

I punched in the button for the first floor, surprised that it didn't pop out of the display panel from the amount of force I used. I'd never have the audacity to ask Josephine to help me prepare for a date with another woman. Yet, there she was, buying my fucking date flowers. I clenched my hand into a fist, trying to quell the rage building toward my mother and her need to overstep her bounds at every turn. I watched the lights on the elevator panel, trying to decide how I could explain everything to Josephine without making her uncomfortable again.

Julian: I wish you were coming with me.

Good, asshole. That's definitely a text you should send to your employee.

I knew I was in the wrong, and yet I couldn't ease off the idea of being with Josephine, really being with her. I'd have given anything to have her on my arm at the fundraiser. Instead, I had Priscilla.

I had to hand it to my mom, she knew how to make a point.

I'd grown up in the same circle as Priscilla. We'd dated briefly at the beginning of college and it had taken me all of one week to realize how hollow she was inside. The hairspray and the makeup and the perfume could only go so far. There was no substance there, nothing to draw me closer, nothing to make me want to lean in and listen, just to be sure I'd heard every word she'd uttered.

Josephine: Obviously.

I smiled.

Julian: Prove it then.
Josephine: Julian. STOP. Every time you flirt with me, I'm going to make you put $5 in a jar.
Julian: I've got money to spend.
Josephine: You're right. Let's scrap the jar idea. Perhaps a shock collar would be more effective?

I shuddered at the thought.

Julian: Point taken.
Julian: Have any plans for the night?

I imagined her out at a bar, sitting by herself, playing with a cocktail napkin while she waited for a man to approach her. He would. She'd sit there for a minute tops before some lucky bastard stole her time for the night. I stared down at my phone while she typed, hoping she'd reply with something boring that involved footed pajamas.

Josephine: Nah, all my orgies fell through.

I laughed and shook my head.

Julian: Multiple?
Josephine: Booked 'em straight from 8:00 PM - 8:00 AM.
Julian: How does one prepare for a twelve-hour block of orgies?
Josephine: 3-day juice cleanse...maybe some carbo-loading the night before. The usual.

I laughed out loud in the lobby of the hotel, not even bothering to watch where I was going as I continued to text.

Julian: Wouldn't the juice cleanse and the carbo-loading counteract one another?
Josephine: You're going to be late to your fundraiser. I'll talk to you later.

My smile slipped away as my fingers hovered over my phone's keyboard. I knew Josephine wouldn't understand my reasoning for going to the fundraiser. She didn't know my mother or understand our relationship. I didn't have time to explain everything to her, but I knew that by cutting off the jokes, she was letting me know she was upset the only way she knew how.

I'd have to find a way to prove to her that going to the fundraiser was strictly business for me.

I didn't pay attention as my driver headed in the direction of Priscilla's apartment. I didn't pay attention as she took a seat beside me in the backseat and I threw her a quiet greeting. I didn't pay attention as we strolled past the step and repeat, cameras flashing in front of my face like overzealous fireflies.

If someone had asked after the event what color Priscilla had worn or what she'd done with her hair, I would have blanked on the answer. Green? Navy? Something dark. Who knows.

I made my way through the event and replied to questions when they were aimed in my direction. I kept watch for my mother, trying to find her so she could see that I'd done as she wished and attended her fundraiser.

I kept one hand in my pocket, clenched around my cell phone, praying that it would vibrate with an incoming text from Josephine.

Two hours into the event, I was antsy and bored. The cocktail hour was about to give way to the dinner portion of the evening and the thought of having to sit still through a four-course meal felt like a death sentence. I excused myself from a conversation I'd been ignoring and went to find my mother. I passed the mayor and his wife, a few celebrities I'd rubbed elbows with at past events, and a few buddies I'd known since private school. I nodded and threw waves as I passed, and then finally I found my mother at the front of the room, near the side of the stage with a microphone in hand.

She was wearing a gold gown with a giant bow situated on the side of her hip. Her brown hair was pulled into a tight knot at the nape of her neck and her skin was covered in a dark fake tan. I knew it was fake because my sister and I had gotten our tan skin from our father while our mother was always the pale one out of the four of us. We'd go on vacation and Lorena, Dad, and I would tan to crisps on the first day. My mom would sit under a shaded umbrella with SPF 90 slathered over every inch of her skin.

She was preparing to step up onto the stage, but I caught her attention just before she could.

"Julian!" she cooed as her gaze slid over to me. "I was just about to do a quick introductory toast."

I leaned in and she did a double air kiss over each of my cheeks. I couldn't recall the last time she'd actually hugged me.

"Hey Mom. I'm actually going to have to head out, but I'm glad I got to see you. The event looks great."

There, that's pleasant. Lorena couldn't be mad at me. I'd attended the event. There was no law that said I had to be there to help clean up at 2:00 AM.

My mother's face fell—barely; the Botox ensured that most of her muscles couldn't move more than a fraction of a centimeter.

"Already?"

She reached out for my arm and pulled me over to the side of the stage, out of the earshot of the friends she'd been talking to when I'd first walked up.

"No. No. That won't do, Julian. You'll stay for my toast and then I'll introduce you to a few acquaintances."

I thought of pulling out my wallet just to ensure that I

was in fact thirty-fucking-one years old and capable of making my own decisions.

I shook my head.

"The fundraiser looks great and so do you. Pass on a hello to your friends for me."

"What about Priscilla?" she asked, her lips pursing together in annoyance. "It would be extremely rude of you to leave your date just like that. Perhaps this is why you're still a bachelor at your age."

Yup. *Perhaps, Mother.*

I stuffed my hands in my pockets. "She can take the car back when she's ready to leave. She has plenty of friends here and many of them weren't coerced into a playdate. I'm sure she'll manage just fine."

"I can't believe you're doing this to me." Her voice wavered. "After everything your sister has put me through this last year. You can't even attend one fundraiser and make your mother happy? Is that too much to ask?"

I flinched back and stared at her, baffled that she could spout such bullshit and manage to live with herself afterward.

"What Lorena has put *you* through?" I asked, hearing the anger taking over my voice.

Her eyes slid to her friends nervously, but I didn't stop.

"How many times have you visited Lorena in rehab? How many of your friends know that she's seeking treatment for drug addiction and that she's not on some extended European vacation?"

She took a breath and cocked her chin in the air as if she were in the presence of someone hardly worth her time.

"How I choose to conduct my relationship with my daughter is none of your business. You don't know the first thing about what I've had to do to keep this family together."

I shoved my hands into my pockets and shrugged.

"Well if you care, she's done really well in treatment and she'll be released in a few weeks. Maybe you can pencil her into your busy social schedule then," I said, turning to scan for the quickest exit. I needed to get the fuck out of Crazyville.

"Where are you even going? What could be more important than this event?" she asked with an incredulous tone as I started to push back through the crowd.

It's not what, it's who.

Chapter Twenty-Four

Josephine

The world isn't fair and I hate it. I'd searched for a night job relentlessly over the last week or so and I'd come back with exactly zero interviews and zero callbacks. You know who gets jobs in the fashion industry? Sons and daughters of people in the fashion industry. I thought there'd be a chance for me. I thought I could prove my worth and start at the bottom. Turns out, even the bottom spots are reserved for those born on the Upper West Side. Unless your surname adorns the front of a public library or is engraved in bronze above a hospital wing, chances are you're not connected enough to land a decent job in New York. It's like the world's biggest sorority and I was definitely not deemed worthy enough to pledge.

After two months of living in NYC, I was just as broke as I'd been when I'd arrived on the Greyhound bus. Every paycheck from Julian went straight to paying my rent and student loans, but it wasn't enough. Not even close. I'd been searching for another position everywhere. Ideally I wanted to stay in fashion, but working retail would at least mean I was around clothing. I'd dropped off my resume everywhere: J. Crew, Madewell, Kate Spade, H&M—none of them needed someone who could only work on nights and weekends. (The ladies at Baby Gap had laughed when I'd asked if they could work around my workweek schedule. Cruel assholes.)

I had fifty dollars left in my bank account. My rent was due in three days, my loan payment was due in four, and I'd passed a delicious-smelling Chinese food restaurant on the way to the subway and had to walk right past it. (Lo mein for $15? Are people just shitting dollars these days? Who can afford that?)

"Oh, wow, what pretty dresses."

I glanced over to the woman sitting in the subway seat beside me.

Her frizzy hair was chopped short to her shoulders. Her deep-set eyes were surrounded by wrinkles, but her lips were coated in a bright red lipstick. She repositioned her circular glasses on the bridge of her nose and stared down at the dry cleaning bag crushed on my lap.

I followed her gaze and frowned.

Yeah, they are pretty dresses. My favorite ones.

I was clutching five thrifted designer gowns I'd collected over the last few years in the hope that I'd have reasons to wear them one day. The gold, shimmery gown at the top of the pile was practically begging me to reconsider my decision. I'd only ever tried it on once.

"Are you a stylist for someone?" she asked. "Is that why you have so many gowns?"

I shook my head, staring hard at the glimmering material beneath the garment bag. "No. I'm going to sell them."

She gaped. "Why would you do that? They're so beautiful."

My chest tightened and for a moment I thought I was going to unload all of my troubles on an unsuspecting stranger. *I will not cry. I will not cry. I will not cry in the middle of a stinky subway car.*

"No room in my closet," I lied, feeling my impending breakdown fighting to break to the surface.

She laughed and shook her head. "Ha. The life of the rich, I suppose."

I didn't bother correcting her.

When the subway arrived at my stop, I tossed the gowns over my arms to ensure they didn't scrape on the concrete. The consignment shop I'd picked had a reputation for finding special vintage pieces. I hoped they would recognize the beauty of the gowns enough to offer decent prices.

The shop was tucked away on the first floor of an old brick building. There were no windows on the front of the shop, and had it not been for the small sign on the door, I would have walked right by it.

I pulled open the door, careful not to let the gowns fall in the process, and a small bell rang overhead, announcing my presence. I stepped through the doorway, breathing in the perfumed air. One look around the space confirmed that

I was in the right place. The same way a candy store brims over with bright sugary treats, the consignment shop was practically overflowing with painstakingly curated finds. An entire wall was covered in vintage scarves and costume jewelry. Directly across the room, there were five floor-to-ceiling shelves completely packed with designer purses. Hermès, Chanel, Rebecca Minkoff, Gucci—they were all there, making me salivate on demand.

"May I help you?" a small voice asked, drawing my attention away from the rows of coveted purses.

I glanced up to see a petite woman perched behind the counter on a small wooden stool. Her bright red hair stuck out in every direction and she had a layer of blue necklaces weighing down her neck. Her black dress did little to hide her frail figure and when I stepped closer, my gaze was drawn to her wrinkled, worn hands clasped in her lap. In front of her, beside the cash register sat an old, abused sewing machine—likely to blame for the way her hands looked.

"Selling those?" she asked gently.

I shifted my gaze away from her hands, up to her gentle smile, and then I nodded.

"Well bring them here and let me see them. We'll see what they're worth."

"The gold is lovely," she said as I laid down the plastic garment bag on the counter, to the side of her sewing machine.

She slid thoughtfully off her chair and reached for the counter to balance herself. I studied her movements with care, wondering just how old she was. Her bright hair and kind eyes seemed to conceal her real age.

"May I?" she asked, pointing to the top of the plastic.

"Yes," I replied as she reached to pull open a drawer.

She pulled out a small pair of scissors and grabbed the end of the garment bag. My stomach sank as I watched her slice through the plastic, from top to bottom, practically cutting my heart right along with it.

"Yes. I knew this one would be lovely," she said, reaching for the gold gown as she let her scissors clatter back onto the counter.

"It's Monique Lhuillier," I said, pointing to the tag for proof.

She hummed and pulled the dress off the stack to inspect it. "Yes. It's beautiful, but not in the best condition."

The top of the bodice had intricate beading that I'd tried my best to conserve over the years. It hadn't been in the best condition when I'd first purchased it, but I'd never had the time to mend it.

She hummed as she turned the gown over in her hands, feeling the fabric between her fingers and carefully inspecting the hemline. I watched her, praying she saw the beauty in the gown as much as I did. When she was done, she placed the gown back onto the pile with a gentle hand and glanced up at me.

"Why don't you look around while I inspect the rest of these, and then I'll let you know what I can offer you for them," she said with a smile.

I swallowed slowly and nodded, even though I'd have rather stayed right where I was, watching her handle my most prized possessions.

"Are those flats vintage Chanel?" the woman asked from behind the counter.

I glanced down at my shoes and smiled.

"Yes."

"Any chance you'll part with those?"

My back stiffened. My Chanel flats would *never* be sold. Even if I ended up on the streets, I'd be the only homeless person in New York wearing vintage Chanel footwear. *Because I have priorities.*

I shook my head. "Not today."

Just the idea of having to part with them made my stomach twist into a ball of anxiety. I stuffed my hands into my pockets and took a step back, confirming to myself that I wasn't allowed to touch a single thing in the shop while I waited for her to finish. Chances were, if I broke something, I'd have to hawk an organ to cover the cost.

I wandered through the store while she inspected the gowns, keeping track of the setting sun through the window on the shop's door. I knew Julian would be picking up his date for the fundraiser soon. Priscilla Kinkaid. I'd googled her the night before, just to rub salt in the wound. She was as pretty and as well connected as I remembered. Most of the photos that popped up in the image search were of her sitting in the front row of various fashion shows, smiling next to the who's who of fashion. She'd apparently vacationed last June with Karl Lagerfeld for Christ's sake.

She and Julian would make a beautiful couple. Their children would be J. Crew models. *Gag me.*

I didn't want to think of Julian smiling at another woman. I didn't want to think of the way he filled out a tuxedo, making it impossible for his beauty to go unnoticed. He was a perfect gentleman, funny and charming. Priscilla would have to be a complete simpleton not to appreciate everything he had to offer.

"Sweetie, I'm ready for you," the woman called from the front counter.

I took a breath and braced myself for the results. Hopefully I'd be able to pay my rent for a few months with the dress money. By selling them, I'd have enough time to find another job and get the loan officers off my back.

She'd hung each of the gowns on a garment rack behind the counter. Gold, black, red, blue, and white. They were all beautiful in their own way, and it was almost more cruel to see them hanging like that, right in front of me but already long gone.

"I would be willing to give you $500 for the Monique Lhuillier and $200 for the rest," she said, pointing to the other four gowns.

My gaze froze on the colorful gowns as my mind tried to process her words. I'd been expecting so much more. That amount would hardly cover one month's rent. My brows tugged together as my gaze shifted back and forth between her and the gowns.

"Do you mean $200 for each?"

She frowned. "No. $200 for them all." She motioned to the last four dresses. "They're not items my clients would pay top dollar for. They're seasons old, but not quite vintage. Most of them need some major repair work before they'd even be ready for resale."

I wanted to throw up. I could feel my anxiety rearing its ugly head, pumping through my body and tainting what little hope I had left.

Fuck this day. Fuck my old dresses. Fuck my massive pile of student loans.

I'd expected to be paid ten times that amount. Hell, maybe even twenty. She might as well have offered me nothing at all for the way I felt. I stood across the counter from her, trying to decide what to do, knowing full well that my mind was already made up. I had to sell them. I didn't have a choice.

I felt like a cheap hooker as I pushed through the shop's

door and made my way out onto the bustling street. Sure, I had $700 in cash stuffed into my wallet, but I felt used and hollow, no better than I had on the way over. Selling those dresses was supposed to solve my problems, but instead, it'd just piled another one right on top, right in the center of my heart.

I was critically close to throwing in my cards. I could feel the pressure rising in my chest, filling every part of me until I thought I'd break right there, in the middle of the sidewalk.

I couldn't have a breakdown; I had things to do. I needed to take outfit photos for a post that should have been up on my blog two days earlier. I needed to email out more resumes and beg for a part-time job. I'd extend my search beyond the school of fashion retail. *Do they have Dairy Queens in New York?* I'd serve up fries and ice cream all night long if it meant I could go one day without wondering if I had enough money to make rent.

"Get out of the way lady!" a deliveryman yelled from behind me just before I felt an excruciating pain shoot up from my foot.

"Shit," I hissed as pain coursed through my foot like a thousand tiny knives stabbing my bones. "Shit. Shit. Shit."

The asshole had rolled his dolly over the top of my foot and all but crushed all my bones to a pulp. I hopped up and down, trying to quell the shooting pain, but it didn't help.

"Are you kidding me?" I yelled as he continued to walk away, not even bothering to acknowledge that he'd almost broken every bone in my foot.

"Who does that?!" I yelled. "And then you don't even apologize?!"

He didn't turn around once. He sped away with his dolly piled seven feet high with boxes, most likely filled to the brim with tiny elephants and lead paperweights. Meanwhile, everyone on the sidewalk shot me glares as if I was the crazy one.

At times I felt as if New York City was trying to kill me. I mean literally crush me under the weight of UPS boxes and overdue rent and rude people. I tried to wiggle my toes, relieved that they didn't feel broken, and then I glanced down to assess the damage.

At that moment I felt a tiny rip in my heart, right down the center.

THE ASSHOLE HAD RUINED MY CHANEL FLATS.

A fat grease stain spread across the top of the leopard print, right where his dolly had rolled over my foot. The double "CC" logo that Chanel was known for had ripped off and was sitting lonely and forgotten on the sidewalk next to my foot.

I knew I was being ridiculous. I knew people were dying because they couldn't eat. I knew people had real problems that didn't include grease stains and designer shoes.

I knew all that, and yet I couldn't stop the tears from slipping down my cheeks as I bent down to pick up the CC logo. I couldn't stop the flood of emotions that hit me.

This was the final straw.

I couldn't do it.

New York wasn't my city. I was not cut out for the hustle and bustle and I was not cut out to make it in the fashion world.

There.

ARE YOU FUCKING HAPPY, UNIVERSE?!

"Sweetie, stop that. You're embarrassing yourself," a gentle voice said from behind me.

I felt a small hand wrap around my waist, tugging on my shirt and trying to pull me back toward the side of the sidewalk.

"Stop that crying."

I looked back to see the consignment shop owner doing her best to drag me back into her shop.

I shook my head and waved my hands, the universal sign for "leave me alone". I knew if I spoke up, my words would come out a babbling mess.

"Come inside for a moment. Come inside and we'll sort this out," she insisted as she dragged me through the shop door. "Are you upset about those flats?"

For a petite old lady, she was remarkably strong. I don't think I could have fought her off if I tried. *Yet another reason NYC isn't for me. I couldn't even fend off an attack from an old lady.*

The bell chimed overhead as we stepped back inside, but I could hardly hear it over the sound of my own babbling.

"Stop that crying. I can fix those flats. That's nothing. With the right solvent, that grease will come right off," she said.

I wiped my face, trying to get a handle on my tears. Her kind brown eyes searched my features, most likely trying to find the origin of my crazy. *Keep lookin' lady. It's there.*

"Does that make it better? Is that all that's wrong?" she asked.

I shook my head.

"What else can I do then?" she asked. "I can't pay you more for those dresses, but I can fix those shoes for free."

I stared up into her kind eyes, took a deep breath, and went for it.

"Are you hiring?"

"What?" She leaned back and narrowed her eyes, obviously taken aback by the question.

"I promise that I'm a great employee," I swore. "Despite what the current circumstances suggest."

She smiled. "You just had a public breakdown on the sidewalk and you expect me to give you a job?"

I felt my lip quiver.

She held up her hands and shook her head.

"Okay. Jeez, just get it together. I can't give you work. The shop isn't ever busy enough for two people, but I have a friend who might be able to help. Are you available for some night work?"

"Yes. Yes! Absolutely."

She let go of my elbows and turned toward the counter. I stayed glued to my spot, watching her pull out an old grey rolodex and dust the top off with her hand. The thing probably hadn't been used since the 80s. She took her time rifling through it until she finally pulled out a worn business card toward the back.

She met my eye as she dialed the number and offered me a reassuring smile.

"It'll be okay," she said. "We all have days like this. Don't you know the old saying: 'When someone ruins your Chanel flats, make lemonade'?"

I burst out laughing, completely caught off guard by her humor.

"I don't think that's how it goes," I said, wiping my nose and finally getting ahold of my sniffles.

She was about to reply when I heard a mumble on the other end of the phone line. She held up her finger to silence me and then spoke into the receiver.

"Hey Margery. This is Beth. Beth Montgomery—yes, yes. I'm good."

There were more mumbles on the other end of the line as Beth and Margery went through the standard pleasantries. Then finally, she smiled up at me.

"I'm glad everything is going good for you. We'll have to catch up for dinner soon," she said. "I actually called though because I have a favor to ask you."

Chapter Twenty~Five

Julian

As soon as I walked out of the fundraiser, I ripped the bowtie from around my neck and shoved it into my pocket. The damn thing had been strangling me for the last three hours and it felt good to finally get a lungful of air.

A hotel attendant rushed forward to greet me. "Sir, would you like me to call you a cab or do you have a driver?"

I held up my hand and shook my head. I needed to walk. I needed to clear my head in the ten blocks it'd take me to get home. It didn't feel good to tell my mother off. She wasn't a malicious person, she was just a bored woman with too much wealth and even more insecurity.

To her, being a good mother meant providing your kids with a prominent last name and the means to succeed. What good was a hug or a kiss? To her, handshakes and air-kisses were the appropriate greetings for everyone from her ladies lunch group to her children. My father had been the affectionate one with us. He was a romantic down to the marrow of his bones. He'd had a way of softening my mother, of rounding out her edges. In the fifteen years since his death, she'd slowly reverted back to her true nature and my relationship with her had taken a turn for the worse. Now, seeing the way she was choosing to handle Lorena's issues, I wanted nothing more to do with her.

A bike bell rang behind me and I stepped aside, out of the way, just as a pedicab flew by me on the edge of the street. The neon lights on his wheels blinked bright in the night, illuminating the girl sitting in the carriage behind his bike. She had long brunette hair that blew in the wind as the driver peddled them farther and farther away. She reminded me of Josephine and I instantly wished that I was with her, that I could talk to her about my mom and she could tell me I was doing the right thing.

I continued walking the path to my hotel, staying right along the edge of the street, with my hands shoved into the pockets of my tuxedo. I was only a few blocks away. I could be tucked in my bed, nursing a glass of scotch in five minutes. Instead, I veered to the right and headed in the direction of Greenwich Village, toward Josephine. I didn't know her exact address, but that seemed trivial in the moment. I just wanted to be near her even if that meant aimlessly wandering around her neighborhood.

Chasing women, stalking their apartments was new territory for me. I'd never been in a situation like it before. Everything prior to Josephine had been black and white. Either I was in a relationship with a woman or it was just a short-term, one night thing. The parameters were laid out early on and the expectations were always made perfectly clear by both parties. This murky swamp I was wading through with Josephine was asking for trouble.

But Josephine was different.

She was my friend.

She was my very hot friend.

She was my very hot, very unattainable friend.

I kept walking through the streets of New York with no real goal in mind and no set destination. By the time I'd arrived outside of an old pizza shop in the heart of Greenwich Village, I still hadn't decided whether or not I was actually going to work up the nerve to call Josephine. I stopped on the curb in front of the pizza place and clutched my cell phone in my hand just as a young couple stumbled out. They had their arms wrapped around one another and just at the end of the curb, the girl stood on her toes to plant a kiss on the guy's cheek. Her date wrapped his arms around her back and dipped her low. I watched them like a fucking creep; they were so happy and in love.

Without another thought, I pulled out my phone and dialed Josephine's number.

It rang three excruciating times, and then I heard her sweet voice on the other end of the line.

"Mr. Lefray, are you calling me from the bathroom at the fundraiser?" she asked, amusement in her tone.

I smiled as the tightness in my chest loosened. She had me wound right around her finger.

"I bailed," I answered simply, stepping toward the wall

of the pizzeria so I'd be out of the way of the other pedestrians.

"With your date?" she asked.

I bristled at the thought. "No. Just me."

"Well Han Solo, you officially win the award for shortest date ever to occur."

I smiled. "It was an hour at least. Maybe two."

"You give a new meaning to the word quickie," she joked.

I laughed and shook my head. "I'm sure she's having more fun without me."

She hummed and I stared out at the street, watching cab after cab pass by in a yellow blur.

"So why are you calling?" she asked.

I took a breath and stared up at the red and white striped awning above me. Time to bite the bullet.

"I'm standing outside Ray's Pizzeria."

"Where?"

"Ray's Pizzeria."

"Uhh, that's only a block over from me. Why are you there?"

"I was in the neighborhood," I lied.

"Mhm. Try again."

I tapped my knuckles against the brick, trying to think of another excuse.

"I really like their pizza. Ray is my godfather."

She laughed.

"Sure. Sure. Why wouldn't you have an Italian godfather that happens to live in Greenwich Village?"

I faked a gasp. "I know, small world, huh? Some might call it destiny."

She laughed and I reveled in the sound of it. Light, easy, carefree. I wanted to hoard the ability to make her laugh for only myself. I was a greedy asshole when it came to Jo.

Silence hung on the phone between us as I waited for her to invite me to her place and she waited for me to push the arbitrary line she'd set up. I knew she didn't want to date her boss. I knew I should have left her alone.

And yet, I didn't.

"You're relentless," she said after a few moments. "I should have ordered that shock collar."

I didn't argue.

"Buy me a slice of pizza and meet me outside my apartment on Grove Street. I'll let you up if you come bearing pepperonis."

I turned to step into the shop, praying they didn't take forever.

"What else do you want?" I asked.

"Whatever looks good. Now hang up so that I can clean up before you get here. I have, like, *unmentionables* in my living room and stuff. I know I come off as really put together at work, but I'm kind of a slob."

Jo wasn't kidding. She lived a block over from the pizza shop and when I approached her building with pizza in hand, I saw her perched right outside. She was on the last step of the stoop, wearing red and white polka dot pajama pants and a University of Texas sweatshirt. Her hair was a mess of curls piled high on her head and she was wearing black-framed glasses.

"We have to stop meeting like this," she joked as I approached.

"I feel so overdressed in a tux. You should have told me the theme for the night was 'eccentric cat lady'." I smiled and handed her the box of warm pizza.

She glanced down at her chest and then back up at me. "Are you kidding? This is my fancy sweatshirt. I only wear it when I'm around royalty and stuff."

I laughed, taken aback by how refreshing she was. I'd already known that about her, but coming straight to her apartment after leaving the fundraiser gave it a stark clarity. The contrast between a woman like Priscilla and Jo was like night and day.

"Stop staring at me and let's go inside," she said with a weird smile.

Had I been staring?

"So this is home?" I asked, glancing behind her.

She lived in a stout, red brick building with iron bars across the first floor windows. It was one of the most worn down buildings on the street, but I knew the rent probably didn't reflect that. Nothing in this area of the city was cheap. She pushed open the front door to reveal a dark foyer leading to a narrow staircase in the very center.

"Yup. It's my home for now," she answered with a shrug.

An older short man was checking his mail on the side of the foyer. A brown yamaka rested on the crown of his head and he moved at a glacial pace as he extracted letters from his small cubbyhole.

"Hey Isaac," Josephine called as we made for the base of the stairs.

"Oh! Hello Josephine!" he exclaimed, turning to face us. "Who is this oysgeputst mentsch with the pitse?" he whispered noisily in her ear.

"Just a friend, Isaac. Goodnight!"

"Friend of yours?" I asked as we hit the second floor landing and started up the next round of stairs.

Jo turned over her shoulder and smiled. "He's a rabbi and sometimes I help feed his goldfish if he's running late. Did you know they have Kosher fish flakes?"

After three more flights of stairs, I peeled off my tuxedo jacket and followed Josephine to the end of the hallway. She stuck her key into the lock, twisted it around, and then turned back to stare at me.

I could just make out her green eyes through the glare on her glasses. She suddenly seemed unsure of herself.

"Once I let you in here, you're not going to look at me the same anymore."

I frowned. "What? Why?"

She smiled. "It's just that my ratmates are really sensitive and I don't want you to insult their home."

I held my hand up in mock seriousness. "Why do you think I ordered extra cheese?"

She laughed and pushed the door open so I could catch my first glimpse inside. It was by anyone's standards a modest studio apartment. In all, it couldn't have been more than 450 square feet, including the tiny patio off the main living room.

"Okay, good, because the rats and I have an understanding. They live rent free as long as we watch Ratatouille every single night. They love the chase scene."

"Jo, seriously it's not that bad."

It was bad. Worse than how I'd lived in college, but she'd done her best to add her charm to the place. One of the walls of the living room was covered with a bright tapestry. She'd shoved houseplants along the windows and multicolored striped rugs covered most of the old wood floors.

"I like it. You have a knack for making the best out of any situation," I said, turning in a circle to get a better look.

"Well at least let me take you on a tour," she said, reaching for my hand. I tried to act casual about the fact that our fingers were twined together, but I was sure she could read the shock on my face.

"Here is the kitchen," she said, taking a step to the left.

I took a step as well, pivoting my body in the direction of the small kitchen area.

"And then here's the bathroom, bedroom, living room, and foyer," she listed off, taking a step to the right and gesturing to the rest of the small room.

I laughed.

"Damn, after all that walking, I think we need some pizza," I said.

"Definitely," she confirmed with a nod.

I pulled her toward the couch. We fell back into the cushions, aligned hip to hip with the box balanced across both of our thighs.

I opened the box so she could reach in for the first slice. The pepperonis were about the size of my head and I could tell from the smell that they used garlic and basil in the sauce. I could have eaten the entire box myself. We each took a piece and folded them in half to keep the cheese from spilling off the edges.

"I like your place," I said.

She stared around at her apartment, chewing her bite. I studied her profile as she processed my compliment.

"Yeah. It's really not so bad. My neighbors are really nice."

I nodded, happy that she had nice people in her building.

"And bonus: technically I get to eat every meal in bed," she joked, patting the black futon beneath us.

I paused, mid chew, and processed her joke.

"You sleep here?" I asked, staring down at the black fabric with a pepperoni slice lodged in my throat.

"Yeah, it pulls out into a twin-sized mattress thing."

Before I could help myself, my brain took a very G-rated comment and twisted it into every R-rated fantasy. *This is where she sleeps. This is where she has sex.*

"Which way do you sleep?" I asked.

"Why?"

"I pride my fantasies on their accur—"

I barely got the words out before I felt a greasy pepperoni slice hit the side of my face.

Chapter Twenty-Six

Josephine

The second I threw the pepperoni slice at Julian, I regretted it, and not because it got pizza sauce on his cheek. No, it was because I really like pepperoni and the pizza place had been stingy bitches about putting it on our pizza. (Four pieces a slice? Might as well order Chinese.)

"Wait, give that back," I said, reaching for the pepperoni.

He jerked out of reach. "Finders keepers."

I watched him pop it into his mouth and chew like a smug jerk. You'd think the pizza sauce on his cheek would have made him look silly, but he looked as sexy as ever, just with a tad more garlic to bring out his tan. His dark eyes were still focused on me, watching me watch him, and before I could think of the hundreds of reasons not to, I leaned forward and licked the sauce right off his cheek.

I thought I was being cute and clever, licking his cheek like it was nothing.

It wasn't.

The tension in the room shifted in an instant. His breath hitched and I realized that I'd pushed him too far. Before I could lean back, he turned his head and his lips met mine in a crash of pizza sauce and lips and garlic and sweet, delicious lust.

He reached for my arm, grasping right below my elbow so I couldn't lean away. At first I was too stunned to do anything. My heart hammered against my chest and my hand shook, trying to keep hold of my pizza slice. Finally, my brain caught up.

Julian is kissing you.

KISS HIM BACK, YOU FOOL.

And then like a magician snapping his fingers, my hesitation disappeared. The pizza box, along with our half-eaten slices, was shoved to the floor like yesterday's news. My eyes fluttered closed and I slipped my hands up over his shoulders, gripping either side of his neck for dear life. He slipped his tongue into my mouth and I twisted my body so that I could face him even more.

He was so in control of the kiss, so much better than me that I felt like I could hardly keep up. I knew I wanted to impress him. I wanted to seduce him with my kiss, but he was too busy seducing me with his.

His fingers skirted the edge of my sweatshirt until he found the patch of bare skin just above my pajama pants. I shivered when his hand pressed up against the base of my spine, tugging me closer until we were chest to chest, heart to heart. He lifted my sweatshirt up, exposing my bare stomach.

I had a moment of hesitation before I lifted my hands up over my head and let him tug my sweatshirt off.

I wasn't wearing anything underneath besides a cream colored bra. There was no lace, no filigree. It was a tad too small, which meant Julian got one hell of show. I couldn't even bear to look down. I knew how unruly my boobs were at times. They were very good at hypnotizing men even when properly contained.

At least Julian seemed to like them.

His finger dragged along the line of my bra, tracing each cup as excruciatingly slowly as possible. I shivered at the sensation and gripped his neck, giving him unspoken approval. Of what? I didn't care. He could have it all. I just wanted him to keep going. I wanted him to unclasp my bra and get on with it.

He leaned back, giving me a second to catch my breath, and I let one hand fall to his thigh, skimming over the silky fabric of his tuxedo pants. It was soft, so much so that it hardly felt like there was a barrier between his tensed thigh and my hand. The higher I went, the more obvious his desire became.

"Holy shit," I gasped, pulling a half-inch away from him and meeting his eye.

He looked like he'd just gone on a long distance run. His cheeks were flushed, his pupils were dilated, and his hair was sticking up in every direction thanks to my wandering hands.

"What?" he asked, out of breath.

"You're hard," I said with wide eyes and a dumbstruck expression.

The edge of his mouth hitched up. "Yeah, that's usually how it works."

I shook my head. "No. You're like, really hard, and…" I couldn't quite pull the next few words out of my mouth, so instead I presented him with a visual. I held my hands up about a foot away from each other and stared up at him with an accusatory glare.

Julian was definitely packing more than six-pack abs. I'd been too caught up in the moment to notice that fact on Dean's yacht, but now? Now I couldn't *stop* noticing.

He rolled his eyes and pushed my hands aside; I swore there was a blush across his cheeks that hadn't been there a few seconds earlier.

"Do you always carry a t-ball bat in your pants?" I asked, too far gone to contain my laughter.

"Jesus, Jo. Can we not talk about youth sports while I'm aroused?" he asked, rubbing the back of his neck.

I reached out to touch the bulge in his pants again.

Yup.

It needs its own time zone.

"Jo?" he asked with a gentle tone.

"Yeah?" I asked.

His hand fell over mine on top of his pants, then he gripped my fingers and pulled them off.

"You can't just hold it like that."

Oh. *Oh!* Right.

Oh my god. I'd just been touching my boss' penis, like it was no big deal. Oh god. *What the hell am I doing?* My vision widened beyond Julian, to the expanse of my tiny apartment, to the stack of hidden bills sitting beneath the magazine on my kitchen counter.

Just like that, the game was over. My responsibilities flooded in like I was a junkie coming off a high. All the signs were there too: I felt regretful, guilty, angry with myself, and—worst of all—I wanted more.

"Dammit!" I jumped off the couch and shoved my hands through my hair. "We just made out, Julian, and—" I paused when I felt air brush over my chest. "You saw me in my bra!"

I glared at him accusingly and he had the gall to flash me his innocent hazel eyes.

"I hadn't realized," he said, making it a point to keep his gaze above my neck. Even still, his smirk gave him away.

I started pacing back and forth across my apartment floor, which was all of ten feet wide. Back and forth, back and forth as my brain tried to work out a plan.

First, I needed a joke to break the tension between us. Why'd the chicken cross the hard body of Julian Lefray?

To get laid.

Which came first?

The chicken or me?

Shit. I was in trouble if I couldn't think of a non-Julian related sex joke. I blamed him. Julian was not supposed to be at my apartment. What gave him the right to show up in Greenwich Village, one block over from my apartment, when he was supposed to be on a date with another woman?

He couldn't expect me to turn him down when he literally showed up at my apartment wearing a tailored tuxedo and holding a box of hot pizza. I mean, that's not playing by the rules.

"Okay, listen," I said, spinning on the balls of my feet and meeting his eyes.

He leaned back against the futon and spread his arms out along the back.

Perfect. He looked edible.

"You can't bring me pizza late at night," I said, trying to get my brain back on topic. "Pepperoni is foreplay to me."

He laughed. "Good to know."

"Also, I think we should set up some other ground rules."

"Rules?" he asked, with one dark brow arched in defiance.

"To prevent future problems like this from occurring." I pointed at his pants. "Exhibit A." Then, I pointed to my bra-clad chest. "Exhibit B."

"I think we should discuss exhibit B first. Maybe let the jury get a closer examination," he said, leaning forward with a devious smile.

"Julian! C'mon, this is serious. Throw me my freaking sweatshirt already."

He laughed and shook his head, clearly disagreeing. I didn't give him time to voice his opinion though. I grabbed my sweatshirt and tugged it over my head as quickly as possible. When I was done, I held up my hand and started counting out rules on my fingers.

"Rule number one: no pizza."

His brown hair was ruffled from our make out and his shirt was missing another button or two up top. *What the hell?*

"Second rule: we can't hang out in my apartment alone. It's too tempting."

"Do I get any say in these rules?" he asked.

"No," I answered quickly as I continued to pace around the room.

"Just to be clear, what are these rules in place for?" he asked, trying to catch my eye as I continued to move.

"It's to prevent the inevitable demise of our friendship," I said. "And to ensure that I still have a job in a few weeks when you're bored of hooking up with me."

"And why would that happen?"

I paused and stared over at him to see if he was being serious.

He looked hopeful and innocent, with his light eyes trained on me as if he actually expected me to believe he was looking for something serious. He hadn't once asked me out on a proper date. He'd never even hinted at it. We were friends who pushed the limits when it was convenient. Nothing more.

I groaned. "The odds are not in our favor. This is a straight up Hunger Games situation. I need to keep my job with you and I'd prefer to keep our relationship somewhat platonic."

His brow quirked. "Don't you think that ship has sailed?"

I shook my head. It couldn't have sailed. If it'd already sailed then that meant I was already screwed.

"Nope. That ship is going back to the marina. To a nice, safe spot."

He frowned.

"Honestly, what do you think my mom and dad will say when I explain to them that I'm banging my boss in New York? I was supposed to move up here and start a life for myself, not shack up with the first guy who befriended me."

To drive the point home, I reached to pull my hoodie down so it overlapped with my pajama pants.

"You and I are friends, Julian. Friends who don't kiss anymore."

Even as I spoke, I scanned his face, trying to decipher

his reaction to my rules. His dimples were hidden away behind a confused scowl. His lips were slightly pouted, just enough that I got hung up on them for a moment before meeting his eye.

For a few minutes neither of us said a word. I waited on tenterhooks, trying to prepare for his reaction, and then he nodded once and leaned forward. He clasped his hands between his legs and rested his elbows on his knees.

"Fine. Do friends go to dinner?" he asked with a curious tone.

"What? We just ate."

I pointed to the open box of pizza on the ground. Our half-eaten slices lay splayed out on the floor, probably soaking grease stains into my rug. Classy.

"I'm talking about sometime next week. Dean and I are going out on Wednesday and you could tag along with us. As a friend."

Oh. Dinner with the guys. Right, maybe I could do that. Maybe it would be good to be around Julian when we had a third person present, someone to act as a sexual-tension buffer. *Although, was Dean really the person for the job?* Maybe we needed a buffer who looked a little less like Ryan Gosling.

And then I remembered my new job and my heart sank. If everything went as planned, I'd be working next Wednesday night. There'd be no time for dinner, with or without Julian.

"I don't think I can," I answered.

"Why not?" he asked, piercing me with a hard stare.

Why not?

Why not?

I hadn't expected him to ask that and I hadn't decided whether or not I was prepared to tell him that I'd had to get

191

a second job, especially when I had no clue what that second job actually entailed. The friend Beth had called helped coordinate the shows for New York Fashion Week; I figured that was a good sign, but I was trying hard not to get my hopes up. For the time being, I was employing the "less is more" approach, at least until I knew what the hell I'd be doing.

"Prior commitment," I said, averting my eyes toward the pizza box once again.

I could see him frown out of the corner of my eye and I wanted so badly to throw away the rules and finish what we'd started. I knew he'd easily be the best lay of my life— he'd already won the best kiss category by a landslide. I knew Julian had the ability to obliterate every guy that had come before him. All the quick, cheesy sex I'd had in college, the bad kisses, the lackluster dates—they wouldn't compare to one night with him.

I studied him as he gathered his things. He pulled his tuxedo jacket back on without a word, shoved the pizza slices back into the box then crumbled it in his hand. He looked so devastatingly handsome, and yet, so defeated. His dimples were tucked away behind a reserved frown. His eyes were downcast, trained on the ground near his feet. He rubbed his jawline as he walked to the door and I followed after him.

He stepped into the hallway, turned over his shoulder, and met my eye. I thought my heart was going to leap out of my chest, rip right out from inside of me.

"I'll see you at work," he said, offering me a small smile before turning down the hallway.

My mouth opened, but there was nothing I could say to make it better. My words were jumbled in my mind, lost somewhere between "I want you, please stay" and "I'm sorry, you have to go".

Chapter Twenty~Seven

Josephine

I'll be honest, I'd assumed the job Beth had secured for me would involve being a high class call girl…or at the very least a *low class* call girl, based on the stinginess she displayed with my dresses.

Luckily for me, the job ended up being much, much cooler than expected, and bonus: I got to wear normal non-stripper clothes. Albeit, a pair of black pants and a t-shirt wasn't high couture, but for two weeks, I'd get to be behind the scenes of New York Fashion Week. I'd get to be up close and personal with all the top models, designers, and bloggers.

The only problem? I'd be holding a broom or a mop at all times.

Yup. That's right. Josie Keller would henceforth be known as Night Janitor. Jealous yet?

For ten days, I'd have to bolt from Julian's hotel at 5:00 PM on the dot and book it to Lincoln Center. I'd have to sneak in the back doors with the rest of the event staff and change into my alter ego, Clark Kent style. There was a small locker room for staff where I'd kick off my heels and slip into converse, slide on a black hat with "NYFW STAFF" embroidered across the front, and grab the broom least likely to break on me.

The pay was terrible, but I didn't care. I could use the extra money while I continued to hunt for a more permanent night job. I saved every penny I earned except for the $5 I used to splurge on a fresh green smoothie every afternoon on the way from Julian's hotel to Lincoln Center. *(And by green juice, I of course mean chocolate cupcake.)*

"Ladies! Ladies, line up, the show is starting in ten minutes!" a stagehand clapped her hands, trying to get everyone's attention—a nearly impossible feat.

I paused my sweeping and stepped to the back of the room to give the models space to run around me. It was only my fourth day on the job and I'd already learned a lot. No matter how organized the event coordinators thought they were, there was always a mad rush ten minutes before the fashion shows started. Fake eyelashes, sticky boob tape, hairspray bottles, high heels—all flying in the air, trying to find their final destination. I'd been hit in the head by enough bras on my first day to realize that I needed to stay as far away from the madness as possible.

And yet, I still *loved* every second of it.

I watched a designer waltz through the room with her nostrils flaring. She paused in the center, cupped her hands around her mouth, and yelled at the top of her lungs.

"Models. Get in line now, or I'm going to rip your hair extensions out. So help me god!"

Some of the designers were a *tad* more pleasant than others…

"You!" a stagehand pointed at me and then waved her hand at the row of salon chairs near the back wall. There was a mess of hair scattered across the floor beneath the chairs. Minutes earlier, a team of stylists had chopped away at extensions to give all the models a similar hairstyle. "Can you pah-lease sweep all that up already? I nearly broke my neck a second ago."

I nodded and jumped into action, pushing my broom out in front of me. I worked quickly to push the multicolored hair into a neat pile, working my magic on the mess. Unfortunately, just as I was about to sweep the first pile up into my dustpan, a model shoved past me on her way to the runway and scattered the hair in every direction. She'd been a force of nature on my small hair mountain.

"Dammit," I hissed as the model waltzed off without a care in the world.

She hadn't even noticed.

I had the *least* glamorous job in the *most* glamorous setting and I was still having trouble wrapping my head around that fact. At times, I got swept up in the excitement of the shows, as if I was somehow a part of them.

After I'd collected all of the hair once again, I swept it into the nearest trashcan and then tried to finish off the rest of my duties as quickly as possible. The sooner I finished, the sooner I could peer out and catch a glimpse at the finale of the show—when all the models paraded down the runway one after another with their dazzling gowns and gorgeous faces. Every time I snuck a glimpse at a fashion show from behind the scenes, I wanted to pinch myself.

Next season's trends were right at the tips of my fingers. Granted, my fingers were sticky and gripping an old broom, but still, it was the closest I'd ever been to my dream world.

I wanted to share my experience on *What Jo Wore*, but I couldn't figure out how to share details without admitting to my readers how I was actually getting my behind-the-scenes look. It was embarrassing, to say the least. Just a few months ago, I'd attended a major fashion gala. The glamorous people from that night were out in the front rows of all the NYFW fashion shows, and where was I? Sweeping up hair.

I found a tiny gap in the curtain off the side of the room and pulled it to the side just a centimeter. I peeked through and held my breath, completely in awe of the show. Strobe lights danced overhead, illuminating each model as they strutted down the runway.

I pulled my phone out of my back pocket and snapped a quick picture so I could send it to Lily.

Josephine: This is my current view.

I clutched my broom and peeked back through the slit in the curtain. The show was in full swing and the photographers at the end of the runway were firing away, snapping hundreds of photos per minute.

I glanced back to my phone after it buzzed.

Lily: What is that? It looks like a cat wearing a top hat.

I smiled.

Josephine: Put your glasses on. It's a fashion show. You can't really see it because the lights are dimmed.
Lily: Hmm, I still see a cat.
Josephine: It's not. You're blind. Go see a doctor.
Lily: How'd you get invited to a fashion show?
Josephine: Turns out that janitors get backstage passes.
Lily: Oh yeah, I forgot about that job.
Josephine: It's still pretty cool though, I must admit.
Lily: Any hot dudes?
Josephine: Just skinny bitches.
Lily: And yet you want me to move there.
Josephine: YES. Gotta go. They're all coming back.

I pocketed my phone and rushed back to work. The shows weren't very long—fifteen, twenty minutes at most. I could usually manage to watch at least five minutes of them before someone noticed.

Once the mess of hair was swept up near the back wall, I went back to my list of duties I had to get done every night. If the models didn't come back and trash the place after the show, I could usually get my work done in about an hour after the show was finished.

That night, I wasn't quite so lucky. The makeup artists had used some kind of glitter eye shadow on each of the twenty-four models. That meant there were twenty-four sets of eyes that left the entire floor of the backstage a glittery mess.

C'est la vie.

• • •

The next morning, I found myself fighting with my eyes to stay awake. I sipped on my third cup of coffee and stared at the email I'd opened ten minutes earlier. It still sat completely blank as the blinking cursor taunted me. I was supposed to draft an email to a general contractor to set up an initial meeting between him and Julian. What had I done? Tried really, really hard not to fall asleep with my eyes open.

"How's it going, champ?" Julian asked.

I blinked and glanced up to see him watching me with a private smile. Clearly, my lack of typing had alerted him that something was off.

"Do you think they've come up with an IV hookup for caffeine yet?" I asked, tapping the inside of my elbow like a junky.

He laughed. "Why are you so tired? Have you been going out without me?"

I yawned and then blinked my eyes a few times, willing away the tiny barbells pulling them down.

"I wish," I said with only a *slight* layer of bitterness.

I hadn't left Lincoln Center until 1:00 AM the night before. The janitor who was supposed to clean the front of the house had bailed and I'd offered to stay and help with the cleanup. The extra hours of minimum wage pay were hardly worth the ache in my back this morning, and best of all, I had to go back that night. *Yippee*.

"You look pitiful," Julian said, drawing my attention back to his lazy smile. He'd dressed down for work that day, foregoing shoes for bare feet. He had on dark jeans and a white button-up. His hair was still styled impeccably, split to the side and combed away from his face. Just a little bit of pomade held the dark locks in place all day. Not that I paid attention or anything. I mean, the man looked edible even on an off day, but right now? All I wanted was my bed and an extra day in the week called LetJosephineSleepday. It'd come between Wednesday and FreeDonutday. (These days would be added if I were President. Just saying.)

"All right, get up. This is unacceptable," he said, setting his laptop down on the couch beside him and standing up.

"No! Don't fire me. Look, I'm typing right now." I started kneading my keyboard with balled up fists, creating gibberish sentences that read something like: ERhwerjkhwejkrhkejryy.

Julian shook his head and held his hand out for me to take.

"I'm not firing you. Why would I fire you?"

"Because I won't let you sleep with me," I answered, shrugging.

He pinched his eyes closed, clearly trying to keep from laughing.

"Yeah, well. I can't exactly fire you for that."

"Look Julian, I like you a lot. I think that's pretty obvious to both of us. I just have a lot riding on this one opportunity, whereas if things don't work out between us, you just have to post another ad on the Internet to replace me."

"Josephine, it's not I—"

"Jul—"

He waved his hands in front of his body so that we'd stop cutting each other off. "Okay. Yes. I get it. I'm not firing you because you've spurned my advances. We're going to see my sister."

"Your sister?" I asked.

"Yes. She wants to meet you and you clearly can't focus on work at the moment. Consider it a little paid field trip."

Chapter Twenty-Eight

Julian

As we walked the few blocks to Lorena's rehab center, I filled Josephine in as much as possible.

"How much longer does she have in the program?" Josephine asked.

"A little over a week."

"Wow. I can't believe she's already almost done."

I nodded. I was proud of Lorena for completing her entire recovery program without any relapses. She'd struggled with substance abuse issues her whole life. In high school she'd dabbled in cheap drugs to pass the time with other rich kids. In college and beyond, it had gradually gotten worse. She lied about it for the longest time, trying to convince herself that she didn't need help. Then one night, she called me crying after watching one of her friends nearly overdose. It had been a wakeup call for Lorena. She entered rehab two days later and I'd moved to New York to help her out.

"She'll always be a little more lost in the clouds than down here on earth with the rest of us," I explained. "But this program has really helped her focus on her career. I haven't seen her this passionate about her clothing line in years."

Even when she first started her brand, it seemed to take the back seat to her addiction, but things were changing. I'd wake up in the morning to an inbox full of emails from Lorena. She wanted to know everything, from how the rental property was coming along to when we'd know the cost of manufacturing for next season's clothing line.

Last time I'd visited her, she had an entire sketchbook full of designs. She was itching to get out of rehab and get back to work. Meanwhile, I was trying to keep my reservations under wraps. I had hesitations about her entering the real world again. Sure, I'd fired all of her noxious employees, but she still had friends and bad influences in her life. I couldn't watch her every second of every day, though I wished I could.

"I'm glad she got help when she did. I can only imagine how big we'll become now that she can focus more of her energy on designing," Josephine said.

I slid my gaze over to her and took in her genuine smile. I knew it had been the right decision to bring her to meet Lorena. My sister needed to know there were other people who still believed in her.

When we arrived outside the rehab center, I pulled open

the heavy glass door and we breezed through the lavish foyer.

"Jeez. Maybe I need to go to rehab," Josephine quipped as we walked past the yoga studio and the coffee bar boasting free chai tea lattes every morning. I supposed it did look like an upscale spa to the untrained eye.

"Don't let the promise of free coffee tempt you into taking up hard drugs," I said, keeping my hand pressed to her lower back to guide her in the direction of the elevator.

"No really, I'm considering it," she joked, gleefully accepting a warm cookie from the reception desk as we passed by.

"This place costs more than most private colleges," I mentioned with a smile.

Josephine paused mid chew and stared up at me with her big green eyes. "Do you think I have to pay for this?"

I could barely make out her question over the gobs of chocolate chips currently shoved in her mouth.

"Definitely," I mocked.

She narrowed her eyes and reached out to pinch my arm.

"Keep it up and I won't give you half."

We took the elevator to the eleventh floor and then I directed Josephine toward Lorena's room. We were halfway down the hallway when I caught the scent of a strong floral perfume. *My mother's signature scent.* It was practically the scent of my childhood.

Fuck.

"Wow. Someone must have stuck a bucket of potpourri in the air vents here or something," Josephine said, scrunching her nose in distaste. "How does your sister stand it?"

I shook my head. "I don't think that's being pumped in.

I'm afraid that smell is a little more menacing."

"What do you mean?"

Before I could answer, my mother leaned out of my sister's room wearing a black silk scarf and a sour expression across her delicate features.

"Nurse! We've been waiting on those drinks for quite some time now. My daughter and I are—"

She paused mid yell when she saw me walking toward her with Josephine by my side. Her sour expression relaxed and then quickly transformed into a confused scowl as her eyes darted back and forth between us. Josephine swallowed the last of her cookie and smoothed the material of her already perfect pencil skirt.

I tightened the hold I had on her waist and drew her closer.

"Mother," I projected.

"Julian! Look how handsome you are in your street clothes. Were you heading out to the park or something?" she asked, scanning over my jeans like they were paint-stained sweatpants.

"Mom, I didn't expect to see you here," I said, ignoring her question and leaning in to give her a kiss on the cheek.

The scent of her perfume was nauseating, but I plastered on a fake smile and motioned toward Josephine. She still had her normal, warm complexion, and her eyes were just as green as they always were, but something was off. Her smile was guarded and her hand shook as she reached out to introduce herself.

"Hi Mrs. Lefray, I'm Josephine Keller."

My mother's mouth slid into a thin, flat smile. "How…charming that my son thought to include you in my family's time of—"

"SHUT THE FUCK UP," my sister yelled from the

inside of her room. "Is that Josephine out there? Get her in here!"

My mother held her palm to her forehead, clearly embarrassed by Lorena's cursing. "Dear, would you mind speaking like the educated woman that you are and not some filthy sailor down by the docks?"

I shook my head, trying hard to conceal my smile as I peeked into Lorena's room.

"Don't you have legs, Lorena? Come see her yourself."

She was propped up by pillows in the center of her bed. Her legs were crossed and she was completely surrounded by magazine clippings. She was at work clipping out another photo when she looked up and saw me standing in the doorway.

"I can't get up right now or all of this painstaking work will be for naught!" she said melodramatically, motioning to the mess around her.

Josephine laughed and stepped up behind me, peering around my shoulder into my sister's room.

"Hi Lorena," she said, offering a small wave. I didn't blame her for being wary of approaching my sister. Lorena's white blonde hair had grown out in the weeks she'd been in rehab so her dark brown roots were showing and she'd forgone makeup for a more natural look. I thought she looked beautiful, though a little crazy with magazines completely covering most of her body.

She looked up at the sound of Josephine's voice and beamed a bright, welcoming smile.

"I would squeeze you so hard if I could stand right now. Do you realize how much I've heard about you?" Lorena said. "And shit, you're gorgeous. My brother insists that wasn't one of the reasons he hired you. If I hadn't known how great your blog is, I daresay I wouldn't have believed him."

Josephine blushed. "Oh, you know about my blog?" she asked.

My mother cleared her throat in the hallway and all three of us turned to look at her. Her bright blue eyes were locked on Josephine as if waiting for her to pay her the attention she was so clearly due.

"So I take it that you're the reason my philistine of a son left my fundraiser so early the other night?" my mother asked with haughty tone. Her arms were crossed and the point she was trying to make was loud and clear.

Josephine turned and smiled wide. "You know I've been dying to meet you, Mrs. Lefray. You've raised such a wonderful son. Did he mention that he's been my only friend since moving to New York? Well, other than my landlady. I met him a few weeks after I moved here and I was already so lonely. If it weren't for him, I'd probably be holed up in my apartment trying to teach myself to knit or something."

I watched my mother's face the entire time Josephine spoke. She wore her frown like armor, but as soon as Josephine started to compliment her parenting skills, she started to crack. Her eyes softened and her arms loosened across her chest.

"Hmm. Where are you from, Josephine?" my mother asked, taking a hesitant step into the room.

Josephine smiled. "This little town in Texas that you have definitely never heard of. Our one claim to fame is when we made it into the Guinness Book of World Records for growing the biggest pumpkin or something."

My mother smiled. "My, how...quaint. So no New York City roots then?"

That question was my mother's way of asking about her

pedigree, as if this were the 18th century and Josephine still needed to prove her maidenhood.

"I wish," Josephine answered. "I mean look at your scarf. I don't think my hometown would know what to do with a woman as chic as you are. They'd probably assume you were a famous celebrity rolling through to film a movie."

At this, my mother laughed. A genuine, loud laugh. I hadn't heard the sound in years.

I knew Josephine was laying it on thick, but she was a smart woman to do so. Having an enemy like my mother didn't do anyone any good. Besides, having my mother like the woman I loved made my life a lot easier.

My gut clenched at the thought.

Love?

Are you fucking insane?

"Okay, stop hogging her, Mother. She's my employee!" Lorena teased from the bed. "Jo, get over here and help me plan my fall collection for next year. I'm thinking army green and navy will be the bulk of my colors. I want to stay away from black for now."

Josephine oohed and awed at the photos spread out across Lorena's lap. Meanwhile, I stood in the corner of the room, trying to figure out when exactly I'd fallen for Jo. When exactly my heart had won out over my head. I watched her lean across Lorena's bed. I studied her smile as they talked, and wondered when it had wound itself so deeply into the very fiber of my happiness. That smile was directly related to me. When Josephine was happy, I was happy.

I felt my mother's stare on the side of my face and glanced over toward her.

She knew.

Moms *always* know.

She'd probably known from the moment we'd stepped off the elevator. I'd had my arm wrapped around Josephine's waist for Christ's sake.

She didn't say a word though. She just tipped the edge of her mouth up and cocked a brow.

An unspoken question clearly asked between us.

Well? What are you going to do about it?

Chapter Twenty-Nine

Julian

I'd just finished the last stretch around Central Park's six-mile running trail and was cooling down with a walk on the way back to my hotel. The morning air still held a crispness to it that I knew the sun would steal in a matter of hours. I loved New York City, but the summer heat was a bitch.

I passed by a bagel shop already packed with customers and contemplated buying a dozen for Jo and I to share throughout the week. My phone buzzed in my back pocket and I paused my *This American Life* podcast and switched over to answer Josephine's call.

"Could you smell the bagels through the phone?" I

asked after the line connected.

She groaned in mock pleasure, but my dick still responded as if she were actually having an orgasm on the other end of the phone line. *Really? At 6:00 AM on the sidewalk outside of a bagel shop? There's a toddler staring at you through the window with slobber dripping down his face. Focus man.*

"Are you at Hot Bagel?" she asked.

"How'd you know?"

"Because it's Saturday, which means you're doing your six-mile loop around Central Park."

Christ I was predictable.

"Yeah, yeah. The sooner you leave me alone, the sooner I can go in and buy us some bagels for next week."

"Okay. First off, make sure you get some cinnamon raisin. Not just a bunch of those gross sesame seed ones. Second, what are you doing tonight?"

I tucked my hand up under my arm as I held the phone to my ear and gave myself a second to calm down. *She's not asking you to go down on her, Romeo. She's asking you a simple question.*

"I was going to meet Dean for drinks. Why?" I was trying hard not to sound over eager, but in reality I just sounded short. I'd never had to try this hard around a woman before.

She hesitated before continuing. "Can you cancel?"

"Depends on what you're about to ask me to do."

"Will you please, please come to a party with me?" She was using her honey-laced tone, the one that had a direct line to my pants.

"Whose party? I thought I was your only friend."

If she was calling to invite me to some dude's party, I was going to lose it. I knew it was only a matter of time before some guy noticed her on the subway or in some deli as she picked out a sandwich. She was too gorgeous to fly under the radar of other men and I was about to have to sit through a night of watching some bass player from Brooklyn try to work his moves on her. *Oh cool, tell me more about your indie band.*

"Well…my landlady is throwing a party tonight and I promised her I'd come. I kind of owe it to her considering how much she's helped me with my blog."

Her landlady?

"I told you I'd help you with those photos," I protested, annoyed that she hadn't taken me up on my offer.

She groaned. "I know. I know. I just feel bad asking you for favors. You already do so much for me and I don't want you to get sick of me."

"Aren't you asking me for a favor right now?"

She laughed. "This is different. This is supposed to be fun!"

"How old is your landlady?"

"I'd say she's closer to seventy than fifty."

"Jo…"

"Okay. You're right. I'll buy you a beer after." She continued before I could reply, "No, wait. I can't afford that. I'll buy you a coke from the nearest vending machine."

I laughed. "Okay. What time should I meet you?"

"Eight."

Eight? What kind of old person starts to party at 8:00 PM?

• • •

At 8:05 that night, Josephine and I made our way up the four flights of stairs that separated her apartment from her landlord's place on the top floor. I'd already memorized what she was wearing: jeans, sandals, and a white tank top. The fabric looked soft, and the spaghetti straps were thin, hardly there at all. The fact that I couldn't see a bra strap made it that much more painful to bear.

"My landlady is a little old school so just say that we're friends. I don't want her to think we're living in sin or anything," Josephine said.

"Isn't that what we are?"

She shot me a sidelong glance.

"Would she really care about that?" I asked, pushing away from the topic of our "are we or aren't we" relationship status.

"Yes. She specifically asked me before I signed my lease if I was going to have any male guests stay over."

"Really? I think that's against the law."

She nodded. "Yeah, well just don't say anything that will upset her. I don't want to be homeless."

I held my hands up, defenseless. "I solemnly swear that I won't get you kicked out of your apartment."

When we arrived on the top floor of the building, Jo knocked on her landlady's door and then offered me a gentle smile.

"Thanks for coming with me," she said, reaching over to squeeze my hand.

Before I could reply, the wooden door swung out in front of us and I came face to face with a very drunk, very sweaty old man.

"Newbies! Welcome!" he said with a grin as his gaze swept over us.

Josephine hesitated before offering him the platter of cupcakes she'd made earlier.

"Barney, don't scare them! Let me answer, let me answer." An older woman rushed forward and smiled wide when she caught sight of Jo on the other side of the doorway.

"My little Josephine!" the woman squealed, enveloping Jo in a hug that at once tipped Jo off balance and allowed the woman to drag her full force into the apartment.

I stepped in after her, trying to stay close. Why was that guy so sweaty? And where was he going with those cupcakes?

"Oh! You brought a friend?" the woman asked with an arched brow. She had red lipstick on that was crusted in the corners of her mouth. Her cotton dress was short, with a halter top that tied behind her neck. It would have looked good on a twenty-two-year-old. On Jo's landlord, I felt like I needed to avert my eyes. There was too much wrinkly, tanned skin on display.

Jo smiled. "Yep. This is Julian. He's just a friend."

I reached out for her hand, but she stepped forward and wrapped me in an awkward hug. Clearly, this woman was the touchy feely type.

"I'm Holly, Josephine's landlady," she said with a wide smile.

"Nice to meet you," I said, stepping back out of her grasp.

Her apartment was much bigger than Jo's. It took up most of the top floor of the building, which meant there was plenty of room for a party, though I hadn't seen anyone besides Barney and Holly. Barney disappeared down the hall, and Holly led us past the entryway into an empty kitchen. An entire bar's worth of alcohol was set out across the island and it looked like a few people had already dipped into it.

Where are they then?

"Grab a drink and then meet me in the living room. It's just down the hall," Holly said, smiling and shimmying her shoulders with excitement.

Barney stepped into the doorway behind her and wrapped his arms around Holly's waist, then pinched her. She squealed and pretended to fight him off, all the while allowing him to pull her from the room.

"C'mon. Gerald wants to play," Barney said, with a hint of something more in his voice.

What the hell does that mean?

I glanced over at Jo to see if she was getting the same weird vibe that I was.

"This is definitely not what I was expecting," I said, stepping toward the alcohol.

Jo shrugged. "It's a little different, but they're nice people, I'm sure."

No, she didn't get it. There was definitely something *off* about this party.

"I think we should head out," I said. My gut was screaming at me to get out while I still could.

Josephine frowned. "What? Seriously? We just got here, and I don't want to offend Holly."

I nodded and tried to tell my instincts to shut up. Sure, Barney and Holly were a little off, but maybe they were just weird old people. New York City is full of those.

"Okay, yeah. We'll stay for a little bit," I relented.

Josephine held up a bottle of Jack Daniels. "Look! They even have your favorite alcohol. It can't be all that bad."

We filled our cups with Jack and Cokes and then clinked them together.

"Cheers," Jo said, smiling up at me.

"Cheers."

"Come on you two! We're about to get started," Holly called from the other room.

I reluctantly followed Josephine down the hall, bracing myself for a night of awkward Monopoly games. If I had to sit by sweaty Barney, I wasn't going to last five minutes.

"What do you think they're playing in there?" Josephine asked just as we stepped into the doorway of the living room and were met by a sight that was so un-seeable, all the therapy in the world wouldn't be able to erase it.

Holy shit.

Holy fucking shit.

The scene we stepped into was straight out of *50 Shades of Grey - Geriatric Edition*.

"JESUS!" Jo cried, letting her cup slip from her hand.

I reached out for it just before it hit the floor, but Jack and Coke still spilled out onto my shirt and jeans. I glanced up and blinked to confirm that my eyes hadn't betrayed me. Nope. It was real and it was too late to leave unnoticed. We were already in the doorway and half a dozen people were staring up at us...

Half a dozen naked, old people. So very naked, and so very, very old.

Candles were lit around the room. Hard rock music played in the background. A woman dressed as a dominatrix cracked a cheap whip in the corner and I flinched as if it were about to hit me. Two old people were going at it on the couch while others stood around and watched. I saw old, flat butt cheeks, and scores of boobs that had been around for the terms of over a dozen different presidents.

"Julian," Josephine whispered. "Am I dreaming?"

I reached out for her hand. "No. We are definitely in the middle of an old person swinger's party right now."

"Josephine," Holly called from across the room. "Come on in, we don't bite!"

Of course you don't bite, most of you don't even have teeth.

"I...um, I think I'm. Have to go. Yeah, actually."

Her words came out as a jumbled mess as her brain short-circuited.

I gripped her hand, ready to drag her out of the apartment, and then Barney held up her tray of cupcakes. He was sitting on the couch with the tray on his lap.

"These are great!" he said, holding one up before he shoved half of it into his mouth.

The fact that he was completely naked as he stuffed Josephine's vanilla cupcakes into his mouth only made the spectacle that much harder to stomach. I was seconds away from laughing until I either pissed my pants or blacked out from shock.

"I'm so glad you..." Josephine murmured with a shaky voice. "I'm just going to um..."

She let her sentence fade out as she stared up at the ceiling, pretending to study the popcorn paint as if it were the most interesting thing in the world.

"We need to back up slowly..."

"Slow and steady," Josephine whispered out of the corner of her mouth.

All eyes were on us. We were expected to join in. Holy hell. Josephine's landlady had invited her to a swaps party. *What the hell has this world come to?*

I saw the dominatrix wind up her whip out of the corner of my eye and I knew she'd provide a welcome distraction in a matter of seconds.

"On the count of three, we're going to make a run for it," I whispered.

"Holly! Come lick this vanilla icing off me!" Barney said, rubbing Josephine's cupcakes all over his naked chest. Josephine whimpered under her breath and I lost it. I couldn't hold in my laughter any more.

The dominatrix cracked her whip and I pulled Josephine back through the hallway, losing myself to a fit of laughter. We broke into a run and Josephine cried out after me.

"You didn't count down!" she yelled.

"It doesn't matter. Just run!"

We ran out of her landlady's apartment and bolted down the stairs. I held onto the banister with one hand and gripped Josephine's hand with the other. We made it back to her apartment in record time. She unlocked the door, I shoved it open, and we both pushed through at the same time.

She flipped the lock and we leaned against the door with a heavy thud. We stood there catching our breath and she slid her gaze to me. I turned to find her smiling from ear to ear as her chest rose and fell. Her cheeks were flushed and her eyes were wide with wonder. I'd never seen her look as beautiful as she did right then.

"So that's why she wanted to know if you would be having male visitors," I said.

I laughed and squeezed her hand. I hadn't even realized I was still holding it.

Chapter Thirty

Josephine

I'd been given one night off in the middle of my NYFW job, and I'd spent it hanging out with naked old people. Not only that, I'd dragged Julian along with me. There wasn't enough eye bleach in the world to clear the memories of that night from my brain, and I knew I had to make it up to Julian somehow.

"I need you to read through that contract the realtor sent over last night," Julian instructed from his perch at his hotel room's dining table on Monday morning. Papers were scattered out around him and we were knee deep into our work for the day. We'd yet to discuss Saturday night and I had no clue how to bring up the subject.

Maybe I could apologize with a tasteful ice cream cake. *"Sorry for subjecting you to old lady boobs. Your best friend, Jo."*

"Jo?" he asked.

I glanced up and racked my brain for the task he'd just asked me to do. Oh yes, the contract.

"I read it this morning and highlighted the sections I think you should take a look at," I answered.

"Good." He nodded, typing away. "And we have a meeting with the general contractor for Lorena's store tomorrow."

I nodded. I may have subjected him to a terrible party, but I was a kickass personal assistant.

"I've scheduled a car to pick us up at 9:00 AM. We'll be meeting the contractor at a coffee shop in Soho."

"And the email Lorena sent over last night?" he asked, peering at me over the top of his laptop.

I smiled. "I replied first thing this morning."

"Looks like you're on top of your game, Keller," he said with a seductive smile.

I stared at him for a moment before averting my gaze and staring back down at my keyboard. *Hey vagina, let's focus on other things right now. Like, oh I don't know, WORK.* It was his fault though. Perhaps I should have added one more rule the other night: no smiling with dimples. Frowning and flat smiles were allowed. Anything more and I couldn't be held accountable for my hands or my lady bits.

"Did you see anyone interesting leaving your landlady's apartment yesterday morning?" Julian asked, barely masking his amusement at my ridiculous life.

I closed my eyes and answered. "No, but Holly left my

cupcake platter outside my door with a note that said 'Thanks for the special treat'. She had washed the dish, but I don't think it will ever be truly clean."

He choked on his coffee.

"Never," he agreed.

He stood up to grab a napkin and I plucked my mug from the coffee table for him to refill while he was up. (We'd established this system early on: if one of us got up, that person was responsible for coffee refill duties. No ifs, ands, or buts.) I used the moment to study him while he was preoccupied; those moments were part of *my* routine. While he was typing an email or making a phone call, I always took a moment to covertly watch him. He always had a warm complexion, but his tan had deepened from his early morning runs. He'd rolled his sleeves up to his elbows and the subtle veins on his forearm were enough to make me swoon. There was something about a guy with strong, defined arms. Or maybe it was just Julian.

"You have to move," he said, turning back to flash a dimpled smile at me.

For a second, I didn't understand what he meant. Like move from his couch? *Dammit, this is why I shouldn't be checking him out at work.*

"Out of your apartment," he clarified when I didn't immediately reply.

Ah, duh.

"Believe me, I wish I could. Unfortunately, I can't find a place that's cheaper than my current lease unless I move to New Jersey or something."

Julian frowned over the coffee cup, and I wondered what he was thinking.

"Don't I pay you enough here?"

I swallowed and thought of how best to reply. Julian

knew nothing about the debt I was swimming in. Sure, this job was decent, but between New York City rent, groceries, college loans, and the damn credit cards I'd used to purchase books and stuff in college, I'd need a lot more than an executive assistant salary to pay it all off. I didn't want Julian to know about my money struggles. It wasn't his concern, and I doubted he'd be able to understand. He came from old money and had made plenty on his own. I didn't want him to look at me any differently.

"More than I'd make breakdancing on subway platforms," I quipped with a fake smile.

Julian laughed and handed me back my mug full of coffee.

"You could always move in here," Julian said, motioning to the master bedroom just off the suite's living room.

I rolled my eyes. "That's the one line you get today. Shock. Collar."

He rubbed his neck with a feigned grimace. "Yeah, yeah. It's just an offer. I'm a noble guy like that."

"Sure you are."

"Like when I rescued you from a swinger's party."

I laughed and covered my eyes, willing away the images that flashed through my mind.

"Let's make a blood pact to never speak about it ever again."

"Okay, but only after we tell Dean about it tonight."

I glanced up and met his eye. "Tonight?"

"Yeah." He frowned. "Didn't I mention that we're supposed to get drinks with him tonight? I cancelled on him for that party we agreed to never discuss again."

I ran through my mind, trying to recall any mention of it. The only thing on my schedule for the day was work,

work, and more work. From 9:00 AM to 5:00 PM I was with Julian, and then I had to run across town to Lincoln Center for a NYFW shift from 5:30 to 9:00 PM.

"I don't think you ever told me about it."

He shrugged. "Well, we're heading over to The Merchant at nine o'clock. Are you interested in joining?"

I should have said no. God knew I'd be exhausted after my shift at Lincoln Center, but the idea of Julian and Dean alone in a bar together was enough to convince me. The two of them would attract women like moths to a flame, and even though he and I couldn't date, it didn't mean I wanted women flirting with him at the bar. No, with me there as a buffer, he'd have a harder time picking up women. I'd make sure of it.

Chapter Thirty-One

Josephine

As soon as I finished up at Lincoln Center, I found the first available bathroom and stood in front of the dimly lit mirror. My appearance was cringe-worthy. *If I asked the mirror who it considered to be the fairest of them all, it'd reply with, "Damn girl, it ain't you. You're a hot mess."*

I pulled off my NYFW cap and inspected the rat's nest on top of my head. I'd attempted to pull it back in a loose knot during my shift, just to get it off of my face. Somehow 90% of the strands were now out of the ponytail and sticking up around my head. My mascara was smudged under my eyes and I had some sort of black substance streaked across my left cheek.

Hey God, if you're up there, this would be a great time for you to work some miracles. Like maybe you could turn this bar of soap into a curling iron.

God's answering machine must have been full or something because the soap didn't change and I was left with what little makeup I'd stuffed into my purse in recent months. In total, I had a small black comb, black eyeliner, and red lipstick. I pulled my ponytail out and ran the comb through my hair. *Not bad, not bad. Starting to look more like a human.* Next, I used a tissue to dab away the mascara beneath my eyes and the black streak across my cheek. I used the black eyeliner to rim the edges of each eye and thanked my lucky stars that my complexion was clear and even on its own. I coated my lips in red lipstick and then braided my hair so that it lay over my shoulder. In a matter of five minutes, I'd gone from a 1.5 to at *least* a solid 5.

It'd have to do.

I pulled my phone out of my purse as I walked through Lincoln Center to the front entrance to catch a cab. I had a few text messages from Lily waiting for me that I'd check later, and Julian had texted me to let me know he and Dean were at the bar; the final text from my mom was the one to catch me off guard. My mom usually preferred to call and leave me voicemails. They were always short and sweet, and had a way of feeling like a dagger to my heart. I opened the text and braced myself for whatever stones and arrows she was wielding that day.

Mom: Josephine, your father's 60th birthday is in two weeks and he'd really like you to come in town for it. I know that you have a busy life in New York, so I don't expect you to stay for long.

Maybe you could just come for the weekend?

Ever since my mom had mentioned my dad's birthday, the guilt of knowing I'd be missing it had started to eat away at me. I thought about it as I lay awake at night, trying to figure out a way to get down there to visit him. I didn't want to miss his birthday, but I'd yet to figure out how it would be possible. After next week, my temporary job at NYFW would be over, which meant I'd need to find another job to help make ends meet. Not to mention, Lorena was getting out of rehab very soon and I had no clue what she planned on doing with my position once she was back at work. Julian had hired me, not her. Would she need an assistant? Would she want it to be me?

If not, it meant I'd be completely unemployed in less than a week.

Perfect.

I was in the midst of some major changes, which meant that I should have been saving every single penny that came my way, not attempting to travel across the country for a weekend getaway. Unfortunately, I didn't think my mother saw it that way. The situation was cut and dried for her: be there for your father's 60th birthday or let him down. Simple as pie. *Southern peach cobbler*.

I headed toward the nearest subway entrance and rang Lily, praying she'd answer.

"JOSIE. Finally!" she screamed into the phone once the call connected.

I hadn't been expecting such an exuberant greeting.

"Hey Lil. What's up?"

She sighed, exasperated by my lack of enthusiasm. "Uh, clearly you have not read the texts I've been sending you."

I cringed. "No, sorry. I was at work. Why?"

"Guess who just put in her two weeks' notice at work?"

I stopped walking midway between steps so that the person walking behind me completely knocked into me. I didn't even flinch when they cursed at me and told me to get out of the way. Who the hell cared? I was in complete shock as I tried to process the fact that MY BEST FRIEND WAS MOVING TO NEW YORK.

"Is this a joke right now? So help me god, do you realize how much I'll kill you if this is a joke?"

Lily laughed. "This is not a drill, my friend. This is happening. I'm about to purchase a Greyhound ticket and everything."

"Lily, you just completely saved the day!"

Yes. Yes. Yes. Things would work out. If Lily was moving to New York, that meant she'd be able to cover half of the rent. I'd have way less expenses when she moved to town and maybe, just maybe, I'd be able to have my peach cobbler and eat it too.

In two weeks' time, I'd head down to Texas to visit my parents and then ride back on the bus with Lily. I'd take her around and show her everything I knew. We'd hit the town together and I'd instruct her on which subway lines to avoid if she didn't want to step in a puddle of urine, which street vendors had the saltiest soft pretzels, and which apartments to avoid if she didn't want to stumble upon a random swinger's party. I could hardly wait.

"We have so much to plan, Lil," I said, unable to contain the giant smile spreading across my face.

She laughed. "Yeah, starting with how the hell we're going to share that damn futon."

Chapter Thirty-Two

Josephine

It wasn't a big deal that Josephine was late for drinks. I didn't watch the door of Dean's bar like she was going to stumble in any minute and I definitely didn't hold my breath every time a brunette stepped through the doorway.

Those would be the actions of a man in love. Me? I was just a regular guy having a regular drink with a regular friend.

"You look paranoid. Do you need another drink?" Dean asked, drawing my attention back to our table.

I held up my scotch, still half full.

He smirked and shook his head.

"Are we expecting someone else?"

"Jo," I answered.

"Ah, the lovely Josephine."

I glared at him over the rim of my scotch.

"I thought this was supposed to be guys' night," Dean said, swirling his glass on top of the teak tabletop.

"She's sorta like one of the guys."

He narrowed his eyes, clearly calling bullshit on me. "I'm fairly sure the double Ds you're so infatuated with make that the most asinine comment I've ever heard."

I shook my head and took another sip of scotch. Agreeing to drinks with Dean had been a bad idea. He loved calling me on my shit, even when I preferred to brush everything under the rug. I guess the apple didn't fall far from the tree. My mother must have had fifty rugs in her palatial townhouse, all with secrets and lies shoved so far beneath that they would never see the light of day again.

"Yeah, well, tonight she's just a friend," I said, putting the cork in the subject.

He nodded slowly, eyeing me with poorly veiled skepticism.

"Have you thought about what you'll do after your sister gets released? Will you still help her with the company?" he asked, moving the conversation on to another subject I hardly wanted to think about, much less discuss.

"I'm not sure. We're right in the beginning stages of building her store. I might stick around for that and then see what other investment opportunities come my way."

"In Boston?"

I stared down at my drink and shrugged.

"Well if you're thinking of staying in New York long term, I have a few projects I'd love your help on. I've been wanting to expand on a restaurant idea, but I need a partner before I even consider it."

My brows perked up at the idea. Would I be willing to extend my stay in New York to hang around and see what sort of trouble Dean and I could get ourselves into? The idea sounded pretty tempting.

"There she is," Dean said with a smile as he held up his drink in greeting.

I turned to the door and watched Jo walk into the bar, stealing the attention of every guy within a ten foot radius.

I had a full grin stretching across my face before I even realized how happy I was to see her. She was dressed differently than usual in tight black pants and a thin black t-shirt. It looked like some kind of work uniform, but I didn't mind the darker look on her.

By the time she'd wound her way toward us, I'd already forgotten my promise to Dean that Jo was just one of the guys tonight.

"I'm sorry I'm late, guys!" she said, coming to stand beside my chair and tossing her purse down onto the table. She seemed worn out, but she looked great. Her bright red lips stood out in the dim light of the bar.

"Long day?" Dean asked.

Jo laughed and scrunched her nose. "Yeah, yeah. I'm sorry, I got caught up."

"With another one of your prior commitments?" I asked with an arched brow.

Jo's smile faltered as she turned her attention toward the bar, strategically ignoring my question.

"What are you manly men drinking?" she asked quickly, waving down a nearby waiter.

I could feel Dean's stare on the side of my face but I ignored him. The bastard could save his judgments for someone else.

"Hi. What can I get you?" the waiter asked, beaming down at Jo with more than just a simple smile. Interest was written across his douchey face clear as day.

"She'll have a Gin Fizz," I said quickly.

Jo peered over at me. "Is that what I got the other day?" I nodded.

She grinned at the waiter. "Then that's what I'll have!"

"Most women would bite my hand off if I tried to order for them," Dean said, watching Jo carefully.

She shrugged his comment off. "Julian's pretty good about knowing what I want."

I watched as the full meaning of that comment took hold for her and then smiled as a blush overtook her cheeks.

"Okay, let's move on," Jo said, waving her hand to change the subject. "What were you two talking about before I got here?"

"I was about to play wingman for Julian here, actually. Maybe get him laid for the first time in months."

I kicked his shin under the table, but his face didn't even budge.

Jo quirked a brow. "Oh really? Months?"

I shrugged and looked her square in the eye.

"Care to help a friend out? I'm sure there's a bathroom we could find," I said with a confident smile.

"Hey, hey. Not in my bar. I just had the floors redone," Dean said, holding up his hand in protest.

I laughed. "It'd hardly be the first time that bathroom would be used for some nefarious deeds."

Jo swallowed and glanced away.

"I'm sure there's a woman here who would take you up on that offer, Julian. We just have to find the right one," she said.

"I think I like the one at this table," I pushed, feeling the effects of my second scotch starting to kick in.

She scanned the room for attractive women and tried to hide her smile. She liked when I flirted with her and yet she pretended to ignore it.

"I'm honored," Dean joked, putting his hand over his chest. "It's just that you're not my type."

I laughed and shook my head.

"What about her?" Jo asked, pointing to the left side of the bar. I turned my attention to where she was pointing. There was a pretty blonde perched on a barstool, alone and sipping on a drink. She glanced over her shoulder as I watched her, and when our eyes met, she smiled and bit down on the edge of her lip—girl code for "come on over".

She was pretty, I'd give Jo that, and her red dress left very little to the imagination, but she wasn't my type. I preferred leggy brunettes who played hard to get.

"Nah, not feeling it," I said.

"Oooookay," Jo said, turning over her other shoulder. "Her?"

She tilted her head to the right, but I couldn't tell who she was talking about. There was a sea of people to our left, plenty of women that I would have picked up back in Boston. Back then my tastes weren't quite so singular. Blondes, redheads, brunettes, tall, short…didn't matter.

"Who?" I asked, squinting toward the crowd.

"The girl with the pixie cut sitting with her friends. She looks like Tinkerbell or something."

Ah, I knew who she was talking about. The girl was gorgeous no doubt, with a sort of Emma Watson vibe. I liked Hermione just as much as the next guy, but she wouldn't do for tonight.

I shook my head and Dean laughed.

"Picky, picky. I'm sure someone here is more than worthy of your attention if you'd only give them a chance."

I scowled at him. "What about you, Dean? Why don't we set you up with someone?"

"Tonight is about you, my friend. Besides, I'm a busy man. I don't have the luxury of dating at the moment."

"Uh oh, then that means you're about to find the love of your life," Jo said.

Dean flinched back. "What makes you say that?"

She laughed just as the waiter set her drink down on the table. She thanked him, took a sip, and then turned her gaze back to Dean.

"Everyone knows that when you're least looking for love, that's when it finds you."

Dean turned to face the bar, slapped both hands over his eyes and called out, "I'm not looking for love!" while making a kissy face.

We laughed and Josephine reached over to grab his arms before the patrons at the bar became even more confused by his antics.

"What about you, Jo?" I asked.

She took a sip of her drink, watching me over the lip of her glass.

"What about me?"

"Are you looking for love?"

She laughed and rolled her eyes. "I plead the fifth."

"Why?"

"Because if I say I am, then your incessant flirting will only become more relentless."

"And if you're not?" I asked.

"Probably the same thing."

I laughed and nursed my scotch. Was she right? Did she

have me so figured out? She certainly had the upper hand: I wanted her and she didn't want me.

Maybe it was time to mix it up, let her know what it felt like not to have me in her back pocket, ready and waiting for a green light.

I sipped my drink and scanned the bar, trying to glance through the crowd of women with fresh eyes. Then I saw her, near the back: a girl with light brown hair, tan skin, and a killer smile. She was sitting with friends and laughing. To be honest, she looked like she could have been Josephine's sister.

Yup. She would do just fine.

Chapter Thirty-Three

Josephine

Most people think of life as a merry-go-round, with highs and lows and slight bumps in the road. At the end of the day, you're riding a pony, so how bad can it be? I looked at my life like a tilt-a-whirl. It spun me round and round until I thought I'd hurl everywhere, and then the carny just kept laughing and kicked it up another notch.

I'd had thirty minutes, maybe an hour tops, where I'd thought things would begin to settle down for me. My best friend was moving to New York. We'd live together and she'd help me pay rent. Life was good, right? No. Life was a pit of snakes.

Julian was going on a date with an adorable girl.

How could this happen, you might ask?

Dean.

Everything bad in my life could be blamed on Dean.

He'd suggested Julian find a girl to date. He'd encouraged him to go over and chat with her.

I hated Dean.

The girl was lovely, of course. Her name was Molly and she'd moved from California the year before. She had this annoyingly cute voice and big green eyes. I hadn't noticed at first, but I swear she and I could have been related. I mean, she would be the pretty sister and I would be the frumpy weird one with a chameleon, but still, the similarities were uncanny.

I couldn't figure out if Julian had picked her on purpose though. He didn't seem like the type to play games, and I knew there were only so many times I could tell him I was uninterested before he actually believed me. The sad part was, I didn't want him to listen. I was selfish, and I wanted him to keep flirting with me, even if it never turned into anything.

Why?

Because I was immature and in love with my unattainable boss, that's why.

The next day, Julian and I were riding in the back of a Lincoln town car, rushing from meeting to meeting. We'd already met with two interior design firms and were on our way to meet with a third. The sooner we picked one, the sooner Lorena's store would go under construction. He'd dressed up for the day in a navy suit with a light blue tie. I loved the way he looked in navy and I loved the way he looked in a suit. The combination was hard to handle all at once. He was staring out the window, his profile a perfect complement to the designer suit: chiseled jaw line, hard cheekbones, hazel eyes staring off into the distance.

"So when are you going to take Molly out?" I asked, peering at him from beneath my lashes.

The edge of his mouth turned down and he kept his gaze steady on the building outside our window.

"Soon," he answered with a half-hearted tone. I'd never seen him so distant.

"How soon?" I pushed.

"Why do you care?" he asked, finally turning to me with a hard stare.

I looked away and swallowed, annoyed with how short he was being with me.

"Because you're my friend and I want you to be happy."

He grunted and pulled a legal pad out of his briefcase. Clearly, the conversation about Molly was over. He uncapped his pen with his mouth and then started scribbling on the first blank page. I had no clue what he was writing, but I didn't dare interrupt him. If this was Julian in a bad mood, I didn't like it.

"You know what pisses me off the most?" he asked, recapping his pen and waiting for me to turn toward him.

"What?"

"That you pretend like it wouldn't bother you if I went out with her."

I rolled my eyes. We were having this conversation? Now? In the middle of a workday, in between meetings, with a driver in the front seat listening to every word?

"I'm just making the best of a shitty situation," I replied, trying to be as honest as possible. "I want you to be happy and I think Molly is a nice girl."

"Bullshit," he said, cutting me off before I could

continue.

"Oh really?" I said, sitting up in my seat and facing him. "You think you have everything figured out, Julian?"

"I think you're lying to yourself and you're lying to me."

I could feel my face growing warm. I was angry and I was two seconds away from letting my temper get the better of me.

"You think this has been easy for me? I moved to New York on my own and you're honestly the only friend I have here. Do you realize how scared I am that you and I will have a fling and then you'll move back to Boston, your sister will fire me, and I'll be left here without you and completely broke? You have no clue what I'm going through so why don't you save the lecture."

"Jo—"

I held my hand up to stop him.

"Not now," I protested.

The tears were already gathering in the corners of my eyes and we were minutes away from stepping into a meeting. I'd look so unprofessional if I walked in with a splotchy face and a choked up voice.

Julian reached out and gripped the patch of skin below my pencil skirt. He squeezed my knee twice, a sort of a gentle apology. I crossed my arms and kept my gaze pinned on the door. I wasn't ready to give in yet.

He took the hint and moved his hand away, brushing my skin with the pads of his fingers in the process. My stomach dipped at the loss of his touch, but there was nothing I could do. I'd pushed him away and now I had to live with my decision. I had a few moments to gather myself before the driver pulled over in front of our next destination. He hopped out of the front seat and rounded the car to open my door. I took a breath and wiped beneath my eyes.

"I'm sorry," he whispered. "To answer your question, I'm not going out with Molly. It didn't seem right to lead her on when I'm interested in someone else."

I froze, absorbing his words and the implications they had. By the time I'd turned, mouth open, ready to speak, he'd already opened his door and stepped out. I wanted to reach out after him and yank him back inside the car. If I were more reckless or if I hadn't needed every single dime I earned working at Lorena Lefray Designs, I'd have jumped on him in a second. I'd have pinned him to the backseat of the town car, straddled his lap, pulled my skirt up, and had my wicked way with him.

If only…

"Are you coming, Jo?" Julian asked, leaning down to peek into my open doorway.

I could have told him everything then. It would have been so easy to come clean. Instead, I accepted his outstretched hand and squeezed my feelings deep, deep down into the pit of my stomach where I could pull them out at night when I lay in bed alone, contemplating how much longer I could get away with pretending that I was anything but hopelessly in love with him.

Chapter Thirty-Four

Julian

I hadn't talked to Jo in almost two days.

I'd gone thirty-one years without knowing her, yet now it felt wrong to even go one weekend without speaking to her. Things had been tense between us since I'd invited her to have drinks with Dean and me. I should have realized that the night was wrong from the very start. Trying to pick up women around Jo had been an idiotic way to try to push her to admit her feelings for me.

In the end, I'd only succeeded in pushing her further away.

At work, we hardly talked. Our conversations were

tense and awkward. Even if I couldn't get her to love me, I wanted things to go back to how they'd been. Being friends with her was better than nothing.

"Bro! EARTH TO JULIAN!"

Lorena snapped her fingers in front of my face and I flinched back to stare at her. She propped her hands on her hips and stared daggers at me.

"I've been calling your name for the last five minutes and you've been off in la la land."

I stared out around my sister's room, at the boxes ready to be moved to the car waiting outside. We'd spent the morning prepping for her departure from the rehab facility and it was time to head out, back to her old apartment in Brooklyn. Our mother had spent the last few days sprucing it up and getting it ready for her to move back in. I'd already gone through a month earlier and thrown away any reminder of her old life, hunting through her cabinets and drawers and tossing anything that could lead her back down the slippery slope.

"Are you ready?" I asked, wrapping my arm across her shoulders and bringing her in for a hug.

She shrugged. "It's strange how much this place has come to feel like home."

"Are you nervous to leave?"

She narrowed her eyes and studied the window on the adjacent wall.

"To be honest, I'm ready to test my willpower in the real world. It wasn't hard to stay clean in here, but I know my friends will hear that I've moved back home and not all of them will support my choices."

I squeezed her shoulder. "They're vultures, Lorena. Let them circle overhead while you keep your life on track."

She frowned and nodded. "I know that, it's just hard to

cut people out of your life like that. Not everything is so simple."

"Well I'm not planning on rushing back to Boston anytime soon. I'll drop by and we can hangout."

She groaned. "Cause hanging out with my big brother is sooo cool."

"Hey! I'm taking you to the final NYFW show tonight. Doesn't that count for something?"

"Hey, you're going as *my* date!" she said with a laugh. "Look everyone, the phoenix Lorena Lefray, rising from the ashes on the arm of her dorky brother."

I wasn't truly excited to go with Lorena to the fashion show. I'd thought of asking Josephine if she'd like to take my place, but it was my sister's first night back in the real world and I thought it'd be best to stick by her side. She'd been invited to sit in the front row and I'd be sitting there right there beside her.

I smiled. "It still counts. Now, c'mon. Let's load this stuff up. The car is waiting and if I'm your date you at least owe me dinner first."

"And here I thought you were easy," she quipped with a smile.

Chapter Thirty-Five

Josephine

My final night of working at NYFW had finally arrived and I walked in the back entrance of Lincoln Center with mixed emotions. The job had definitely had its rough moments, but I loved being behind the scenes of fashion shows and I was really going to miss the extra income.

With Lily moving to New York soon, I'd be able to make ends meet with just one job, but I still had to help her out until she found a job of her own. She'd been working in restaurants her whole life and had started a food blog a while back. She wasn't so much a chef as she was a critic.

She loved eating good food and prided herself on knowing which restaurants were the best ones in town. New York would be the perfect city for her if only she'd just hurry up and arrive.

I stepped into the dressing room for the final show of the season. Marc Jacobs. Everyone who was anyone would be sitting in the audience and I was backstage working as a glorified janitor. A janitor surrounded by couture wearing black pants, a t-shirt, and a black baseball hat with "NYFW STAFF" stretched across the front. *God, why have you forsaken me?*

Models, hair stylists, makeup artists, stylists, and designers were running around like worker bees in the center of a hive. Elbows, knees, arms, fists—at any given moment, various body parts were colliding with me as people rushed to finish their jobs. I went back to emptying the trashcan in the corner of the room just as I heard someone start to yell at the front of the room.

"Where the hell is Gillian Grace?" a man spat, spinning in a circle and flailing his arms wildly. "Do these models think contracts are a joke?!"

He was short and completely bald with circular framed glasses perched on his nose. He was dressed in all black, like me, except his clothing probably cost more than all of my organs combined would go for on the black market.

He clapped his hands and started yelling again.

"So help me god, if she doesn't arrive in three seconds, I will murder her entire family."

I reached for my broom and took a step back, lest he catch sight of me and direct his anger at me.

Wrong move.

He whipped around and narrowed his eyes on me. I froze as if I were trying to fend off a bear. *Don't let him smell your fear!* He scanned over me once, all the way up and all the way down, and then he took a step closer.

"You," he yelled, pointing in my direction.

Every single person in the area paused and turned toward me. I whipped around to see if there was someone behind me; there wasn't, only a black concrete wall and craft food services. (Which I'd been sneaking food from for the last ten days. What? It's not like the models ever touched it.)

"Don't play dumb. I'm talking to you," he said, stepping another foot closer.

I gripped my broom tighter and smiled tentatively.

"Uh, yes?"

"Who are you?"

His question felt philosophical, like I was supposed to respond with a treatise on existentialism. Instead, I just replied with my name.

"Josephine."

He waved his hand with impatience. Clearly my name wasn't what he was looking for.

"What are your measurements?"

I glanced from him to all the other people watching me and waiting for my reply. I was supposed to say my size in front of a room full of models? *I should not have eaten that Chipotle burrito last night.*

"Uhh—it depends on what I'm wearing. Usually I can pull off a smaller size in pants—"

His patience wore out somewhere between the "u" and the first "h" in "uhh".

"You're literally boring me to death. Enough. I need you to model. Take off that heinous uniform and see Nikki for sizing. Tell her you're filling in for Gillian Grace."

I laughed. Cracked up, in fact. Wow, this was a really

bad reality show. He wanted me to model in a Marc Jacobs fashion show during the finale of New York Fashion Week? I didn't even know where to begin with my protests, so instead I stood mute, with deer-in-the-headlight eyes.

He wasn't pleased by my reaction. "I know. Believe me, I wish this were a joke. Now stop sweeping and go get changed. I don't have time for this."

With that, he turned and walked away. His departure acted like an on/off switch for the insanity in the room. The second he walked away, the room returned to chaos and I determined that my life had taken a sharp turn into Crazyville.

I was still clutching my broom when a short Latina woman with purple cropped hair and dark lined eyes stepped up in front of me and pursed her lips.

"I'm Nikki," she said, giving me a onceover, much like the other guy had just done.

"Josephine," I said, pressing my hand to my chest.

"Are you like a custodian or something? What's with the hat?"

I reached up to feel the brim. I knew the bright white NYFW letters illuminated my lower-middle class status.

"Yeah. Uh, I work here and I don't think I fully understand what's going on."

She popped her hip out with a touch of attitude. "Martín is down a model, so he's enlisted your help. We'll get you fitted and push you through hair and makeup as quickly as possible."

"No. No. I don't think that's a good idea."

"So you're turning down $3,000 and the chance to model in New York Fashion Week? What, do you love your current gig that much?"

Hold the phone.

No one said anything about three grand! I'd do a whole hell of a lot for three grand and most of it was illegal in Texas and New York. Walking in a fashion show for money hadn't even seemed like an option.

"You'll receive a check before you leave tonight. They hand them out before the after party. I'm sure someone will fill you in on everything, but there's no time for me to explain it all right now."

Nothing she was saying made sense to me and worst of all, I had no time to argue. In a straight up movie montage scene, ten things happened around me at once: someone pulled the broom from my hand, another person ripped the shirt off my head, a measuring tape appeared around my boobs, and two women crouched down in front of my legs. HEYO.

"Nice tits," one assistant said as she finished measuring my chest.

"Uhh, thanks," I replied as she ran in the opposite direction, having acquired the measurement she needed.

"Is this your natural color?" a hairstylist asked as she ripped the hat and ponytail from my head.

"Yes," I said, squinting from the pain. *Well, it was my natural color before you ripped all of it out*

She ran her fingers through the tangles, yanking as she went.

"It's beautiful. Yes, we'll leave the color. No time to change it. I'll freshen up the cut and style it while they do your makeup. Let's go."

She wrapped her hand around my bicep and began to pull me after her.

"Hold on!" the woman between my legs protested. "I'm getting her inseam."

Her hand was two millimeters from my vagina and I'd

never seen her in my life.

"What exactly will I be wearing?" I asked the gaggle of people swarming me.

No one appeared to hear me.

In ten seconds flat, I'd gone from Josephine to Cinderella. Except, while Cinderella had evil stepsisters and one fairy godmother, I had Martin and fifteen bitchy birds flitting around me.

There was no time to reflect or consider the sharp turn of events my life had taken. While one woman did my makeup, another woman attacked my haggard nails. I had a woman sizing my feet as another sewed me into a dark blue couture dress.

"I don't actually know how to walk down the runway," I admitted after being sewn into the dress. I'll be honest, a part of me purposely waited to tell them until after they'd sewn me in so that they'd feel pity and let me keep it.

"Honey, how old are you?" the makeup artist asked.

"Twenty-four."

"So you've been walkin' for at least twenty-three years. Keep your head up, take confident steps, and look where you're going. Don't look down, you'll only trip yourself."

"But my gown is really short."

She met my eye in the mirror and shook her head. "They just tailored that dress to your body specifically. It's the exact length it should be for you to walk just fine. Now stop complaining."

Alrighty then. That was that. I stayed quiet, trying to conceal my nerves as they finished up working on my face. When I opened my eyes after they'd finished with my eye makeup, Nikki stood behind me in the mirror. I met her eyes and she smiled, seemingly impressed with how I looked.

"It's time to line up, let's go."

I tried to talk some reason into her one more time.

"Are you sure there's not an actual model they could get for this? I am honestly the least qualified person in this place."

She laughed. "Yeah, well, when you're gorgeous, people forgive you. They sure as shit ain't puttin' my ratchet-ass cankles out there."

She yanked me to the side and I almost tripped in my three-inch heels.

"This is your spot."

I looked to where she was pointing and my heart leapt in my chest. I was positioned among half a dozen super models I stalked on Instagram at least once a day. Charlie Whitlock stood in front of Gigi Hadid. Cara and Giselle were taking a quick selfie. Me? I looked back toward Nikki to find that I was now utterly alone; I wanted to throw up everywhere.

"Places, everyone! The show is about to begin!" Martín yelled from the front of the line. "Walk slow. DO NOT SMILE. Own that runway and then line up quickly for the finale. There is no time for delays."

He glanced down at his clipboard and I took a final breath as deep bass started bumping through the speaker system. I *loved* the song.

"Oh!" Martín yelled, drawing our attention once again. "Most of all, remember that you're all fucking supermodels."

I felt the vomit rising in my throat.

There's no way this could end well.

Chapter Thirty-Six

Julian

I skimmed my hand over the breast pocket of my suit, right where my phone lay hidden away. I knew as soon as I pulled it out, the show would begin. Even still, I itched to pull it out and check in on Josephine. All day I'd tried to come up with some sort of casual way to reach out to her: *How is your Saturday going? Hey, that song you like just came on the radio. What's up with the unrest in the Middle East?*

Thanks to my better judgment, I'd yet to send any of the texts I'd drafted throughout the day. She'd see right through my veiled attempt to pull her back to me. I had to give her space and hope that by Monday, she'd be ready for things to go back to how they'd been before. (That is, us pretending to be friends while subtly eye-fucking the shit out of each other.)

My sister and I were front row center at the Marc Jacobs fashion show. I was mostly out of my element, but I was wearing a new navy suit and Lorena assured me that I fit in just fine. She'd conveniently left out the fact that I'd be one of only a handful of men in attendance. There were beautiful women surrounding me, celebrities I recognized from the latest blockbuster hits, pop stars, and other faces I vaguely recognized from TV, but all I cared about was the phone in my suit pocket and its lack of text notifications.

"You look really handsome," my sister said from the chair beside me, nudging me with her shoulder.

I peered over and smiled. I may have preferred to be watching a basketball game, but at least I was in good company. My sister looked like her old self for the first time in months. She'd spent the entire afternoon getting ready with people in my hotel. I'd stayed down in the hotel bar, far away from the smell of hairspray and nail polish. They'd delivered a dozen dresses up to my room and she'd picked a beautiful, long green gown that was as unique as she was.

"You look beautiful," I said, wrapping my arm around the back of her chair and kissing her forehead. Maybe I'd made a mistake staying so far away in Boston. Lorena needed family support, and while my mother appeared to be coming around slowly, there was no replacement for a big brother.

"Thanks," she smiled. "Are you going to come with me to the after party?"

I frowned, thinking of all the alcohol and other

substances that would surely be supplied in abundance at an event like that. "Do you think that's a good idea on your first night?"

She pressed her hand to my arm as reassurance. "I won't go for long. I just want to say hello to the designers and then I'll get a cab back to my apartment. It just feels like I've been away from the fashion world for a while and I don't want people to forget about me."

I nodded. I could see why she wouldn't want to miss it. It'd be a good networking event for her, especially in a world that thrived on relevance, but it definitely wasn't my idea of a fun Saturday night. I could imagine someone asking me about my favorite look from the show and me having to scramble for the name of some fancy item of clothing. *What exactly is a blouse? A fancy shirt?*

"We can go for a bit," I relented.

She beamed and then her gaze darted to the front of the theater.

"The show is starting soon!" she said, clapping her hands with excitement.

I sat back in my chair and scanned the room. The first few rows were dominated by young women, some of them probably bloggers like Josephine. They were dressed to the nines, some in eccentric outfits that I couldn't quite wrap my head around.

The woman on my right was an older woman with sunglasses on. Lorena had whispered about her being the editor of some big magazine. Everyone seemed to be impressed by her—a few young women had even asked for her photo—but all I cared about was the amount of perfume she'd sprayed on. I was starting to get a headache from the overwhelming scent of roses.

There was a convoy of photographers near the end of

the runway, shouting over one another to be heard. At least a dozen of them had lenses the size of my head, all lining up to get a good shot of the runway.

I was still watching them when the house lights dimmed around us and loud music started pumping through the speakers. There was no real introduction before the first model started down the runway with an angry expression on her face. She looked skeletal in a white gauzy dress. Maybe her face was so scrunched up because her dress was so tight. Seriously though, soaking wet she couldn't have been more than ten pounds.

The photographers went crazy, snapping away as she approached the end of the runway. The next few models that strolled out after her were just as lithe with sharp cheekbones and confident walks. Some of the outfits were sexy as hell, but most of them I didn't understand. Some of them wore hoods not attached to anything. What was the point of that? Everyone around me was oohing and awing, including Lorena, but I just adjusted my suit jacket and pretended to be interested. Lorena was going to owe me after this one.

And then Josephine walked out from backstage.

Wait.

My mouth dropped.

What the hell?

Josephine.

Why was Josephine walking in the fashion show?

I blinked and then squinted to confirm that she wasn't some kind of mirage. She looked different, more made up than usual, with a polished edge to her usual girl-next-door beauty. She was in a midnight blue strapless dress that cut off way too short. She had on heels that strapped up around her ankles and made her long tan legs go on for miles.

Maybe to everyone else, she looked like a standard model, but I could see the nerves lurking beneath the surface. She clenched and unclenched her fists as she walked and every few steps, she glanced down at the runway as if to ensure it wasn't going to slip out from beneath her.

As she passed in front of me, I resisted the urge to reach out and touch her, to pull her close and ask her why she was modeling in a fashion show. She'd never once mentioned the fact that she was a model.

Instead, I sat in shock, following her walk down the runway in utter awe. My heart was beating in step with the up-tempo bass. She walked to the end of the runway, propped her hand on her hip, turned toward the cameras, and then strutted back just as quickly as she'd come. She'd been on stage for less than a minute, but I could have sworn time had stopped all together.

Lorena leaned in and whispered, "That model looks just like your assistant!"

I nodded and followed Josephine's figure as she walked off the stage.

"It was."

Suddenly it looked like I had a very good reason to accompany Lorena to the after party.

Chapter Thirty-Seven

Josephine

I'd walked in my first—and most likely last—New York Fashion Week show and I could hardly wrap my head around the insanity of it. I'd been sewn into a dress, had my makeup done and my hair professionally styled, and then they'd shoved me out from backstage like a mama bird pushing her baby bird out of the nest…and I'd SOARED.

I didn't trip once, I posed at the end of the runway, and a ton of photographers from giant magazines had snapped my photo as if they were actually going to do something with it. *(I'll probably share the next US Weekly cover with Kate Middleton and her new baby.)*

A few of the kinder models had adopted me into their group and I'd made sure to snap a ton of photos with them for my blog. My readers wouldn't believe the story when I finally got around to sharing the juicy details about my night. Of course, I'd probably dedicate an entire month to posts about the show. *Oh that picture? That's just me and GISELLE, chillin' in designer duds like it's the most normal thing in the world.*

And the dress? I wasn't ever going to take it off. Ever. The sturdy midnight blue material was structured and tailored to my body so that it emphasized my curves. It accentuated my breasts without needing a bra (which, for us well-endowed females, is practically a miracle in and of itself). The fabric wrapped tightly around my waist and there was a sharp slit that ran up the center of my left thigh. It was seductive and beautiful, and as I walked into the after party, I actually felt like I belonged.

I followed the group of models to a table off to the side, taking in the party as I went. Drinks were flowing and waiters were carrying around silver trays of hors d'oeuvres that I stared at longingly but didn't dare touch.

We crowded around a small cocktail table and I listened to the other models discuss their own versions of fashion week. They tallied up the shows they'd walked in and the number of couture outfits now sitting in piles back at their apartments. I listened with wide eyes, practically melting on the spot. I considered bragging about some of the more picturesque dust piles I'd swept up in my prior NYFW experiences, but I feared that most of the models didn't share my sense of humor.

I was about to combust at the sheer awesomeness of the night when I felt a hand wrap around my arm, just above my elbow. I knew the grip, knew the feel of those fingers on my skin.

I stepped back to turn just as a seductive voice whispered against my ear.

"I didn't realize you moonlighted as a model."

Goosebumps bloomed down my arms as I registered the familiar voice. I inhaled a breath and glanced over my shoulder to find Julian standing there. A sharp navy suit stretched across his broad shoulders and chest. Black hair framed his sharp features and his eyes shown like two fiery embers in the club lighting. Desire spiked my veins as my eyes slid over him.

When I didn't respond to his comment, he arched a dark brow.

"Jo?"

I swallowed and wet my lips.

He didn't let go of my arm and when I turned toward him, my body brushed right up against his. His fingers tightened on my arm as my hip grazed his.

"It's a long story," I shrugged, trying to make the last four hours seem far simpler than they'd actually been.

He glanced down at my red lips and then his gaze lowered farther. The sweetheart bodice on my dress was likely his favorite part of the design. When he met my eyes once again, there was a faint smile where there hadn't been one before.

"What are you doing here?" I asked, trying to slow my racing heart. Having him there, this close to me, felt like it might be too much for me to handle. Usually I was around him in controlled environments. This? With me in a dress that was made for sin and him in a suit that I wanted to rip right off? He was temptation personified.

"Lorena dragged me to the show," he explained. "She and I were invited to the after party as well. When I saw you walking in the show, I couldn't very well turn it down."

I smiled and glanced over his shoulder to see if she was still around.

"She just left in a cab a minute ago," he said, answering my unspoken question.

I glanced back at him and swallowed slowly. So there we were. Alone. He looked divine in his navy suit. It was the perfect complement to his immaculate bone structure. He was sharp lines, hard edges, subtle lips, and inviting eyes. Every detail blended into an alluring combination, one that called to me like a bad habit.

"So now you're here all by your lonesome?" I asked, just to confirm my suspicions.

He smiled. "If you won't have a drink with me, then I guess I am."

I glanced down to give myself a reprieve from his stare. Truth be told, a drink with a man dressed like James Bond sounded too good to pass up.

"I'd love one."

He directed me toward the bar with utter confidence: a firm hand on my lower back, his hip touching mine as we waited in line. I bit my lip to keep from turning toward him and saying something I'd regret. He didn't feel like my friend, Julian. He felt like a devil in disguise.

"What would you like to taste?" he asked, rubbing a slow circle in the small of my back.

I smiled with understanding. "Whatever you're having."

He nodded and turned toward the bartender. "Two gin and tonics."

We stepped to the side to allow the next guests to order, but Julian stayed close.

"I haven't told you how beautiful you look yet."

I blushed under the weight of his compliment and glanced away. "You don't have to, it's just all the makeup and stuff they put on me before the show."

His finger skimmed over my shoulder, down the length of my arm. My stomach clenched in response and for a brief moment, I closed my eyes, letting his touch consume me.

"I know it's more than that," he said, just as I heard our drinks placed down in front of us.

I sipped mine like a man dying of thirst, hoping the burn of alcohol would quiet my nerves.

"What'd you think of the show?" I asked, trying to keep my gaze on anything but him. Not that it mattered; his entire appearance was already burned into my memory. That slicked-back dark hair, tan skin, defined jaw. There was no point in reminding myself of how hard it was to deny my desire for him.

"The show was lovely, but I didn't care to watch anyone but you," he replied before taking a long sip of his drink.

I looked over my shoulder, careful to see if anyone was watching us. We were in the corner of the venue, by far the least entertaining people in the room, and yet I felt like we were on full display.

"Julian, is this a good idea?" I asked.

He arched a brow.

"Is what a good idea?"

"You and I testing the limits like this? Things worked best when we were just keeping things platonic. Wouldn't it be easier that way?"

His jaw clicked in annoyance at my questioning and instead of answering, he finished off his drink, took my empty cup, and dropped them both on a table beside us.

"You know what?" he asked, skimming his hand down my arm until his fingers were entwined with mine. "I don't think I care anymore."

He gripped my hand and dragged me out of the room after him, almost too quickly for me to keep up. I had to pick up my pace and even then he wouldn't slow down.

"Julian. Slow down. Seriously."

He acted as if he couldn't hear me.

"Where are we going?" I asked.

He didn't reply and he didn't let go of my hand. We stepped through the door of the club and were met with brisk night air. I crossed my free arm over my chest, trying to shield as much of my skin from the chill as possible.

Julian walked to the line of cabs, nabbed the first one, and held the door open for me.

"Are you getting in?" he asked with a dark gleam in his eye. There was no please, no sugarcoating. He wouldn't tell me where we were going and he wouldn't promise to be a perfect gentleman when we got there.

I could get in the cab and see where he'd take me or I could step away and go back into the party, maybe even push Julian away for good.

The edge of his mouth curved up as he watched me wrestle with indecision. I think he knew I'd already made up my mind. What was there to decide anyway? How many times could you deny yourself a craving that you fantasized about day in and day out? Why should I care about keeping my life on a perfectly straight course when it kept throwing wild curves at me?

Instead of giving him an answer, I stepped closer, wrapped my hands around his neck, and kissed him. Hard. I tilted my head and bit down on his bottom lip. He wrapped his arms around my biceps and held me against him. His tongue slipped into my mouth and I moaned, pressing even closer to him. I could feel his heart beating in time with mine. This was it. I was getting in that cab and I'd find out if Julian Lefray was worth the days and days of agonizing over him.

"Are you two getting in or what?" the cabbie asked.

I pulled back, out of Julian's reach, and pressed the back of my hand to my lips. Julian smiled apologetically at the driver as he ushered me into the back seat. He held my hand, assisting me as I slid to the opposite side and watched him slide in after me. The scent of his cologne swept in alongside him and I had to grip my hands together in my lap to keep from mauling him.

My dress rode high on my thighs, just inches away from revealing too much. Julian directed the driver toward his hotel and I skimmed my finger along the hem, wondering just how long we were going to have to contain ourselves in the back of the cab.

Then again, why did we have to contain ourselves?

I didn't want to stop. Who knew how long it'd take us to get to his hotel. I'd just had the best kiss of my life and I wanted more. I knew we couldn't have sex in the back of the cab, but the driver was more than occupied with his eyes on the road. Short of slipping off my dress, I knew he wouldn't notice what we were doing. I could tease Julian a bit, just enough to drive him mad.

As soon as we pulled out into traffic, I dropped my hand to Julian's knee.

He shifted an inch closer and met my eye. He didn't speak, but the question lay in his eyes all the same.

What do you think you're doing?

I smirked and let my hand drift higher.

He gripped my wrist to stop me, but I pushed on,

R.S. GREY

dragging my nails along the inseam of his suit pants.

"Have a fun night?" the cabbie asked.

Julian cleared his throat and nodded.

I smiled and inched farther up his leg. I couldn't unzip his pants—it'd be too loud—but I could drive him crazy through the thin material just fine.

"What was your favorite part?" I asked, wanting to hear the lust in his voice again.

He slid his gaze to me and narrowed his eyes. His grip on my wrist lessened, but I could still feel my pulse against the pads of his fingers. It was my tell. Each thump let him know just how much I was craving him. My heart rate was frenzied because of him.

"I don't think it's happened yet actually," Julian replied, watching me with interest.

"Oh, is there another party or something?" the cabbie asked.

I laughed and skimmed my hand an inch higher.

"Something like that," Julian said, clamping down on my wrist as soon as I met my goal. I smiled. He was just as hard as I'd been anticipating, but I couldn't move my hand with him gripping my wrist as tightly as he was. I jutted out my bottom lip. *Bastard.*

"Is this all right?" the cabbie asked.

I glanced outside and realized we were already at Julian's hotel. I wasn't ready for the cab ride to be over; I wanted to keep teasing him. I wanted to drive him crazy with my hand so that he could repay the favor later.

Julian reached for his wallet to pay the cab fare, but he never loosened his grip on my wrist. Whether it was conscious or not, it felt like he was doing it so that I wouldn't bolt at the last minute. We'd come to these crossroads before, but this time there'd be a different outcome.

There was *no* turning back now.

Chapter Thirty-Eight

Julian

We were civilized as we walked through the lobby. I held her hand and we walked fast, keeping eye contact with the bank of elevators at the end of the lobby. The woman behind the front desk greeted us and I threw her a wave before picking up the pace.

I pressed the call button as Josephine slid her gaze to me and revealed a slow, private smile. I squeezed her hand tighter as the doors to the elevator slid open and we stepped inside.

The moment the doors closed, I pushed Jo to the wall. All civility was lost. She bit my lip as I slammed her hands against the wall over her head and she ground her hips against mine. I was tracing the top of her dress with my finger when the elevator dinged and the doors swept open twenty floors below our final destination.

I jumped back, giving us space to breathe as a couple dressed in cowboy boots and rhinestone hats stepped into the elevator.

Jesus Christ.

Jo's chest was rising and falling as if she'd just finished a marathon. Her cheeks were flushed and she had her hand pressed to her stomach, trying to calm herself down.

The couple didn't even seem to notice. The woman glanced from her to me and then smiled wide.

"Are you two real New Yorkers?" she asked with wide, curious eyes.

Odd question for a hotel elevator.

Jo smiled and nodded. "Do we look like it or something?"

The woman pulled her purse off her shoulder and dug inside of it. "You're both just so glamorous. Could we get a picture?"

Jo met my gaze and I arched a brow.

"Just of us two?" she asked the woman.

The woman stopped digging and pulled out a giant camera. She handed it off to her husband—who didn't seem at all phased by his wife's request—and stood on the other side of Jo.

"I'll be in it too," she replied jovially.

I laughed. Only in New York.

I stepped closer to Jo and she wrapped her hand around my stomach. I could still feel the excitement surrounding her. Her body practically hummed with desire. I had my hand on her hip as the man positioned the viewfinder in front of his eye. Then, as he was about to snap the photo, I slid my hand down over Jo's ass, dangerously low. She pinched my side to stop me, but it was too late. The man snapped the photo and Josephine practically came apart in my hands.

They thanked us for the photo, stepped off after a few more floors, and then Jo turned her angry gaze on me.

"Really cute, Julian. They totally knew what you were doing."

I smiled. "No they didn't. I was watching her husband's face. He was oblivious, including the fact that they came all the way from Texas to get a picture of a Texan."

She crossed her arms and leaned back against the elevator wall.

"Besides, it's payback for the cab ride over here."

She arched her brow and studied me from across the confined space. There was an unspoken war taking place between us—one that I wasn't sure I could win. I thought she was about to argue with me when she bent forward and slipped her hands underneath the bottom of her dress. The slit on her left thigh pulled wider and I clenched my fists to keep from slamming the emergency button on the elevator panel. She reached up, took hold of her black thong, and slid it all the way down her legs. I watched the material descend her long legs as a rush of blood swept through me.

She held it out on the tip of her finger and smirked.

"You wanted to feel it so badly while they were taking the photo, so here you go," she said, tossing it at me.

I caught it in my right hand and smirked.

She crossed her arms over her chest, pushing her breasts up even higher. I loosened my tie and slid my suit jacket off my shoulders. She watched me start to undress as the elevator pulled to a stop on my floor. The doors slid open and I gestured for Josephine to step out first. She narrowed her eyes, clearly untrusting of my motives.

"I can be a gentlemen sometimes." I smirked.

She laughed and headed in the direction of my hotel room. I pulled my keycard out of my wallet and stepped up behind her.

"Though I know you prefer when I'm not," I said as I unlocked the door.

She turned around, gripped the two ends of my tie and pulled me into the suite. The lights were off, the city was our torch as she tugged the tie from my collar and tossed it over onto the couch. My jacket was next and then she stood there, eyeing me up and down with excitement.

She reached behind her to the zipper of her dress and I stepped up and gripped her hand to stop her. I wanted to take it off her. The midnight blue fabric was the last defense between us. Her breasts pressed against me with every inhalation, and she waited there with bated breath for me to release the dress and let it fall to the ground. I wrapped one hand up around her neck, at the base of her skull. I used the leverage to tilt her head back and then I stared straight into her eyes, watching for any last scrap of insecurity.

"Will you be honest about how badly you want me right now or do I need to slide my hand between your legs to get the truth?"

A rose blush bloomed from her chest, up over her cheeks.

She wrapped her left leg around me and the slit in her dress pulled open just like it had in the elevator.

I let my hand run from the inside of her knee, up over the smooth skin of her inner thigh. Her breath picked up as I skimmed higher, up to where her thong should have been.

I watched her features as I slipped my finger between her thighs. She was completely lost to the moment. Her eyes rolled closed and she bit down on her bottom lip. I pressed a finger into her, watching her cheeks flush with color, and then I contemplated taking her right there, up against the door of my hotel room.

I slid another finger inside her and moaned at how amazing it felt to finally feel all of her. I could have stayed right there all night, teasing her with my fingers, but I wanted our first time to be different. I wanted her to remember it as the best sex she'd ever had.

I pulled back and unwrapped her leg from around my waist. She opened her eyes and glared at me, surprised by my quick departure.

"Uh, you'll have to try a little harder than that. I wasn't even close."

I laughed and stepped back.

"Take the dress off, Jo."

She propped her hands on her hips and narrowed her eyes. "I've already done everything for you. This is the only thing you have to take off."

"Your bra?" I asked.

She smirked. "I'm not wearing one."

I ignored the shot of adrenaline that accompanied that confession.

"What about your shoes?" I asked. They were laced up like gladiator sandals and looked like they'd take an hour just to untie.

"I assumed you'd ask me to leave them on or something."

I smiled, but didn't confirm her suspicions. "I have a feeling this will be a little rough and I don't exactly want scars on my back from those heels."

Her smirk widened. "Oh, you're going to be rough?"

I shook my head at her incessant questioning. "Jo, lay down on the bed."

She looked back at the king-size hotel bed, perfectly coifed by the afternoon maid.

"But my dress is still on."

I dragged my hand through my hair and kicked off my shoes. "Then take it off."

"Bossy, boss man."

I stepped forward and reached behind her for the zipper on her dress.

"They sewed me into it," she said, lifting up on her tip toes to kiss the edge of my jaw. "You'll have to—"

Her words were drowned out by the sound of fabric ripping.

"Julian!"

"I'll pay to get it fixed," I assured her before she could throw a hissy fit.

Her green eyes locked on mine with a flare of attitude and then she reached for the collar of my shirt. She clenched her fists and pulled as hard as she could. The first button on my shirt flew across the room, but none of the others even budged.

"That was far less dramatic than I thought it would be," she laughed.

Her dress slipped down as she laughed, exposing a few more inches of supple skin. I gripped the dress at her hips and pulled the material down even more, all the while thanking the bra gods for their absence.

She worked on the buttons of my shirt while I ran my hands over her chest, down her flat stomach. My eyes raked over her skin, following the trail of my hands. I hardly noticed when she slid my shirt over my shoulders, but as soon as it was gone, I pushed her back toward the edge of the bed and climbed up on top of her.

Her hair fanned out around her head. Her lips parted and her chest rose and fell in quick successions. The longer I looked, the longer I cupped her curves, the rosier her skin became beneath my touch. I smoothed my hand down the curve of her hip, down between her legs. She arched her back and dug her nails into the backs of my arms.

"Julian," she moaned.

I nudged her legs apart with my knee and watched her green eyes squeeze shut.

"Are you nervous?" I asked, curious about her reaction.

She scrunched the bed sheets in her hand, opened her eyes, and stared up at the ceiling.

"A little bit. It's just been a while and the last time I did this, it was dark and I was a little drunk and he definitely didn't touch me the way you're touching me."

I smiled and scanned down her body, watching my finger slip higher up her inner thigh.

"Like this?" I asked.

She squirmed beneath my touch and kept a tight hold on the sheets. "I'm about to spontaneously combust if you don't…"

I smirked. "Do what?"

She pushed up onto her elbows and her gaze flitted back and forth between my eyes.

"Julian Lefray, please put me out of my misery. Do you realize how long I've waited for this?"

I laughed and pressed my hand to the center of her chest, pushing her onto her back.

"I've waited just as long, Jo, but you have to relax. You have the most beautiful body I've ever seen. Just let me touch you."

She groaned and let her body fall back onto the bed. I gripped her hips and pushed her up higher on the bed. Her head hit the pillows and she watched me with a curious stare.

I scooted down and skimmed my hand down across her chest and stomach until I could grip her thighs and spread her legs even wider.

"Oh, Jesus," she whispered, throwing her arm over her eyes.

"Jo, relax," I whispered, pressing one hand to her stomach to hold her on the bed and using the other to keep her legs open. If I was about to put my mouth between her legs, I didn't want her to buck up and break my nose.

"Okay. Okay," she said, taking a calming breath. "I'm relaxed, I promise."

Liar. Her body was still humming with nervous energy, but I loved the way she felt. She was so easy to touch, so full of beautiful curves that I'd been fantasizing about for the last few months. I was mesmerized by every part of her. The soft skin over her hip bones, the dip of her belly button, the arch of her back as I dragged my hand up her thigh and then pressed a finger inside of her.

Her lips parted and I gave her a second to still, then I followed the path of my finger with my mouth.

There was no point in waiting for her to remain still. Jo laughed and talked the whole way through the night. Every time I pushed her a little further, she'd slink back and make a joke, trying to lighten the moment.

She watched me with curious eyes as I slipped off my pants and boxer briefs. It was the first time she'd stayed silent the entire night. I crawled back on top of her and kissed up her chest, over the swell of her breasts, and up the side of her neck.

"I'm not nervous anymore," she whispered as she wound her fingers through my hair. "I want this so badly."

I leaned back to catch her eyes and we stared at each other in silence. If I stopped then, Monday morning wouldn't be any less awkward. We'd already gone so far. I'd already seen every inch of her skin and I'd already heard a symphony of moans from her supple lips. No amount of time could erase those memories. I knew that, but as I slipped inside of her and she shook beneath me, I realized there was so much left hanging between us. She was completely open to me. For once, there were no pretenses or expectations. She wasn't pushing me away and I wasn't pretending that she was just a friend. No more playful, witty flirtation. Just lust, distilled.

Josephine

He took his time with me, winding his fingers through mine and pushing them out to the sides. He ground his hips against mine, watching and studying my reactions so he could discover what really drove me mad. I must have been so easy to read, because he could do no wrong. When he skimmed the tops of my breasts, I squeezed his hands tighter. When he caught my earlobe between his teeth, I moaned softly against his cheek. When I came apart beneath him, my whole body shook. My eyes squeezed shut and my nails dug into his skin so hard I was sure I'd draw blood.

In that moment...

I knew I was his.

Chapter Thirty-Nine

Josephine

Monday morning was monumental for two reasons.

First, we had to decide which architecture firm to hire for Lorena's new offices. This was a big deal and would ultimately shape the entire design of her store.

Second, there was the little fact that Julian and I had made love on Saturday night and now we were going to have to work together. *No biggie*.

I woke up early on Monday, stood in front of my mirror, and applied a thin layer of makeup—mascara to hide my nervous eyes, red lipstick to give me false confidence. The entire time I got ready, I replayed the previous day and contemplated how easy it'd been to wake up in Julian's bed.

"Dude, you're basically crushing me right now," I said, *pushing him off of me at the crack of dawn.*

Julian was a cuddler, a suffocating cuddler. I woke up with half of his body on top of my mine. I was practically suffocating and when I rolled over, my lungs thanked me for the extra air.

"Mmm…again," he murmured, still half-asleep. His *hand found my left boob and I rolled my eyes.*

"You don't get sex before I get breakfast. Now get up and let's go find a bagel."

"You're so high maintenance." He laughed, rolling *over and stretching his arms above his head.*

HELLO, NAKED JULIAN.

The man was all toned, tan skin and six-pack abs. I wanted to lick him from his toes to his forehead, but more than that, I wanted a bagel and some damn cream cheese.

"C'mon, c'mon, c'mon. I'm hungry."

He groaned and threw the blankets off, and my eyes bulged out of my head a little bit. The man needed to warn people before he just stripped down like that. I was momentarily dumbstruck as I took in the contour of his abs and the curve of everything that lay below.

"Jo, my eyes are up here," he joked.

My face turned the color of a Cherry Icee and I promptly turned away from him to examine his hotel closet.

"I'm stealing a t-shirt and then I'm going to leave this apartment to hunt down food. My stomach is eating itself as we speak."

Julian's hand wrapped around my waist and then he pulled me back against his chest. His palm splayed out on my stomach and then he inched lower. My stomach dipped and my knees buckled. Traitorous body.

"Nope. No," I said, resisting the temptation to give in to his pursuit. "If that hand moves any lower, I'm going to karate chop you."

It moved lower and my body betrayed me. My stomach was like, "Meh, I can wait to eat," and my girly parts were like, "HELL YEAH, this is a great idea." And that's the story of how Julian banged me on the floor of his closet with his suits and ties judging us from above.

Our breakfast turned into a stroll through Central Park and then a lunch. I eventually made an excuse about having to do laundry (yeah, right) and cleaning (ha ha) and we parted ways after a breath-stealing kiss.

As soon as I stepped away from him and walked to the subway, the last twenty-four hours started to set in. The same parts of my brain that had pushed me to sleep with Julian were now firing off insecurities and worries at a pace of 1000 thoughts per second. Were you sexy enough? Did you make enough sexy sounds? Did you make too many sexy sounds, thus coming across as a crazy porn star? Did giving him a blowjob seem cool and hot or just plain desperate? Did you come across too needy or were you cool and casual?

Cool New York girls can have sex without emotions. They are confident and strong. They don't second-guess their decisions and they don't question what a man wants. YES. That's me! I'm cool and confident!

I walked a little quicker to the subway after that with my head held high and my shoulders pushed back. I could have broken out into a choreographed dance routine if only I'd had backup dancers with me.

Unfortunately, that confidence had dwindled sometime during my various REM cycles because by Monday morning, my take-no-shit attitude was gone.

After I finished getting ready, and stuffed a breakfast bar and an apple into my purse, I opened my laptop to check my email. I had fifteen minutes to spare before I needed to head to Julian's hotel, and I definitely didn't want to show up early.

I hadn't had time to check my email over the weekend, and it definitely showed. My inbox was overflowing with emails from my bank and various spam coupons that I never got around to unsubscribing from. A few emails stood out. The subject lines all pertained to the Marc Jacobs fashion show or interview requests. I kept scrolling, losing count of how many there were. ABC News, The Today Show, Late Night with Jimmy Fallon, and People Magazine were at the top of my inbox. My first instinct was to assume that all of the emails were from spam accounts. How could they not be? There could not have been an email from Vogue sitting in my inbox.

My hand shook as I hovered my mouse over the subject line. By the time it finished loading, I thought my heart was going to beat out of my chest. I checked the email address to confirm it wasn't something like VogueMagazineEditorISwear@gmail.com. *Nope*. The email was from ElizabethPHope@Vogue.com.

Holy shit.

I scrolled down and started to read, trying to remain as calm as possible.

Dear Ms. Keller,

My name is Elizabeth Hope and I'm the Social Media Team Leader here at Vogue. First of all, congratulations on your runway debut last week. You were quite the talk of the show afterward. I'm sure you've seen the news around the Internet since then, but I wanted to reach out and contact you personally. Vogue has been looking to hire an in-house blogger, someone to expand our readership to a younger generation. Our ideal candidate would be a fresh face, someone new to the fashion scene, and someone willing to team up with Vogue to expand our readership—

I zoned out after that. Straight up spaced out in the middle of my apartment. I think my brain short-circuited midway through her email. I backtracked and reread what she'd typed. *I was the talk of the show? News on the Internet?* Truth be told, I hadn't checked my blog, YouTube, or Twitter since Saturday morning. Julian had been quite the distraction…

I paused midway through her email and pulled YouTube to check my notifications. Last I'd seen, I had somewhere around ten thousand subscribers. Now? Well over two hundred thousand. *What the fuck?* In twenty-four hours? My hand shook as I refreshed the website, just to confirm my eyes weren't deceiving me. Nope. No error. My Twitter was the same and when I went to check the hits on my blog, I had thousands upon thousands of new readers.

How?

How had these readers found me so quickly?

I went back to Twitter and searched my tags. The culprit for my stardom wasn't hard to find. One particular photo from the fashion show had spread like wildfire. It was a photo of me standing at the end of the runway with my hand on my hip and a devious smile on my lips. I looked far sexier than I ever had before, owing to the lighting and dress, I'm sure. Marc Jacobs had posted the photo first and after that every major fashion magazine had reposted it with #FashionWorldsCinderella. Apparently someone had leaked the fact that I wasn't actually a model, and people everywhere had found my story endearing, so much so that Vogue was now offering me a job.

The chime of another incoming email pulled me out of my thoughts and my eyes scanned to the clock on my microwave. *Shit.* I was going to be late. I closed my laptop and ran to grab my purse on shaky legs. I didn't have time to finish reading Elizabeth's email, but I already knew that my life was about to change. Interview requests? A possible position working with Vogue as an in-house blogger? This had been my dream for as long as I could remember. I wanted to be a fashion blogger and I wanted to make enough money blogging that I didn't need to moonlight as a janitor.

I still hadn't fully processed the sharp turn of events in my life when I knocked on Julian's hotel door fifteen minutes later.

"Coming!" a female voice sang from the other side of the door.

I let my hand fall back by my side and stared at the hotel room number, completely confused. Why was there a woman answering Julian's door less than twenty-four hours after we'd had sex?

So help me god.

Chapter Forty

Josephine

The door to Julian's hotel opened wide and I was met with a bright smile and white-blonde hair twisted into a polished bun.

Julian's sister was standing on the other side of the door and my heart was no longer in danger of pounding out of my chest. Jeez, my organs couldn't take much more excitement this early in the morning.

"Cinderella!" She beamed, stepping forward to boop me on the nose with an imaginary wand.

"Lorena, it's so good to see you," I said as I hugged her before scanning down to get a good look at her outfit. I was used to seeing her in casual clothes, but now that she was out of rehab and back in the real world, she looked far more glamorous with a slight bohemian edge. Her arms were covered in bangles and she had a gold tribal-inspired statement necklace laying against her simple white dress. Her Valentino heels were so beautiful that I had to clasp my hands together to stop myself from bending down and stealing them right off her feet.

"It's good to see you too. Did Julian tell you I'd be working with you guys starting today?"

I shook my head. "He didn't, but I should have realized you would be."

Speak of the devil…

Julian stepped out of his bedroom freshly-shaven with wet hair and a devilish smile. He was putting the finishing touches on his red tie and conjuring up memories that I wished I wasn't thinking about right in front of his sister.

"Morning Jo," he said, coming closer and bending to kiss my cheek.

I inhaled his cologne before he stepped away and pushed aside the wave of desire that came with it.

"Ah, are you a cheek kisser now, Julian? When did you become such a European dandy?" Lorena asked, glancing back and forth between us.

"Jo has a way of bringing out the gentleman in me," he said with a wide smile.

I grunted. "Do not believe that, Lorena. Just last week we went out for lunch and he almost let the restaurant's door slam shut on me."

Julian held up his hands. "No! I thought you'd stopped to look at magazines a ways back, so I didn't hold it open. Not to mention, the door was really heavy."

I laughed and shook my head.

"Is this what it's going to be like to work with you two? How do you even manage to get anything done?" she questioned.

"Usually we institute quiet time," I offered. "We aren't allowed to talk until we've checked off at least three items on our to-do lists."

It sounded like a joke, but it was true. If Julian and I had it our way, we'd distract each other with photos of dogs and YouTube videos all day. Obviously things would change now that Lorena was back. We'd have to adjust to a third person and something told me Lorena wouldn't care for dancing cat videos as much as Julian and I did.

When I strolled farther into his hotel room, I saw that Lorena had already set up shop at my normal spot on the big couch. Julian's laptop was across from her, which meant I was left with the hotel desk. This wasn't a bad thing—in fact most normal people work from desks—it was just that I knew I wouldn't get away with sneaking my normal glances at Julian all day. Things were already changing.

Lorena took her seat at the couch and jumped right into work. Her enthusiasm was infectious and I knew she'd been waiting months to finally get back to her company. We had a final meeting with a design team in the afternoon and I needed to finish a few things before then.

I opened my laptop and laid out my pen, phone, and notepad in a neat row. The setup wasn't as comfortable as the couch, but it would do. I had a view of Central Park right out the window. Sure, I'd have preferred my standard view of Julian, but maybe the new setup would help my productivity.

My computer was still booting up when Julian held a warm cup of coffee out in front of me. I hadn't even heard him approach; I'd been too lost in the craziness of the morning. I reached out to take it from him and then he squeezed my shoulder, a small gesture of reassurance.

"Thank you," I said over my shoulder.

He gave me a knowing smile and then headed back to his spot on the couch. If Lorena noticed the exchange, she didn't say anything about it.

"Jo! You have to give me all the details about Saturday night. I've seen your photo everywhere this morning! You're seriously famous now," Lorena said, clapping her hands in excitement.

I glanced over to Julian and he smiled.

"By all means, tell her about the fashion show or we'll never get any work done today." I laughed and proceeded to give her every juicy detail of the show. After all, I could tell her the insanity of the first half of my night without including the details of what happened after. With her brother. In this very hotel room.

She'd pestered me with questions, but I didn't mind. It was mid-morning by the time Julian heavily suggested we actually start to work, but even then, I had to promise to tell her more during lunch.

By the time we'd all settled down to work, I had too many conflicting thoughts swirling around my head to actually focus. I couldn't even decide what should take top priority: the fact that Vogue had emailed me about a job or the fact that I wanted to jump Julian's bones at that very moment.

I glanced over my shoulder and snuck a peek at Julian. He was firing away on his keyboard with his brows subtly tugged together, a sign of concentration. I loved watching him while he worked. He hit enter on whatever he was typing, leaned back on the couch, and caught my stare.

An earthquake would have taken a backseat to that stare. My heart leapt in my chest as a slow, seductive smile spread across his lips. The breath of my lungs, the beat of my heart, the basic ability to pull my gaze away from him—they were all under his control. The connection between us was stronger than any willpower I could have mustered.

"Julian, what's the website for the architecture firm we're meeting with this afternoon?" Lorena asked, interrupting our moment.

Oh right, maybe stop eye-fucking Julian while his sister is around.

I closed my eyes, took a deep breath, and turned back to good ol' Central Park.

Concentrate. Open your email. Pretend to type something. It can be gibberish, just stop sitting there like you're frozen.

I'd managed to get through half an email when Lorena stood to use the restroom a few minutes later. My fingers froze over my computer keys as I processed that she'd be gone for a few minutes. There was absolutely no way I would let the opportunity slip by me. The second the door to the bathroom locked into place, I pushed off my chair and ran to Julian as quietly as possible. He shoved his laptop aside, stood, and reached for my face. He cupped my cheeks in his palms as our lips met.

That kiss.

That kiss was a sucker punch to my gut. That kiss was Julian laying claim to my soul. I was on the fringe of insanity, swept up in the feel of him. I was wholeheartedly convinced that we could have a quickie while Lorena was in the bathroom, and then I heard the toilet flush.

Julian and I flew apart like we'd just been caught red-handed. My heart hammered in my chest as I glanced to the bathroom and then back to Julian. His devilish smile didn't help matters. I laughed and shook my head, giving myself another foot of distance between us.

Damn. *Would it kill Lorena to take her time? Get comfortable in there. Read a book!*

"I'm going to ask her to grab us lunch," Julian said, running his hand down the length of my arm before tucking it away in his pocket.

I tilted my head. "Why?"

"Because I want fifteen minutes alone with you before the meeting with the architecture firm this afternoon," he said, bending to steal one last kiss before the bathroom door opened.

Alrighty then.

"Are you guys okay?" Lorena asked with a skeptical tone. When she'd gone into the bathroom, we'd been sitting down and working quietly. Now, we were standing together in the center of the room, panting as if we'd just finished a triathlon.

"Yeah," I nodded. "Julian and I are doing our work yoga."

What?

She arched a brow. "What's that?"

I laughed as if she was crazy, my brain working overtime to come up with an answer. "Oh. Uh, you just pause every hour on the hour and do five minutes of stretching." I turned to Julian. "Go ahead, Julian. Show her your downward dog."

Chapter Forty~One

Josephine

I stared at my open laptop in front of me, wondering how I'd managed to sit at my kitchen counter for an hour and not type a single word. I had three blog posts to write for the coming week, a Greyhound ticket to purchase, a giant check to deposit in my account, and a hundred or so emails to respond to, one of which was from Vogue.

I'd yet to tell Julian that I was heading home to Texas for a few days. It wasn't because I was purposely keeping things from him, we just hadn't had a moment alone to talk where we weren't attacking one another. Since Saturday, I'd had interview request after interview request from blogs and news channels wanting the inside scoop about the "Cinderella of New York Fashion Week". It was all a bit surreal, but with each passing day my social media followers continued to double. I was supposed to have had dinner with Julian the night before, but I'd had to cancel last minute to do an interview with People Magazine. It was just a short piece, not the front page or anything, but still! I couldn't very well turn down People Magazine. I knew the timing of everything was terrible. Julian and I had finally decided to sleep together, and the very next day, my life had exploded into chaos.

I reached for my phone, knowing I'd have a better chance of getting everything out if I texted him. I drafted a short and sweet message and hit send before I got distracted by another incoming email. My inbox was currently hovering at around 132 unread messages, all from important people, all vying for my attention.

Josephine: Hey, my dad is turning 60 next week, so I have to head home to Texas to celebrate with him. It won't be for long.
Julian: What? When do you leave?

I glanced at my calendar hanging on the front of my fridge.

Josephine: Three days.

How had the days crept up on me?

Julian: Way to give a guy some warning…
Josephine: Are you mad?
Julian: No. Why would I be? I just wish your dad

lived in New York.

The image of my dad wandering around the streets of New York was almost too comical to consider.

Josephine: Believe me, you don't want him living here.
Julian: How long will you be gone?
Josephine: Just for a few days, but I'll be bringing Lily back with me. She's moving into my apartment.
Julian: Sounds like trouble.

I smiled. With Lily moving in with me, there definitely would be trouble…I just hoped it was the good kind.

Chapter Forty-Two

Julian

"Julian, how did my shoe get stuck in the lamp?" Josephine asked as I buttoned up my pants.

I turned to look over my shoulder. Sure enough, Josephine's high heel was wedged between the wall of Dean's boat and the bedside lamp. A few inches to the left and I would have busted the light bulb.

"I think I was just ripping stuff off you," I explained. "I don't have great aim when you have your shirt off."

She glared at me and then bent to retrieve her shirt from the floor. I'd wanted to just throw it overboard but I knew she would have killed me. Even still, as she buttoned her blouse back up, I took every opportunity to get my fill of her while I could.

"They're breasts, Julian," she laughed. "You can literally type 'boobs' into Google and see half a million of them."

I smirked. "None quite as perfect as yours though. I know; I've tried to find them."

She reached to throw one of Dean's pillows at my head and I realized I'd underestimated her ability as it clocked me in the side of the face.

"Oh my gosh, I'm sorry!" she said, rushing toward me. "You were supposed to duck."

I laughed. "It didn't hurt, Jo. It's a pillow."

She held my hands back so she could get a good look at the side of my face and I made the most disgusting face I could imagine.

"It's okay, right?" I joked.

She rolled her eyes. "Even with pillow-face, you're still the hottest guy I know."

I smiled. "Is that why you let me sneak you down here?"

We'd both had a free Saturday afternoon and I'd come up with the brilliant idea to sneak onto Dean's boat to finish what we'd started weeks ago. Fortunately, I knew where Dean hid a spare set of keys to the cabin. We'd decided to skip over the boat's bed; laundering sheets isn't really my thing. Instead, we started out in the cabin and then made our way to the bathroom and beyond. Dean's boat had officially been christened.

She let go of my hands and turned back to retrieve her pants from the floor.

"To be honest, I have zero willpower where you're concerned," she admitted.

I grinned. "Good. That works in my favor."

We spent a few minutes cleaning up Dean's boat and ensuring we left it in the same state that we'd found it. Dean was a stickler for order. Every single piece of furniture had to be in an exact spot. His obsessive behavior extended into all areas of his life, which is probably why his businesses were so successful.

"Seriously, the cabinets in here are labeled," Jo yelled from the bathroom. "He has little tags that say 'towels' and 'toilet paper'."

I laughed.

"I feel bad for the girl who ends up with him," she said. "Could you imagine living with him?!"

I tried to recall one of Dean's girlfriends. There were dates every now and then, but I couldn't recall a single woman who'd managed to hold his attention or met his standards for more than a few weeks.

"I don't think he's planning on settling down anytime soon anyway. He's too busy taking over the earth," I said.

She walked out of the bathroom a few minutes later after declaring it clean.

"And what about you?" she asked.

"Am I too busy to settle down?"

She nodded and watched me carefully.

I smiled. "I care more about enjoying earthly pleasures. You can put the towels and toilet paper wherever you want, so long as you keep doing that thing with your tongue."

She stepped forward and kissed me. I reached out to hold her against me to prolong the kiss as long as possible, but she was too quick.

"Why am I not surprised by that answer?" she asked.

I shrugged and attempted to concentrate on much more pressing matters, like my stomach.

"I'm starving. Are you hungry?"

Her smile faltered. "I have to head home and pack."

"Pack for what?" I asked, forcing a calm demeanor. In reality, it felt like someone had hit me in my gut as hard as they could.

She crossed her arms.

"I'm going home for a week to visit my dad for his 60th birthday, remember? Stop giving me that look!"

I immediately changed my face. *What? Was I frowning or something?*

"Already?" I asked, confused by how quickly time had passed in the last few days.

She nodded.

Another punch to my gut, this time a little more on its mark. I tugged my hands through my hair, trying to calm down. Why did it feel like she was leaving for good? Maybe because in the last seven days, she'd hardly had any time for me. Part of the reason I'd stolen her away to Dean's boat was because I knew she wouldn't be able to get cell service out at the marina.

"I leave tomorrow."

WHAT?

Calm down, asshole. It's only a few days.

It's nothing.

"I wish you weren't leaving tomorrow."

You were supposed to calm down before you spoke...

She furrowed her brows and crossed her arms tighter. Her green eyes, usually clear and inviting, were warning me to relax.

"I'm sorry," she said, though she didn't sound like she actually was. "I didn't think it'd be that big of a deal."

Shit. Shit. Shit. I was fucking all this up. It wasn't a big deal.

I stepped closer and reached for her hands; she kept them wrapped around her waist until I pried them away and clutched them tightly.

"What if I got us some takeout and came to your place to help you pack?" I asked.

I didn't care if I sounded desperate. I *was* a little desperate, and what did it matter as long as Dean wasn't around to hear me sound like a sad sap?

Her face softened. "Chinese?"

I smiled. "Whatever you want."

She nodded. "Okay, but I seriously have to pack. I leave at 6:00 in the morning and haven't even printed out my ticket."

I held up my hands as a sign of innocence.

She arched her brow and I smiled. She knew me better than that.

"All right, I'll be honest. I had plans to take advantage of you once you were in a wonton-induced haze, but now, I promise I'll keep my hands to myself."

Chapter Forty-Three

What Jo Wore

Post #1270: Welcome!
Comments: 1,340   Likes: 23,009

Hello to all my new followers! Many of you found me from the Marc Jacobs show, but I'd like to invite you to relax and stay a while. I hope you'll find that my blog is full of great advice for the beauty obsessed on a budget. You can check out my past beauty guides, fashion posts, and hair style guides in the archives section of the site.

Once you're done with that, I just posted a new video on YouTube highlighting a few of my favorite homemade lip stains. I'm a MAJOR fan of lip stains!

They have the same dramatic effect of lipstick without the mess. Not to mention, I've learned from experience that they withstand even the hottest make-out sessions. More on that later though ;)

For now, check out my video below.

Until tomorrow,
XOJO

● ● ●

Josephine

I told myself I couldn't miss Julian while I was in Texas because we weren't really dating, but my brain wouldn't listen. We'd had sex eleven times. (Twelve if I counted the time he went down on me on my couch. That had been an out of body experience. Mouth-finger coordination was one of his fortes.) On top of that, he'd taken me out for exactly three frozen yogurts and five pre-coitus meals. What the hell were we doing if it wasn't dating? I refused to think of it as friends with benefits—I have a vibrator for that. His name is Larry and he's much lower maintenance than Julian.

I was nervous about my trip to Texas, not only because I was leaving things with Julian a tad up in the air, but also because in the last few months, there'd only been a handful of days that we hadn't seen each other. A week straight would be a new test—one I knew I wouldn't easily pass.

I stared out at the bus terminal through my tiny window and wished I could fast-forward seven days ahead. I wished that instead of sitting on the bus, waiting to start my journey to Texas, I was already back and about to meet up with Julian for some steamy reunion sex. *(Because, duh, that's gonna be awesome.)*

"Lady, is this seat taken?"

I glanced over my shoulder to find an older woman wearing a yellow muumuu and clutching a giant fabric bag that reminded me of my grandmother's old curtains. She reeked of cigarette smoke and what I could only assume was the faint stench of cat pee.

Oh no. Nononono. This isn't happening.

I glanced around the bus to see if there were still vacant seats. There were plenty, at least ten or twelve near the back, yet she wanted to sit right beside me.

What was I going to do? Lie? I had two days of traveling on the bus with her. She'd clearly find out if I lied and then I'd have to suffer her death stares for the rest of the ride. No thanks. I didn't want to be found dead on the side of some highway.

I nodded and smiled timidly, ensuring that my carryon bag was tucked between my legs so she'd have plenty of room. She took the seat beside me and I held my breath, wondering just how long I could get away with breathing through my mouth.

"I brought a tuna sandwich for lunch," she said. "They never stop enough and my doctor says I have to watch my blood sugar like a hawk."

I swear my eye twitched as I tried to kccp from saying something obviously rude in reply. She didn't notice my silence and kept right on talking. There were fifteen minutes of people filing onto the bus and her sentences just kept on coming.

"I have disc issues in my neck, so I like to rest my head on my neighbor so that I can get some good shuteye. Don't worry though, you can do the same to me, I don't mind."

Awesome.

"If I pass gas while I'm asleep just nudge me awake. I think I let this sandwich sit out a little too long this morning."

Perfect.

"You don't mind if I take the middle armrest, right? My elbow is arthritic."

Great. I'll just wedge myself against the glass and pray for death.

With each passing word, I slid down lower and lower in my chair. I'd walked the runway of NYFW a week earlier and yet I couldn't afford a plane ticket home. Instead I had to spend 46 hours next to this bag of bones as she farted on my face?

How is this my life!?

I didn't give myself another second to sit in self-pity. I pulled out my laptop, logged on to the Greyhound's wifi (thank god for that), and pulled up the email from Vogue—the email I'd been avoiding for the past week. I knew Elizabeth was waiting for my reply, and I'd drafted one right away. I'd actually drafted fifteen, I just didn't think any of them were good enough to send yet.

I reread the first part of the email and then checked through the items she'd requested I send: cover letter, resume, and a portfolio filled with my best blog posts, Instagram photos, and Twitter posts. They wanted proof that I could create new, interesting content for their readers, so I also had to include a short presentation of what I could offer the Vogue team that would differ from the other applicants.

All in all, it didn't seem so bad. I jotted down a list of things to get done during the bus ride, praying my laptop would stay charged long enough for me to finish. Then, I scanned back down the email and froze as I caught sight of two words:

Signing. Bonus.

My stomach dropped.

Ms. Keller, I'd also like to inform you that you would receive a one-time signing bonus. This isn't standard protocol, but our social media team really has their eye set on you and we've come up with a number that we hope adequately reflects our interest.

I stared at the sum listed at the bottom of the email, counting the zeros three or four times before I decided that they were actually there. The signing bonus she'd listed was more money than I'd ever had in my bank account at one time. It was more money than I hoped to save in the next five years. It would cover the rest of my student loan debt and then leave me with a few thousand left over. Most importantly, it was far too much money to ignore.

As the Greyhound bus pulled away from the terminal, I started typing away on the items Elizabeth had requested. By the time I'd nailed down my cover letter, the city skyline was long gone and we were well on our way to Texas.

Heehaw.

Chapter Forty-Four

Julian

Dean and I had a lunch meeting scheduled for the day Jo left for Texas. I wanted to call and cancel on him, but then I realized it would be a welcome distraction. He and I could talk about business, and I could pretend that I wasn't having Jo withdrawals less than twelve hours after she'd left.

The presentation he showed me took all of five minutes. He was opening up a new restaurant serving high-end blah, blah, blah. Good food was good food and everything Dean touched seem to turn to gold. He showed me the numbers from his previous restaurants (which were ridiculous for the food industry) and I cut him a check. I'd been to enough of Dean's restaurants to trust his judgment. The man was a restaurant wizard, and I was happy to invest in his next venture.

I held up my half-empty glass of bourbon.

"Here's to becoming rich old bastards."

He laughed and clinked his glass to mine. "Cheers. I look forward to doing business with you."

I reclined in my chair and glanced at the TV above the restaurant's bar. The NBA playoffs were in full swing, but I'd missed most of the games thus far thanks to Jo's uncanny ability to distract me. Honestly, when she took her shirt off, it was game over, literally.

"Where's your girlfriend?" Dean asked with a smile.

I glanced away from the TV. "My what?"

He shook his head. "Josephine."

I didn't want him to bring her up. I'd barely lasted twelve hours without her. How many more did I have left? Over a hundred. Fuck.

"She's in Texas."

He straightened his tie, unbuttoned his suit jacket, and then relaxed back to mirror my pose. He'd been such a surfer kid in college, so it still felt strange to see him wearing suits every day. His blond hair was cropped short now, but back in the day it'd hung long over his forehead. The girls in college had flocked to him like he was their lifeblood. Annoying bastard.

"I take it from your shitty ass attitude that things aren't going well with Ms. Keller?" he asked with a knowing smirk.

There they were again: memories of Jo and I having sex in my hotel. I thought of the sex Jo and I'd had after she'd finished packing. I know. I'm a bastard. I'd promised her I was going to keep my hands to myself, but then she sucked a noodle through her come-fuck-me lips and I was a goner. She'd straddled me on the floor and I'd nearly choked on my egg roll. And that's not a euphemism.

I could feel the shit-eating grin spread across my face. "Things are going very well."

"So then you're dating?"

Dating?

My smile faltered.

It was like he'd just asked me if I believed in an afterlife. Dating? Jo and I hadn't talked about that. Why hadn't we talked about that? We were definitely dating. *Right?* Do adults even make it official like that anymore?

Like a slow, slithering snake, doubt started to sink in. She had been really quiet the night before and seemed to have a lot on her mind. She'd hardly given me any notice about Texas, and she'd never given me a definite day for when she was getting back...

"I think?" I answered.

He tilted his head and arched a brow. "You think? That's not really an option. It's yes or no. Especially for women."

"Oh really? When's the last time you actually dated a woman? What makes you the authority on the subject?" Yup. He was right about my shitty attitude. I was all but yelling at him.

He smiled and took a sip of his drink. "I leave the dating to poor schmucks such as yourself." He pointed across the table at me. "Even still, I know that until you both discuss it, whatever you're doing isn't a real thing. She probably thinks you're going around town playing the field."

I shook my head and laughed. "No way."

I glanced back to the TV and took another sip of my drink, pretending to watch the sportscasters replay clips from the night before. The screen went hazy as I realized I had absolutely no clue what Jo was thinking.

Did she think this was just a fling? Did she honestly think I was sleeping around?

When the hell would I have time for that? I was with her all day, every day.

"Bet you didn't know you were coming to lunch for a business meeting and a therapy session," Dean said, trying to lighten the mood.

I grunted. He'd just dropped a bomb on me and I had no clue how to clean up the mess.

I needed to talk to Jo.

Chapter Forty-Five

Josephine

My computer had 2% battery life left when I finally attached every document to the email for Elizabeth. I tapped on my keyboard impatiently, watching the loading bars creep along as the files uploaded. *C'mon Greyhound wifi, don't fail me now.* My battery hit 1% and I all but screamed with frenzy. It'd already been a week since Elizabeth first emailed me. She'd most likely given the job to someone else. I couldn't go another day without replying to her and I probably wouldn't be able to charge my computer again until I got to Texas the next day.

My gaze shifted back and forth between the battery

percentage and the loading bar as I prayed for the battery's juice to last just a little longer. Right as the final document finished loading, I hit send on the email and watched my computer's screen turn black.

Dead. Right in the middle of sending the email.

"Fuck!" I yelled, pounding on the power button over and over again, demanding that the computer magically come back to life.

"Gladly sugar!" someone called from the back of the bus.

I turned to Gladys and shook her awake. How the woman was still alive after all that snoring was beyond me. She blinked her eyes open and glanced over.

"Do you have a cell phone I could borrow to check my email?" I asked with a kind smile. My shitty phone didn't connect to the internet because I couldn't justify spending that much on a phone when I could hardly pay my rent. Of course in that moment, I wished I'd sprung for the damn iPhone.

She shook her head. "Never been one for those cancer boxes. You can't be too careful with your health," she said as she dug into a bag full of Cheetos.

I stared at her for another moment and then had the overwhelming urge to scream. I'd been stuck on a bus for twelve hours and I still had another twenty-four to get through. My neck ached, my butt was numb, and my stomach was growling like a hungry lion since I'd skipped going off the bus for dinner so I could finish up the email to Vogue.

"Okay, thanks anyway," I said, turning back to my computer and closing it. Whatever happened, happened. There was nothing more I could do about it while I was stuck on that bus. I turned to the wide window and pressed the side of my head against it. The sun had set a little while ago, but dusk still illuminated the drab landscape. I watched cities pass by me as I tried to find the silver lining in my day. I'd be home soon, and home meant getting to see Lily.

I knew I'd feel better if only I could contact Julian. I pulled my phone out of the front pocket of my purse, turned it on, and stared at the lack of bars in the top left corner of the screen. Nothing. Nada. Wherever the hell we were, there was no cell signal. No cell signal meant I couldn't talk to Julian.

Instead of texting him, I imagined what he was probably doing back in New York. It was Sunday, which meant he'd probably gone on a run in the morning, maybe stopped somewhere for breakfast afterward. I imagined the attention he probably received from women on a daily basis. A cute guy like him eating alone in a coffee shop? Just hand him an adorable puppy and call it a day. The man was a catch. I could only imagine a woman sitting down to chat with him, admiring his dimples the same way I did every morning. They'd think they'd scored big time; not many men were more attractive than Julian. But then he'd open his mouth and he'd make them laugh and they'd find themselves as mesmerized by him as I'd been for the last few months.

I closed my eyes.

Good going, Jo. You were supposed to find a silver lining. Instead, you imagined Julian on a date with another woman.

I crossed my arms, kept my eyes shut, and tried to distract myself with ideas for my blog.

It didn't work.

With an hour left on the first leg of my bus trip, Gladys pulled out her tuna sandwich and I truly contemplated what it would be like to hurl myself out the window of a moving bus.

Yup, there's my silver lining.

Chapter Forty-Six

Julian

"You've reached Josephine Keller. Sorry I can't come to the phone. Leave a message after the beep."

I hung up and threw my phone on the couch. *I'm going crazy.* I'd never been crazy over a woman, and there I was, at the ripe age of thirty-one, finally having my ass handed to me by one Josephine Ann Keller.

I knew I was going crazy because that's the only excuse I had for calling Josephine ten times in the last three hours. I'd already left two voicemails. The first one was calm and normal. The second one? I was pretty sure I'd sounded a little off my rocker.

I left lunch with Dean feeling like the floor had been ripped out from under me. I thought Jo and I were on the same page. I knew she was crazy about me, but now I suddenly needed to hear her say it and I wanted to say it back. I needed to tell her that I loved her, that I wanted a real relationship.

As luck would have it, Dean *would* knock sense into me during the one day Josephine was off in the middle of Texas and therefore incommunicado. *Do they have cell service in Texas?*

My phone vibrated on the couch and I lunged for it. Lorena's name flashed across the screen and I resisted the urge to groan.

"Hey Lorena."

"Top o' the morning to you too, sunshine. How about a little excitement when your little sister calls you?"

I forced a smile even though she couldn't see it.

"I am excited you're calling me. What's up?"

"I have something important to ask you."

I sank down into the couch. "What?"

"What would you say if I asked you to stay on at my company and take over as the official COO?"

"But—"

"Just hear me out first. You already own nearly half of the company, and you're much better at the business side of things than I am. I should have asked for your help years ago, but I was too proud."

"Are you sure?"

She laughed. "Believe me, it won't be easy to work with your baby sister every day, but I promise to give you lots of space."

I tilted my head back and stared up at the ceiling. A few months back, when I'd received word that Lorena needed me to step in and help with her company, I'd been less than keen on entering the fashion world. It still wasn't my thing, but I'd enjoyed my time in New York more than I'd thought I would. I liked helping her find a new office space and interviewing architecture firms. I liked helping her rebuild her company from the ground up. Obviously, most of all, I'd enjoyed working alongside Josephine.

Which made me consider the idea that if Lorena still needed me, would she still need Josephine too?

"What about Jo?"

She hummed, mulling over my question. "I love Jo and I think she's really been an asset over the last few months."

"So you'll keep her on?" I prodded.

"Yeah, if she wants to keep working for me. She's really blown up since that runway show last week. Even if I just pay her to wear my designs, it'd be really good for the brand."

"What other positions are you having people apply for?" I asked.

"Ideally, I'd like to find two good interns and an assistant designer. Obviously I need to really vet every applicant, but if I expect to create a new line by next season I need way more manpower."

"Yeah, I agree."

"We can start to tackle that on Monday though. I just wanted to call you and get your opinion on staying on while I was brave enough to do it."

I laughed.

"Do you think you'll miss living in Boston?" she asked.

I narrowed my eyes as I thought over her question. "It was pretty nice to have some distance from Mom."

She laughed. "Yeah, I bet. Did you get her invitation for dinner tomorrow night?"

My mother had sent us both formal invitations for a family dinner. The card was like an inch thick and embossed with our family crest. It was all too pretentious for me, but it made my mother happy to cut down trees for dinner parties, so whatever.

"Yeah, and I have to go or I'll look like an asshole."

"You're the prodigal son finally back in New York City! She's probably going to parade a line of fertile females for you to select from."

I cringed. "You make it sound like she's running a brothel."

She laughed. "Yeah, I guess you're right. That's pretty gross."

"You know what though, I was surprised she came down to visit you in rehab."

It'd taken guts for my mother to face the music. She'd always lived in eternal la la land where the only thing that could go wrong was that she'd arrive five minutes after a sale ended at Bergdorf's.

"Yeah. I know. She's called and checked in on me every day since then too. I really do think she's coming around. We need to go to dinner tomorrow."

I groaned. "Fine. I'll start ironing my three-piece suit now."

"That's the spirit!"

• • •

By the following morning, Josephine still hadn't called me back. Ten calls, two voicemails, and still no call back. She was either avoiding me or kidnapped in the middle of

Texas. I clutched my phone and resisted the urge to call her for the eleventh time. Instead, I changed into workout gear and hit the long trail around Central Park. Exercise always cleared my head and I figured that by the time I was finished, Jo would have finally called. I left my phone on the couch in the hotel and hit the trail.

As I ran, I thought of what I'd do if I moved to New York full time. Helping Dean with his new restaurant wouldn't take up all of my time, hardly any in fact considering he had a team set up around him to do most of the legwork. He just needed me as an investor, which meant I'd have plenty of time on my hands.

I definitely wanted to stay on with Lorena. I liked working with family and I had good ideas on how to make her business profitable. I could find a new place to live near her new shop and start to really lay down roots in the city.

When I finally made it back to my hotel room, my lungs were burning and my legs were threatening to quit. I ripped my shirt off and walked straight for my phone. There was no call from Jo, but I had a voicemail waiting for me from an unknown number.

I hit play on the voicemail, kicked off my shoes, and headed toward the shower.

"Hi Mr. Lefray. This is Elizabeth Hope from the social media team here at Vogue. I just have a few questions pertaining to your work experience with Josephine Keller as we're considering her for a position in our Vogue offices. Would you mind giving me a call back at your earliest convenience? Thank you."

What the fuck?

I replayed the message twice, trying to determine if I'd heard it right.

Jo had applied for a position at Vogue?

She wanted to leave Lorena Lefray Designs?

I stared down at my phone and scrolled to Josephine's name on my contact list. I knew if I called her she wouldn't answer; I'd already tried to get in contact with her every way that I knew how. Doubt settled in my stomach like a heavy rock. *Fuck.* Dean was right. I should have told Jo what I wanted from the beginning. I shouldn't have assumed she could read my mind. If we were together, really together, I wouldn't have to worry that she was getting cold feet and pulling away, applying for jobs elsewhere and heading down to Texas to put some distance between us.

I needed to call Elizabeth back, but I gave myself some time to process her message first. I jumped in the shower and ran the water until it was hot as sin, dipping my head beneath it and closing my eyes. I could count the number of times in my life when I'd felt out of control on one hand:

1. When Jimmy Sanders knocked my hotdog to the ground in elementary school and I was too chickenshit to stand up for myself.

2. Right before I jumped out of the plane the first time I went skydiving.

3. When I'd had a one-night stand with a woman who showed up at my place the next day with a suitcase in tow. She'd assumed she was moving in. After one night together.

4. Right fucking now.

I was supposed to get out of the shower, don my suit, go to my mom's dinner, and sit across from her at the table while she rambled on about something I couldn't care less about. Meanwhile, the first woman I'd truly come to love was in Texas, completely out of cell phone range and completely unaware of my feelings for her.

I turned off the water, wrapped a towel around my waist, wiped the fog off the mirror, and stared good and hard at my reflection. My eyes stared back at me, challenging me. *This is it. She doesn't know how serious you are about the relationship, and she doesn't know how valued she is at the company. You either grow a pair and go get her or you regret it for the rest of your life.*

By the time I stepped out of the bathroom, I was ready to call Elizabeth back. That is, right after I called my sister. I dialed her number and then pulled my suitcase out of the hotel closet.

"Hey, I can't talk right now," she answered with a frenzied voice. "I'm scrambling to get ready for dinner. I just got back to my apartment."

"That's fine. I'm just calling to let you know that I won't be at dinner. Tell Mom I'll make it up to her."

I pulled open my dresser drawers and reached for a few pairs of boxer briefs and socks.

"What? No! Why the hell are you canceling last minute?"

I dropped my running shoes into my suitcase, straightened up, and took a breath.

"Because I'm going to Texas."

Chapter Forty-Seven

Josephine

By the time I stepped off the last Greyhound bus, I felt like a baby giraffe learning to walk for the first time. My knees were wobbly and my feet had lost all feeling at about hour 20 of my 36-hour drive. I needed to charge my phone and check my email, but first I needed to retrieve my suitcase from the growing pile beside the bus.

I'd lost Gladys somewhere around Lubbock, but worry not, for she left me clear instructions to find her on "that internet yearbook". I'd assured her I'd find her on Facebook and we'd parted ways. For the next few glorious hours, I'd had two seats all to myself. I'd stretched out and stared out at the Texas hill country, wondering what Julian would think of all this wide open space. New York City can be overwhelming; the concrete jungle seems to never end. I was beginning to think that a week back in Texas would do me some good.

"Oh my god. Oh my god. Oh my god!"

I turned toward the squealing voice just in time to catch my best friend as she hurled her full body weight at me. Lily wrapped her arms around my neck and her legs around my hips, nearly toppling me over. I stepped back and caught my balance, but she still clung to me with her full strength.

"You're like a flying squirrel," I laughed.

She loosened her grip around my neck and stepped back, flailing her arms.

"I cannot believe you're here right now," she said, beaming from ear to ear.

Getting a good look at her made me want to cry. I'd missed her so much over the last few months—especially in the last few days—and now there she was, standing in front of me in her full glory. Lily had clearly been out in the Texas sun. A smattering of freckles ran along the bridge of her nose and across her tan cheeks. Her blonde hair was streaked with honey highlights. Whereas I was tall and on the slender side (hence why Marc Jacobs had pulled me up onto the runway), Lily had been the adorable one growing up. I'd always envied her heart-shaped face and bee-stung lips. Our small town boys were never sure what to do with my height, but Lily was always the center of every adolescent boy's heart.

"Do you understand how happy I am to see you?" she asked. "This town is slowly crushing my soul."

I laughed and passed her my backpack so I could grab

my suitcase from the top of the pile near the bus.

"I'm sure it's not that bad," I contested, though I knew she wasn't really exaggerating.

She shot me a pointed stare.

I laughed and trailed after her toward the parking lot. Her beat up red car sat in the very last row, backed into the spot just in case it didn't start and needed to be jumped. Our high school and college years had been marked by continuous failings on the part of her old car. Even still, I was happy to see it. I tossed my luggage in the back and slid into the passenger seat. It still smelled like the Ocean Breeze air freshener she hung from the rearview mirror and the pealing upholstery clung to my skin as soon as I took my seat.

"That was the longest bus ride of my life," I said as she pulled out of the parking lot and onto the gravel drive.

"Well at least you'll have me beside you on the way back."

I smiled.

"We'll have to find someone to drop us off though. I'm selling this bad boy tomorrow afternoon."

I glanced back. "What? Really?"

She slid her hands across the steering wheel and nodded. "Yup. I'm only getting a few hundred bucks for it, but it's better than nothing."

I frowned and glanced around the car. The dashboard was cracked and peeling off near the corners. The numbers on the radio had chipped off years ago and the CD player had never worked. The cloth covering on the ceiling had lost hold a while back and it dipped low in some parts. Even still, I'd kissed my first boy in the back of this car. Lily and I had tee-peed quite a few houses in high school using this bucket of bolts as the getaway vehicle.

"I'm kind of sad to see ol' hoopty go," I admitted.

She grunted. "That makes one of us. I can't wait to get rid of it."

"Well thanks for picking me up. I was scared you weren't going to show up since I couldn't call and remind you."

She turned off the main highway and pulled onto a dirt road, toward our small town. We still had miles to go before we'd be home.

"Yeah, I tried to call you this morning, but I figured you didn't have signal."

I nodded.

"I'm assuming you have to eat dinner with your family tonight?" she asked.

I nodded. "Yeah. Today is my dad's birthday so I can't miss it. I'm going to help my mom with the cake and stuff."

Her eyes lit up. "I just put together a bunch of good cake recipes for my blog. You should test one of them out."

I smiled. Typical Lily. "I'm pretty sure my mom is just going to make a box cake. We aren't fancy like you."

She cringed. "Why do people have so little creativity in the kitchen?"

I reached out and gripped her shoulder. "Have no fear, Lil. Soon you'll be in New York City and there will be crazy restaurants galore. You'll have so many restaurants to review for your blog, you won't know where to start."

She smiled. "If only I could afford to eat at one of them."

I let my hand drop to the car console and stared out the front window. We were two broke bitches, but that wouldn't always be the case. Lily was so talented and she knew food. She'd gone to culinary school instead of a standard college. She didn't want to be a chef. She wanted to be a restaurant reviewer for the masses, a trustworthy version of Yelp with easy to read reviews posted weekly with photos and interesting tips.

"We'll figure it out," I promised, offering her a smile.

By the time she pulled into my driveway to drop me off, I was wholeheartedly confused on what I was supposed to do about the Vogue position. A part of me didn't want to tell Lily about it until it was a sure thing. I'd already be upset enough if I didn't get it, maybe it was best if I didn't have to spread the bad news around.

"Call me tomorrow and we'll go over plans for New York," she said as I leaned down to close the passenger side door.

"Sounds good. Thanks for the ride!"

She pulled out of the driveway and I turned to the house. Nothing had changed in the months I'd been away. My mom still had roses in the front flowerbeds and my dad was a few days late on mowing the grass, as usual.

I smiled and headed for the front door just as it swept open and my mother appeared. She wiped her hands on her apron and stepped onto the porch. God, we looked so much alike. Her brown hair was chopped off in a short, blunt bob and she was wearing a sundress that was a familiar staple of my life growing up. Her face was makeup free, as usual, but she didn't need any. Her green eyes were rimmed with dark lashes, like mine, and her smile was infectious enough not to need any lipstick.

"My Josie," she beamed, pulling me in for a tight hug. I inhaled her scent and wrapped my arms around her, letting her envelop me in a much-needed hug.

"Hey Mom," I said as she released me to grip my shoulders and get a good look at me.

Her smile faltered. "Are you eating up there in New

York? You look too thin, sweetie."

I resisted the urge to roll my eyes. "I promise I'm eating a lot. I just walk everywhere."

She pursed her lips, not quite sure if she wanted to trust my answer or not. I was sure by the time I left on Friday I'd have a heaping amount of food to take back with me, "just in case".

"Where's Dad?" I asked, dropping my bags in the foyer and stepping farther into the house.

My dad poked his head over the leather recliner in the living room, waving the remote control in greeting. "Hey sweetie!"

I smiled and bent down over the chair to give him a hug.

"Happy birthday, Dad."

"Oh, thanks. It's not every day that your old man turns forty."

I laughed and kissed his cheek. "Whatever you say, pops."

"C'mon, Josephine. You can help me with dinner while Dad finishes watching golf."

When she turned, I made a gagging motion toward my dad. He laughed and shook his head.

"Go help her. She misses you, y'know."

"Yeah, yeah."

I dropped my luggage in the hallway and followed my mom into the kitchen.

"Bet you don't get many home cooked meals up in New York," she said, handing me an extra apron from the back of the pantry door. Our kitchen hadn't changed at all in the last twenty years. Old floral wallpaper still covered the walls. Dark wood cabinets sat above weathered countertops. The refrigerator was still covered with drawings and photos of me from when I was younger.

I smiled at the sight.

"Actually, I fixed spaghetti for a friend just last week."

Julian had complained that the noodles were so al dente that he chipped a tooth, so we'd tossed it out and gone for takeout instead. But technically, I cooked.

"Oh, so you're finding friends? I've heard it can be pretty hard to get to know people up there."

She passed me the pepper grinder and together we added salt and pepper to a chicken dish that was about to go into the oven. Carrots, peas, and onions were stuffed around the chicken inside the casserole dish. My mouth was already watering.

"Yeah. I have some friends."

"Where'd you meet them?" she asked, glancing up at me over the chicken.

"Work," I replied, dropping the peppershaker back onto the counter.

She went to work chopping up green beans and I stood to the side, trying to stay out of her way.

"And they're good people?"

I laughed. "From what I've seen so far."

She pursed her lips. "Well. I just want you to be careful. Don't get swept off your feet by some guy. You need to focus on what's important."

I rolled my eyes when she turned to toss the green beans in a big pot to boil, deciding it was best to just stay silent. She hummed as she added spices to the green beans and I plopped down on one of the bar stools.

"Do you remember Sonya Foster?" she asked, glancing over her shoulder at me.

I quirked a brow. "She was in my graduating class. Why?"

She turned back around and shrugged. "She's really made something out of that little salon downtown. People travel from all over to get haircuts from her. Her parents were bragging about it during dinner the other night."

She waved the spoon in the air and kept on rambling.

"I think it's just great that she's brought something to our community like that."

I gripped the edges of my stool. "Did you mention my career at dinner?"

She turned to reach for the salt and met my eye for a moment. Shame burned behind her gaze, plain to see.

"Your father and I told them you were in New York, but I couldn't remember what your exact job title was and I didn't want to get it wrong." She shook her head. "The Fosters wouldn't know anything about that sort of thing anyway."

Of course, because country folk are incapable of learning things. Right.

"Y'know if you wanted to come home, I really think you could do something like Sonya has done. You could maybe even work for her for a little bit and get your bearings again."

I scooted my stool back so that it scraped against the wood floor.

"Jo?"

I shook my head.

"Honey?"

Maybe if I hadn't just sat on a bus for 36 hours and didn't smell like tuna fish, I would have brushed my mother's comments off, but I had and I did, and I couldn't take it anymore. I couldn't stand their shame any longer.

"You and Dad don't get it. Do you know how hard it is to make it in the fashion industry? I've been busting my ass every single day and I'm finally starting to thrive in New York City. Vogue—VOGUE MAGAZINE—wants to hire me for a job. My blog has started to take off, and I have thousands of people reading it every day. More people than Sonya will ever meet in her life! More readers means more advertisers. I could really make a name for myself, but you and Dad can't seem to believe in me for even five seconds. You want me to throw in the cards and move back here? To do what? Cut hair?"

I pushed away from the counter and held her gaze. This was the last time I'd talk about this and if she wanted to listen to me, she would. If not, I'd said my piece and I could move on.

Chapter Forty-Eight

Julian

Josephine lived in the middle of nowhere.

452 Cherry Street in Nowheresville, Texas.

I'd found that out as soon as I'd stepped off the plane. As I was renting a car from the Dallas airport, I'd asked the two older women behind the counter if they'd heard of her town. The one on the left with the 70s style hair had scrunched her nose.

"Loretta, is that where they shot Fridee Night Lights?"

Loretta shook her head. "No, that was out near Austin. This is some other small town. I could look it up on Bing or sumthin' if you'd like."

I said no thanks and they shrugged, handed me the keys to my rental, and sent me on my way.

I'd tossed my bag over my shoulder and headed out with the idea that I'd get a few hours of driving in before I crashed. That was a terrible idea. I'd already sat through a late night flight out of New York, so by the time I reached the outskirts of Dallas, I was having trouble keeping my eyes open.

I found the first hotel on the right side of the highway, pulled in, and called it a night.

That was my first mistake.

Blue Star Hotel would have ranked at about a .5 on the 5 star scale. I had mattress springs sticking into my back for half the night, and the other half of the night the neighbor's shouting next door was impossible to drown out. I'd forgotten to set an alarm, and at 10:49 AM, I shot up in bed with one question:

Where the hell am I?

My disorientation subsided as I recognized the dilapidated hotel furniture and the popcorn ceiling that was chipping off and decorating the carpet with white flecks. Ah, right. Good ol' Blue Star. I threw the hotel blankets off and hopped in the shower. (I nearly pulled the showerhead off as I tried to angle it for my height.)

I sat in the parking lot of the seedy hotel, staring at Josephine's address. I had no clue how much longer I had to go before I reached Josephine's hometown, but I wanted to get on the road as soon as possible. I plugged in her address and put the car in reverse.

It said I had nearly three and a half hours to drive.

I slipped on my Ray Bans, hit play on a Willie Nelson playlist, and set out for greener pastures. And greener pastures. And greener pastures. The one thing that continued to shock me about Texas was how fucking big it was. If I set out in a car in New York, I'd end up in another state in no time. Hell, I could go through three or four states in one morning. In Texas? I could drive for a full day and still not make it to the other side.

By the time my playlist looped back for a third time, I was ready to call it a day. I'd already stopped for gas, and somewhere in the middle of my drive I'd missed a turnoff from the highway and had driven over an hour in the wrong direction. I'd cursed the high heavens, u-turned off the side of the road in a ditch, nearly gotten my rental car stuck, and then finally got headed back in the right direction.

By the time I pulled into the outskirts of Josephine's town, I'd managed to turn a three and a half hour drive into a six hour drive. My stomach was shouting at me for food and my bones ached from sitting for so long. I ignored the fact that I was about to piss my pants and continued on the highway past the "Welcome" sign, which, by the way, noted that the population of the town floated somewhere around 300. Yup. As in less people than the graduating class of my high school.

I kept driving until the highway gave way to a two-lane street that looped around a town square. A limestone courthouse sat in the center of town with businesses surrounding it on all sides. Most of them had their lights off and shades drawn, so I assumed they were already closed for the day. I pulled off to the side of the street in front of a dark butcher shop and checked the navigation to Josephine's house. She couldn't be far from Main Street. Right?

I refreshed the map and a screen popped up that read, "No network connection, try again."

I did. I tried it three more times with the same result,

and then threw my phone onto the passenger seat.

Well, awesome. I had no clue where to find Josephine's house, I had to piss, and I was hungry as fuck.

The things people do for love…

After I gave my phone another ten minutes to prove to me that it was definitely not going to pick up a cellular signal, I pulled back out onto the road and looked for the first open gas station.

I passed a dozen churches—at least—before I found a gas station a few miles down the road, heading out of town. The parking lot was deserted except for a black Bronco parked to the side on the grass. All but one of the pumps was covered with an "out of order" sign. I pulled up to the one working pump, cut the engine, and ran inside like my life depended on it.

A kid that looked to be between 13 or 14 at most sat behind the counter eating a hotdog. I ran past him toward the restroom and then he shouted with his mouth full.

"You need the key!"

I looped back around and held my hand out, but the kid shook his head.

"Payin' customers only."

He stuffed another bite of hotdog in his mouth and chewed slowly, watching me with beady little eyes.

I rammed my hand into the candy bin in front of me and then dropped three Snickers and a Butterfinger onto the counter.

"There," I said, pulling out my wallet and handing over my card. "Can I have the bathroom key now?"

He shook his head. "There's a five dollar min'mum on cards."

I resisted the urge to strangle him and instead shoved my hand back into the candy bin. After he rang up my order with excruciating laziness, I held my hand out for the key.

"Are you gonna get gas too?" he asked, pointing to where my car was parked haphazardly in the spot.

I waved my hand.

"After. I just need to piss."

He shrugged, slid off his stool, and bent to retrieve a tiny key hanging off a giant plastic keychain. I reached for it and ran for the door. Had I cared, I would have contemplated the origins of the sticky film coating the plastic keychain, but I honestly didn't give a fuck.

Once I'd gone pee, found enough shitty food to fill me up for the time being, and paid for a full tank of gas, I nodded to the kid behind the counter.

"Do you know where Cherry Street is?"

He laughed. "Sounds like the name of a porno."

I resisted the urge to ask his age.

"Is that a yes?"

He shook his head. "I'm from over near Whitewater. I don't know anything 'bout Cherry Street."

I assumed Whitewater was a neighboring town.

"Do you have any maps around here?"

He pointed to a cardboard rack near the door that was all but empty except for a Texas State Parks pamphlet that looked like it'd been used a few times, crumbled up, and put back.

Perfect. I'll camp my way through the Texas hill country instead of finding Josephine.

"Thanks anyway." I nodded as I pushed the door open.

"I'd try McAllister's bar," he called out. I turned and he pointed in the direction I'd just come from. "It's a block off Main Street, just behin' the courthouse. Most nights there's a few guys in there. One of 'em should be able to help ya."

Chapter Forty-Nine

Josephine

I had my face squashed up against the window as I concentrated on not throwing up. Every twist and turn we took in the truck made my stomach's contents jostle in the worst way possible. I was about two seconds from throwing up all over my dad's upholstery.

"Do you have to drive like a wild woman?" I moaned, clutching my stomach.

Lily glared over at me. "I'm literally going ten miles an hour, your highness."

I stared back out the window, wishing I was back home, in my bed, sleeping off the beers I'd just downed like there was no tomorrow. It was the day after my father's birthday and I'd needed some space from my family. I'd picked Lily up, grabbed a six-pack from a gas station in town, and together we'd driven out to the middle of nowhere so I could down them all.

"If you're going to throw up, at least hand me your phone first," she said.

I was still clutching it against my stomach. I hadn't let it out of my sight since arriving in Texas in the hopes that it'd pick up a signal. The thing hadn't buzzed in days.

"Fine. Take it. I have zero service in this godforsaken wasteland anyway."

I huffed and tossed the phone in the center cup holder.

"I just want to call Julian! I haven't spoken to him in two days. TWO DAYS!"

We passed the "Welcome" sign and continued on toward Main Street. Lily turned to the right and we drove down the side street, right past McAllister's bar. There were two or three cars out front, not many. Near the door, under a street lamp, I noticed two guys talking. One was Louis Calhoun, the manager of the bar, and the other one was tall and dressed in black slacks and a button-up. He *had* to be from out of town. I squinted as Lily drove by, trying to make out his profile, and then suddenly, I recognized him.

"Julian!" I shouted so loud that even my own ears started to ring. "That's Julian!"

Lily slammed on the brakes. "What? Where?"

"At McAllister's! Turn around!"

She shook her head.

"If you think Julian is at McAllister's then you really are trashed. I'm taking you home."

"But if Julian is here, that means...where is New

York?" I asked, turning back to the window and starting to roll it down, cranking it lower with both hands. "I'll ask him."

"JULIAN!" I screamed, practically throwing the top half of my body out of the truck. "JULIAN! Lily won't turn around!"

Lily put the truck in park on the side of the road and yanked me away from the window.

"Dude, shut up. People are sleeping and you're yelling like a madwoman."

I didn't care. I unlocked the passenger door and hopped out, ready to run. Instead of the smooth ground meeting me at the base of the truck, I kept falling until my feet landed in a muddy ditch. I tried to pick up my feet, but they were stuck under a foot of muddy water. I'd somehow wedged myself in so far that I couldn't get out.

"Lily! Help! I'm stuck!"

I tried to pick up my feet and kick off the mud, but there was no use. It was like quicksand and I needed Lily to help me if I was going to get out without getting even dirtier.

"Jesus Christ. I cannot believe you just did that," she said, hopping out of the truck and slamming the door behind her. "I should just leave you in there after how you've acted tonight."

I swatted at the gnats swarming my face and I swore two or three of them actually made it into my mouth. I tried to spit them out, but there were too many to keep track of.

"No! Please, you have to save me," I begged, feeling tears building in the corner of my eyes.

I was so close to seeing Julian. He was at McAllister's and I was going to die in a ditch before I got to him.

"Julian!" I yelled again.

A dog started barking and then porch lights flipped on

behind me. I twisted around to see who it was as Lily slid down the ditch, careful not to get caught in the mud herself.

"If you don't shut up, I'm going to leave you in here. You just woke up the Jensens and I really don't feel like explaining this situation to Randy right now. That man is mean."

On cue, Randy poked his head out of the front door with an angry scowl marring his features.

"Hurry! Hurry!" I said, reaching for her hands so she could help pull me out.

"Josephine? What the—is that you?"

I glanced up toward the deep voice and my heart dropped.

Julian was standing up on the street, right behind the bumper of my dad's truck. Light from a distant streetlight encased him from above. His hair was disheveled and his shirt was half-untucked. He looked a little worse for wear, but he was there, standing less than five feet away from me.

"Julian?" I asked, holding my hand over my eyes to get a better view of him. "What are you doing here?"

Lily glared back and forth between us. "Wait. Are you kidding me? Julian was actually at McAllister's? You're Julian?"

He nodded, not taking his eyes off me.

"I'm stuck in a ditch," I said.

The side of his mouth hitched up in an adorable smile. "I can see that."

"Get off my lawn right now!" Randy Jensen yelled from his front door. "You hear me?! Imma go get my shotgun!"

Lily and I both screamed and Julian slid down the side of the ditch to grab my hand. Between him and Lily, it only took me a second to crawl my way back up to the street. We scrambled up to the truck, flinging mud behind us as we went. Lily flew around to the driver's side door and Julian and I climbed in on the passenger side. I held my breath the whole time, waiting for the sound of a birdshot blast.

"Go, go, go!" I yelled, pounding the dashboard.

Lily stepped on the gas and the truck tires squealed against the concrete as we made our getaway.

"Did he really have a shotgun?" Julian asked, turning to look back.

I started to laugh, and then I couldn't stop. Lily flew down the street, putting as much distance between us and Randy's house as possible. I sat on the center of the bench seat with Lily on one side and Julian on the other, lost in a fit of laughter. The last twenty minutes had been too funny to be real. Randy Jensen had almost shot me. What a way to go.

"Can you believe that just happened?" I asked, trying to catch my breath.

"Your stupid ass almost got us killed," Lily said, shaking her head.

"Me?!"

She shot me the evil eye. "Yes, you!"

Laughter gave way to a shit-eating grin as I stared out the front window. The night sky was expansive, surrounding us from every angle. Lights flashed by us like shooting stars, one after the other, granting my wishes one by one. I fell back against the seat and turned to find Julian watching me with his steady gaze. I found his hand on the seat and laced my fingers through his.

Not ten minutes earlier, I'd been daydreaming about him, wishing I could somehow talk to him, and suddenly there he was. He was sitting beside me, studying me with a bemused smile. Before I'd finished my thought, I was leaning closer, inhaling his cologne and pressing my lips to his. We fell into each other like a person falls into bed after a long day: with a heavy, happy sigh. I grasped the front of his t-shirt and pulled him toward me. He inhaled sharply. The kiss was soft and sweet. He tilted his head and gripped the back of my neck, holding me steady.

I wanted to climb onto his lap and wind my fingers through his hair. How else could I get closer? I wanted to touch him from every angle, put all the pieces together, and prove to myself that he was really sitting there beside me, that he'd come to Texas for me.

He gripped my shoulders and pulled back, breaking the kiss and staring down at me. I could feel my heartbeat in my stomach. I couldn't ignore the kick drum feeling of excitement at having him right there in front of me.

I stared up into his hazel eyes and whispered, "You're my knight in shining armor. I love you."

And then I promptly clutched my stomach, leaned forward, and threw up all over his lap.

Chapter Fifty

Julian

I'll be honest, I hadn't anticipated that my trip to Texas would involve so much throw-up. I mean, sure, some throw-up is a part of life. However, the amount of vomit Jo could apparently produce seemed disproportional to her size.

I also anticipated meeting Jo's parents over a quiet dinner, not while delivering their daughter home drunk after a crazy night out.

Yup. That's right. I had the pleasure of delivering Jo back home, completely drunk and only half lucid.

I stood on her parent's front porch and knocked,

thankful to have Lily standing beside me for backup. My gut clenched when the porch light flipped on and a very tired woman answered the door with a confused scowl.

"Lily? Is everything all right?" the woman asked, shooting a glare in my direction. "Who are you?"

I squeezed my eyes shut, trying to comprehend how the situation could possibly look any worse.

Oh right. I was covered in throw-up and smelled like last week's trash.

Her mom was still glaring at me, waiting for a reply.

"Oh, hi. I'm Julian. I work with your daughter."

Her brow quirked in curiosity, but she didn't ask for me to elaborate.

"Is she drunk?" Mrs. Keller asked, glaring at me as if I was the one who'd put her in that state.

In turn, I glared at Lily. *Now would be a great fucking time to speak up.*

"She and I were just hanging out and she had one too many beers. Julian found us and helped me get her home."

Mrs. Keller stared down at Jo with clear disdain and then pulled the door open so I could carry her inside.

"C'mon," her mom said, waving me down the hallway.

I dipped past the doorframe and did a quick onceover of Jo's childhood home. My mother would have hated it. Unless a home had curated antiques from floor to ceiling, she thought it was tacky. I didn't agree. Sure, the furniture was old, but there were photos of Jo covering every spare surface. She was framed around the room in various stages of life. As I trailed down the hallway after Mrs. Keller, I caught one gem of a photo where Jo was sporting braces AND lopsided pigtails. I held in my smile and locked the image away for blackmail purposes.

"Lily, you can go," Mrs. Keller said with a tone that

definitely warned against argument.

I glanced back and met her eye. *Don't leave me with her,* I begged with my gaze.

"Uhh." She froze and shot me an apologetic look. "Okay."

I shook my head. No. She'd made this mess and she was not about to leave me to clean it up without her.

"Well, I'll come back and check on her in the morning then…"

I mouthed, "Do not leave."

"Julian? Are you coming?" Mrs. Keller asked, clearly annoyed.

I squeezed my eyes shut, worked up the nerve, and then turned back to continue carrying a now sleeping Jo to her childhood bedroom.

I turned the corner into Jo's room to find Mrs. Keller pulling out pajamas for Jo. I walked toward her bed so I could set her down. She stirred as I placed her against her pillows but stayed asleep.

"How fortunate that my daughter had you to help carry her home," Mrs. Keller said with a tone that said the exact opposite.

"I found her when she was already drunk with Lily, but yes, I'm glad I was there too."

She tsked and shook her head. "Is this normal behavior for her in New York? She never acted like this when she lived here."

I crossed my arms. "She's never once been this drunk with me."

Her eyebrows rose. "Oh, and is she with you a lot?"

"Nearly every day."

She glared at me and I knew she wanted me to elaborate.

"We work together. I hired Josephine when she first moved to New York."

She grunted and dropped Jo's pajamas onto the corner of her bed. "So then why are you in Texas? Do you regularly follow your employees when they travel cross country?"

"Carrie, everything okay in there?" a gruff voice called from the back of the house.

Shit. Was I about to have to explain myself to Jo's dad too? *Lily is going to owe me so much.*

"Yes. Go back to bed, Rick."

She glared back at me and crossed her arms. "Why don't you let me know what's really going on between the two of you? You have my daughter's throw-up all over you, so either she's fired or you're in love. Which is it?"

I had to hand it to her. I'd been in meetings with some of the toughest guys in business and I hadn't sweat as much as I was in that moment. I snuck a peek at Jo and watched her chest rise and fall gently. She looked so angelic in her sleep, completely unaware of the havoc she'd caused.

"I'm in love with her," I said.

There was a long pause as her mom and I stood and processed my declaration. I'd yet to admit my feelings aloud to anyone, not even Dean. Suddenly, my love had roots. There was no turning back.

When I glanced up at her mom, she was watching me with a wistful smile.

"All right then, I'll grab a new shirt for you and then you can help me get her cleaned up. I think it's time for you to experience all the joys of loving my daughter: the good, the bad, and the ugly."

337

Chapter Fifty-One

Josephine

I knocked on the door of room 208 and inhaled the scent of coffee and donuts. It was a winning combination by anyone's standards, but it'd take a lot more than breakfast from Suzie's Sweet Shack to earn Julian's forgiveness. My mother had delivered the Cliff's Notes version of the night as soon as I'd stirred from my beer-induced slumber. I'd tried to ignore the sledgehammer banging against my brain as she spoke, but as soon as she'd broken the news of what I'd put Julian through, I'd known I had to make it up to him before it was too late, even if I couldn't exactly walk straight.

I'd inhaled two Advil, two cups of coffee, and two glasses of water, and then finally felt semi-human once again. After a shower and some makeup, I felt nearly good as new.

I knocked on the motel door again and then heard someone stir in the room. A few seconds later, the door opened to reveal Julian: shirtless, disheveled, and squinting to keep out the harsh glare of the sun.

I smiled and held up the supplies in each hand.

"I come bearing gifts," I said, tipping the donut bag left and right so that the aroma would hit him.

Who can pass up donuts? *Seriously.*

He ran his hand through his hair, grunted some form of greeting, and then opened the door all the way for me.

I stepped into his motel room and glanced around. The bed was a mess, with covers thrown to the side and pillows splayed out in random directions. He must have showered the night before because I could smell his body wash over the normal stench of the motel.

"Fitful night of sleep?" I asked with a perked brow.

He shot me a glare and then took the coffee from my hand.

"Okay, here." I dropped the bag of donuts on the TV stand and pulled out a chocolate iced donut with a napkin. He was sitting on the edge of his bed, watching me as I turned and handed it to him.

"You just sit there and drink your coffee and eat your donut as I talk. Okay?"

The edge of his mouth lifted in a half-smile as he glanced down to the coffee. I was definitely winning him over, but he wasn't going to make it easy for me.

"Okay, well first off," I said, straightening my back and preparing myself for the speech I'd rehearsed in my dad's truck on the way over. "I'm so sorry that I, uhh, threw up on you last night."

I glanced over his bare chest. It was tan, broad, and toned with no remnants of throw-up anywhere. Still, the memory would haunt me for the rest of my life.

"That was admittedly not one of my finest moments."

He nodded and stayed silent, clearly giving me the stage.

"Okay, also, I'm really sorry that you had to take me back to my parent's house after Lily ditched you. It's hard enough to meet someone's family for the first time, even under the best circumstances."

His brows perked up as he took a giant bite of donut. *Good, let that sugary goodness sink in.*

"On the plus side, my mom really likes you. She said that most men wouldn't have had the balls to bring me back home like that."

He laughed. "Did your mom actually say 'balls'?"

I smiled. "No. Not exactly."

He nodded and finished off his donut.

"Okay, I apologized about the throw-up and my mom," I said aloud, trying to think of what else I had subjected him to the night before. "Oh, and sorry for almost getting you shot by Mr. Jensen."

"Is that all?" he asked, tilting his head and watching me.

"All that I have to apologize for?" I asked.

"No," he said, shaking his head.

He stood from the bed and stepped closer to me. I watched him approach, curious what he was about to do. He leaned forward and dropped his coffee and donuts on the TV stand behind me. His chest brushed against mine as he moved and I pressed my lips together to stay quiet.

He slipped his hand around the back of my forearm and

then slowly dragged it up around my bicep.

"All that you have to say."

I swallowed, recalling the declaration I'd made in the truck the night before. I'd been drunk and exhilarated by the fact that Julian had flown to Texas for me. Could I be blamed for telling him the truth about how I felt?

Julian and I could go back to being friends, just the same as before. We could have amazing sex without the labels and responsibilities.

This didn't have to end just because I'd accidentally told him I loved him.

I could take it back.

He leaned forward and wrapped both hands around my arms, pulling me against his chest. His mouth found my ear and he whispered the next few words against my skin.

"Tell me what you told me in the truck last night."

I closed my eyes and pictured two scenarios: one where Julian and I were together and happy, and one where I told him my true feelings and he pulled back, slowly at first, and then all at once. Gone.

"Jo, tell me," he said kissing the side of my cheek.

I wanted to tell him the truth. I wanted to throw myself at fate and live with the consequences if he decided he didn't want me anymore.

My voice shook as I spoke. "I think you and I should be more than friends."

My heart leapt in my chest. *There. I said it.*

"Mhm," he hummed.

I smiled.

"And I think you should take me on a date to a restaurant and we'll order an appetizer and dessert. No, two desserts."

He laughed. "I agree, but why should we do that?"

I kept my eyes closed, focusing on the feel of his lips against my cheek, the grip of his hands on my arm. I knew what game he was playing. I knew he was calling my bluff and I wasn't ready to give in just yet.

"Because you're very funny," I whispered.

"And?" he asked, peeling away the layers of my resolve.

"And you're very nice for taking care of me while I was drunk."

"And?"

"You've got a cute butt."

I could feel his smile against my cheek.

"Jo…"

"And I love you."

He leaned back and stared into my eyes. A triumphant smile coated his lips and I resisted the urge to kiss it off.

"I love you too," he said.

Warmth spread through me as I held his gaze.

"Is that why you came to Texas?" I asked.

He glanced to the side, gathering his thoughts before catching my gaze once again.

"It seems silly now, but Dean scared the shit out of me after you left. I thought you were pulling away, and then I got the call from Elizabeth about the Vogue position. I assumed you hadn't told me about it because you wanted to let me down easy."

I flinched back. Vogue? He knew about Vogue?

"Elizabeth contacted me for a reference," he explained.

"She did?" I asked.

"Yes," he said, leaning back to get a better look at me. "I told her she would have to discuss your recommendation with Lorena, since I obviously might be biased, but I also told her that you've been a wonderful employee.

Dependable, organized, and hardworking. I told her that she was crazy if she didn't hire you."

My eyes widened in shock. "You didn't. Did you?"

He smiled and his gaze fell to my lips. "Of course I did. It's the truth."

"What'd she say?" I asked, alarm bells ringing in my head.

"She said that she'd notify you about the position first thing upon your return to New York, but that if I spoke with you first, I was allowed to congratulate you first."

I covered my mouth in shock. "Julian! ARE YOU KIDDING ME?!"

He laughed and shook his head. "It looks like I won't be your boss anymore."

I stared down at his chest, contemplating his words. I'd landed the job at Vogue. I would be working at Vogue. Vogue would be my employer.

No matter what way I spun it, it didn't sound right.

How was that possible?

And why was I a tiny bit sad about it?

I liked my job working for Lorena Lefray Designs. I loved being with Julian all day, every day.

"Jo?"

"Yes?" I asked, keeping my gaze on his chest.

"This is a good thing."

I bit my bottom lip and collected my thoughts.

"I know that. I do. I want the job, it's just…the reason I didn't tell you about the position earlier was because I wasn't sure I wanted it. I really like working with you and if I leave…"

"We'll still see each other every day," he said.

I flicked my gaze up to him and smiled.

"Because you and I are dating," he said. "Together. In

love."

I smiled and let his words sink in.

"You know what that means?" I asked. "We're going to go out on dates, and I'm going to leave a toothbrush at your house, and we're going to bicker about dumb stuff like where we want to eat, and then we'll throw in the towel, order pizza, and have sex on the couch."

He smirked. "I have to say that sounds pretty nice actually."

"You know what else it means?" I said.

"What?"

"You definitely have to share half of that donut with me now."

Chapter Fifty~Two

Josephine

I lugged my backpack through my parents' house, confused about how I was somehow leaving Texas with fifty extra pounds of luggage. I'd taken a trip to Sally's Thrift Shop the day before and had left with a pair of kickass cowboy boots for $5, but they weren't that heavy. It was probably the five boxes of homemade cookies my mom had insisted I take back to New York with me. *Twist my arm, why don't you?*

"Josie? Are you headed out?" my mom asked, popping her head out of the kitchen.

I glanced up from my bag to see her scanning over me,

worry clouding her gaze. We'd had a long chat about my choice to get plastered the other night. I'd assured her that I wasn't a crazy alcoholic, and she'd forced me to promise that I would be honest with her if I ever did have a problem. I'd all but promised to provide her with weekly blood screenings just to ensure her that I was okay. Even still, I knew she wasn't wholeheartedly convinced that I should be going back to New York.

"Julian is going to swing by and pick me up after he gets Lily."

She nodded and gripped a tea towel between her hands, staring hard at my torso.

I leaned my bag against the wall and stepped forward to give her a hug. I'd already said my goodbyes to my dad the night before. He couldn't stand to see me driving away. It was easier for him to pretend I was just going off to a sleepover or something like I was still in high school. Big softie.

My mom gripped the back of my shirt and I pressed my face into the crook of her neck. I leaned my cheek on her shoulder and inhaled her scent.

"Take care of yourself, okay?" she said.

I nodded and stepped back, trying to keep my feelings at bay.

"It'll be better now that Lily is coming with me. We'll have a little family in New York."

She smiled, but it didn't reach her eyes. I knew she was putting on a brave face.

"I'll try to visit more often too. Maybe I can come back down for Christmas?"

She sniffed and glanced away. "That'd be great."

I heard a car pull up onto the gravel drive outside and I glanced through the front door to see Julian's rental car. I reached down for my bag and gave my mom another quick hug.

"I'll call you when we get to New York," I promised, starting to head for the door.

"Jos—"

I turned back over my shoulder.

She wrung the tea towel through her hands and swallowed hard.

"I want you to know that your dad and I are really proud of you. Not many people around here are willing to go after their dreams the way you have." She met my gaze and smiled. "I think at first we took it a little personal—the fact that you wanted to leave this town so badly. It was all you used to talk about, but now I finally understand that this place has never been big enough for you."

My fingers loosened their hold on my bag and it clanked to the floor.

"Just promise me that you'll keep your head on straight. We raised you as a Texas girl." She pointed at her chest. "Make sure you always keep that in your heart."

I bit down on my lower lip, confused by the tears clouding the corners of my eyes. I clenched my teeth and blinked, considering how profoundly her words had hit me. In the back of my mind, I'd been holding out for her acceptance and blessing for the last few years. I'd known I was taking the path less traveled, but I'd still held out for the day when my mom would finally understand.

"I just want you to be happy," she said as I stepped forward and wrapped her up in another hug.

"I know that. I promise I won't let you down," I whispered against her chest as tears slid down my cheeks.

The doorbell rang three times in quick succession and then I heard Lily's voice on the other side of the door.

"Let's go, Jos! The plane leaves in four hours and it's going to take us at least two hours just to get to the airport."

Her shouting was punctuated by more pounding and when I turned around I saw her face squashed up against the glass, trying to see inside. Such a scoundrel.

My mom laughed and held me back at arm's length.

"You'd better get going," she said.

I nodded and tried to compose myself as best as possible. I hadn't been expecting that speech from my mom. I'd prepared myself to leave without my parents' blessing once again, but it felt so much better walking through the front door knowing that I was making them proud.

I walked to the edge of the porch and squinted to block the sun shining overhead. The jasmine around the perimeter fence of my parents' house was swaying in the breeze, filling the air with a sweet aroma. Lily ran to the car, opened up the passenger door for me, and then popped the trunk. Julian stepped out of the car and held his hand up to his brow to shield his face from the sun. When our eyes locked, he grinned and shook his head. The message was clear: *Your best friend is a maniac.*

Lily ran toward the porch, cursed me for being so slow, and grabbed the bag out of my hand so she could take it to the car.

"Don't you realize how close I am to finally moving to New York City?!" she asked. "Hurry your ass up!"

I laughed as she tossed my luggage into the trunk.

Julian rounded the back of the car and dipped down to give me a quick kiss. The scent of his body wash momentarily masked the jasmine as he wrapped his arm around my back. I wrapped my arm around his neck and held myself against him for a moment, immersed in the feel of him.

"I can't believe I let you buy us plane tickets," I whispered before stepping back.

"Consider it a going away present from Lorena Lefray Designs. Besides, I bought them with points. It's not a big deal."

Our original plan had been to ride the Greyhound back to New York, but Julian had quickly put the kibosh on that idea. (Telling him about Gladys *might* have had something to do with that.)

A loud honk pulled me out of my moment with Julian. When I turned toward the car, Lily was leaning across the front seat with her hand poised over the center of the steering wheel.

"Let's go you love birds. I'm about to leave you both behind!"

She slammed her hand down on the horn again, this time for a solid ten seconds.

"Stop it! We're coming," I shouted.

Before she could honk again, I rounded the front of the car and pushed her into the backseat, far away from the horn. She had the audacity to give me a cheeky smile.

Julian slipped into the driver's seat and pulled back out of the gravel drive. I saw my mom standing in the kitchen window, watching us back up. I waved as we hit the end of the drive and she waved back, offering a final goodbye.

"Do you have to buy a pass for the subway or do you carry quarters around all the time?" she asked, leaning forward.

"You get a reloadable card. Definitely don't carry quarters around with you," I said, visualizing a weighed down Lily pulling mountains of quarters out of her pockets every time we took the subway together.

"Oh okay. That makes sense."

"What are you planning on doing for work?" Julian asked, peering back at her in the rearview mirror.

She picked at her thumbnail as she stared out the window with narrowed eyes.

"Eventually I want my blog to be able to support me, but I know that I'll have to get a full-time job for the time being."

Julian glanced toward me. "Blog?"

I smiled. "Yes, Lily has a blog too, but it's all about food."

She beamed in the back seat. "It's an 'everyman' food review blog. I post lists like 'Where to Get the Best Burger in Texas' and stuff like that, but I want to switch gears when I get to New York and really start to review more restaurants."

"Have you told her about Dean?" Julian asked.

Lily leaned forward. "Who's Dean?"

"One of my friends from college. He's a restaurateur in New York and I'm sure he'd have room for you at one of his restaurants if you don't mind serving."

Lily pinched the back of my arm. "How could you have kept this information from me."

"Ow!" I yanked my arm away and flashed her a death stare. "To be honest, I did it on purpose. You and Dean are going to be like oil and water. I already know it'd be a disaster if you worked for him."

Julian laughed. "Can't say I don't agree. Dean's pretty headstrong."

"Yeah? So what? I am too."

Julian and I exchanged a knowing glance. We both knew the facts: Dean and Lily were both annoyingly good-looking and annoyingly stubborn. The chances of them getting along were slim at best. The chances of them tearing each other's clothes off at first sight were much more likely.

"Honestly, it sounds like fate that you have a friend in the restaurant industry. Promise me you'll put in a good word for me?" Lily asked.

Julian nodded. "I'll see what I can do, but you should know that Dean's a smug bastard."

I peered back at Lily out of the corner of my eye.

She wasn't the least bit deterred by Julian's warnings. On the contrary. She was leaning against the back seat with her arms crossed and a confident smile across her lips. She looked like she was plotting something diabolical and I didn't want any part of it.

"I'm sure I'll be able to handle him," she said. "Besides, most guys are all bark and no bite."

Epilogue

VOGUE BLOGS

Seasoned Designer Returns to the Spotlight
June 28, 2015
By Josephine Keller of *What Jo Wore*
Comments: 3,008   Likes: 55,434

Forget everything you thought you knew about Lorena Lefray Designs. In the past, she's been known for dark, grungy styles best worn with crimson lipstick and paired with a serious gothic attitude. Next season, she's taking her collection—and her brand—in a whole new direction.

I've been honored with a sneak peek of the designs that will hit runways in September. Three words: tribal, colorful, daring. This collection will not be for the faint of heart. There are no neutrals. She wants her clothes to speak volumes, and THEY DO.

In sync with her first runway debut in two years, she'll be opening up her very first storefront in Chelsea this fall. I was a part of the beginning stages of this project and I have to say, you have never seen a store like this. Imagine walking into Chanel and having Karl Lagerfeld handpick a dress just for you. Now imagine that you're listening to hip music and sipping on some amazing (complimentary) champagne while he does it.

It's going to be EPIC.

I'll be sitting down with the designer for a one-on-one interview closer to the opening of her store, but for now, I'll leave you with a first look at the Lorena Lefray Designs 2015 Fall Collection. (I'd recommend you start saving up for it now!)

Until tomorrow,
XOJO

Acknowledgements

To my readers. I write these books to make you smile. I hope that they're a light spot at the end of a long day. Whether this is the first book you've picked up from me or the sixth, I appreciate all of your support.

To Lance, who has become quite a writing partner. Thank you for taking my words and making them funnier than I could ever imagine. We make quite a good tag team!

To my mom & dad, thank you for your unconditional support. I would have never had the courage to pursue writing without you two.

To my street team, aka the women who put up with an author who is scatterbrained 95% of the time, thank you for supporting me when I need you all the most! This book was written during quite a crazy time in my life, and I would not have been able to finish it without you guys there to support me along the way.

To my editor, Caitlin. Thank you for being eternally patient and flexible. I'm so proud to have you as a part of this process.

Big thank you to my proofreaders! Jennifer Van Wyk, Amanda Daniel, & Erin Spencer—I can always count on you three for support during crazy release schedules! I would be completely LOST without the help of you three.

Also. BIG THANK YOU to everyone who accepted an ARC edition of this book for hanging with me for all the tweaks and changes!

Other Books by R.S. Grey:

Scoring Wilder
USA TODAY BEST-SELLER
New Adult Sports Romance

What started out as a joke--seduce Coach Wilder--soon became a goal she had to score.

With Olympic tryouts on the horizon, the last thing nineteen-year-old Kinsley Bryant needs to add to her plate is Liam Wilder. He's a professional soccer player, America's favorite bad-boy, and has all the qualities of a skilled panty-dropper.

* A face that makes girls weep - check.

* Abs that can shred Parmesan cheese (the expensive kind) - check.

* Enough confidence to shift the earth's gravitational pull - double check.

Not to mention Liam is strictly off limits. Forbidden. Her coaches have made that perfectly clear. (i.e. "Score with Coach Wilder anywhere other than the field and you'll be cut from the team faster than you can count his tattoos.") But that just makes him all the more enticing...Besides, Kinsley's already counted the visible ones, and she is not one to leave a project unfinished.

Kinsley tries to play the game her way as they navigate through forbidden territory, but Liam is determined to teach her a whole new definition for the term "team bonding."

Recommended for ages 17+ due to language and sexual situations.

The Duet
Adult Romance

When 27-year-old pop sensation Brooklyn Heart steps in front of a microphone, her love songs enchant audiences worldwide. But when it comes to her own love life, the only spell she's under is a dry one.

So when her label slots her for a Grammy performance with the sexy and soulful Jason Monroe, she can't help but entertain certain fantasies... those in which her G-string gets more play than her guitars'.

Only one problem. Jason is a lyrical lone wolf that isn't happy about sharing the stage—nor his ranch — with the sassy singer. But while it may seem like a song entitled 'Jason Monroe Is an Arrogant Ho' basically writes itself, their label and their millions of fans are expecting recording gold...

They're expecting *The Duet.*

Recommended for ages 17+ due to language and sexual situations.

Available on: AMAZON

The Design
Adult Romance

Five minutes until the interview begins.

Fresh on the heels of her college graduation, Cameron Heart has landed an interview at a prestigious architecture firm.

Four minutes until the interview.

She knows she's only there because the owner, Grayson Cole, is her older sister's friend.

Three minutes.

For the last seven years, Grayson has been the most intimidating man Cammie has ever had the pleasure, or *displeasure*, of being around.

Two Minutes.

But the job opportunity is too good to pass up. So, Cammie will have to ignore the fact that Grayson is handsome enough to have his own national holiday.

One.

After all, she shouldn't feel that way about her new boss. And, he *will* be her new boss.

•••

"I'm not intimidated by you," I said with a confident smile.
"Perhaps we should fix that, Ms. Heart. Close the door."

Recommended for ages 17+ due to language and sexual situations.

With This Heart
New Adult Romance

If someone had told me a year ago that I was about to fall in love, go on an epic road trip, ride a Triceratops, sing on a bar, and lose my virginity, I would have assumed they were on drugs.

Well, that is, until I met Beckham.

Beck was mostly to blame for my recklessness. Gorgeous, clever, undeniably charming Beck barreled into my life as if it were his mission to make sure I never took living for granted. He showed me that there were no boundaries, rules were for the spineless, and a kiss was supposed to happen when I least expected.

Beck was the plot twist that took me by surprise. Two months before I met him, death was knocking at my door. I'd all but given up my last scrap of hope when suddenly I was given a second chance at life. This time around, I wasn't going to let it slip through my fingers.

We set out on a road trip with nothing to lose and no guarantees of tomorrow.

Our road trip was about young, reckless love. The kind of love that burns bright.

The kind of love that no road-map could bring me back from.

Recommended for ages 17+ due to language and sexual situations.

Available on: AMAZON

Behind His Lens

Adult Romance

Twenty-three year old model Charley Whitlock built a quiet life for herself after disaster struck four years ago. She hides beneath her beautiful mask, never revealing her true self to the world... until she comes face-to-face with her new photographer — sexy, possessive Jude Anderson. It's clear from the first time she meets him that she's playing by his rules. He says jump, she asks how high. He tells her to unzip her cream Dior gown, she knows she has to comply. But what if she wants him to take charge outside of the studio as well?

Jude Anderson has a strict "no model" dating policy. But everything about Charley sets his body on fire.

When a tropical photo shoot in Hawaii forces the stubborn pair into sexually charged situations, their chemistry can no longer be ignored. They'll have to decide if they're willing to break their rules and leave the past behind or if they'll stay consumed by their demons forever. Will Jude persuade Charley to give in to her deepest desires?

Recommended for ages 17+ due to language and sexual situations.

Available on: AMAZON

Made in the USA
San Bernardino, CA
22 January 2016